AFTER EVERYTHING

ANDREA NOURSE

After everything we've shared
After everything we've lost
We haven't been worth the cost
I gave you my heart; I gave you my soul
It used to be you, we used to be us
After everything is gone
I finally have it all

CHAPTER ONE

I touched the tip of my finger to the cool glass of the window and stared down at the busy street below. Drops of rain raced down the pane, chasing each other toward their final destination. As the heat from my finger transferred to the glass, the droplets diverted and created a new path, avoiding me altogether. Moments like this, I wished I were the rain.

"Abby," my mother said and cleared her throat. "Are you listening to me?"

I nodded but didn't speak. She, of course, couldn't see this through the phone but I kept nodding anyway.

"How's the *'songwriting thing'* going?" If it were possible to hear air quotes, my mother would be the perfect person to narrate them.

"Great," I replied. The lie slipped out far too easily. "Everything is great."

Nothing was great, but I couldn't tell her that. I couldn't admit that my lack of planning combined with my impulsive decision to run away from my hometown, family, and husband had all been a mistake. She didn't need to know the full extent of my failures. Otherwise, she'd never stop rubbing them in my face.

"You've always been a terrible liar," she said with a snorted laugh.

"How long do you intend to mope about your apartment? Have you done dishes this week? Last week? Do you have on clean underwear?"

Rolling my eyes, I bit back the sarcasm that bubbled inside my throat and said, "Yes, Mom, I'm wearing clean underwear. The apartment is clean. Everything is fine."

Fine. The most loaded word in the English language. Fine wasn't fine and neither was I.

"Don't roll your eyes at me, Abigail Grace." Never mind that she couldn't see me. She knew me better than anyone. Just as I'd known she air quoted "songwriting thing," she knew I was rolling my eyes as I said "fine." I flinched at her tone and shook off the feeling it brought on. I wasn't sixteen. She wasn't in control anymore. My life was mine and mine alone to fuck up, and I was doing a mighty fine job of that all on my own. I didn't need her meddling to make things worse. "Abby, are you there? I can't hear you."

"Sorry, it's raining." I yawned.

"Let me guess," she said with a small laugh. "You're staring out the window and wondering which raindrop will win the race."

"You know me well," I said. Niles, my cat purred and rubbed against my bare legs. I reached down and scratched his head. He climbed into my lap and curled himself into a tiny ball of black and white fluff. "Listen, Mom, I know you're worried or whatever, but I'm fine. I can take care of myself. This is just a small setback."

"You were fired, Abby, I'd call that more than a setback."

"I wasn't fired, I was let go. The agency downsized." She was right, though, I'd been fired, but they were also in the midst of a downsizing after losing a big client. I might have survived the downsizing if I hadn't shown up for the most important meeting of my life fifteen minutes late and with a hangover the size of my hometown—small, but invasive. My performance in that meeting is what lost us the big client. So, technically, we were both right. She knew me well enough to know I'd somehow managed to fuck up this golden opportunity. I'm nothing if not predictable.

"Have you told your—" she said, pausing to swallow her distaste before finishing her question. "Your father?"

"Do you really want to know?" I asked.

"Nope, I don't."

"Great, then I won't have to lie." I hadn't called him, nor did I plan to. I'd missed our coffee date on Monday, being hungover and late and all. He'd called, but I'd never called him back. I wasn't in the mood for a litany of "I told you so"s or "you just know how to let me down don't you"s. The two things I'd recently learned that my father excelled at. Well, that and pretending he'd never had a wife or two daughters in Missouri.

"Maybe it's time to tuck your tail between your legs and come home," she said as if she were simply suggesting a small tweak. Her casual tone dug under my skin.

"And do what?" I asked without bothering to hide my annoyance.

"There are plenty of jobs here," she said.

"I can't come home, Mom, you know that."

Mom sighed and then paused as if she were seriously debating her next sentence. As soon as she spoke it, I wished she thought harder and kept it to herself.

"You know he won't wait forever, right?" she asked.

"I don't want him to," I said. As I said the words, the all-too-familiar tug of home pulled me away from the comfort of my cozy Nashville condo. I took a deep breath and said, "And what would I do for work? Ed at the radio station made it clear my old job wasn't an option."

"I'm sure there are marketing jobs here," she said.

"In Wishing, Missouri? They don't even know what marketing is." Moving home wasn't an option. I'd sell myself on Dickerson Pike before I moved back to Missouri. No, failure wasn't an option. It didn't matter that I was already halfway there.

"Or, I bet Rayna would let you come back and sing a few nights a week at Lace & Grit or bartend. She did you good when you got that hair up your ass to go to college."

I bit my tongue. I'd sung at the tiny dive bar more times than I could even remember but I was fairly certain neither the town nor

Rayna would welcome me back with open arms. Not after what I did to Jacob. Not after I left like I did. "Just, no," I mumbled to myself.

"What was that?" she asked, her voice suddenly sounding a thousand miles away.

"Nothing, Mom." I didn't have the energy to defend myself or my move to Nashville anymore. I wasn't coming home. Even if it meant groveling for more handouts from my father.

"Sorry, I've got to run. Your sister just pulled up with the twins," Mom said. Her voice kicked up an octave. It always did that when Lindsey was around. My older sister was her pride and joy. I was her biggest disappointment.

"Give them hugs and snuggles from Auntie Abby."

"Come home and give them out yourself."

I sighed and said, "I love you, Mom. Talk soon?" She hung up without returning the sentiment.

I dropped the phone onto my lap and closed my eyes. The rain pelted the window. Each one hitting a new note and continuing the song no one asked it to sing. I laid my head against the window and waited for motivation to strike. I should be looking for a new job or heading out for a songwriter meet up or writing a song. Or anything other than moping around my overpriced condo in three-day-old pajamas. But I hadn't touched my guitar in months, not once in the months since I'd left home. I'd moved to Music City and lost my will to write.

A knock at the door pulled me from my brief moment of reverie. Niles leapt from my lap and rushed to the door, eager to see what was on the other side. I'd gotten a cat because they were supposed to be chill and quiet. Somehow, I'd managed to adopt a lap cat that thinks he's a dog. I slipped off the window seat and padded across the floor. Before I pulled it open, I swiped my hand through my mousy blonde hair. When was the last time I'd combed it? Monday? Had I even done it then?

"Abigail Rhodes?" a young man asked when I pulled the door open.

"Yes?"

"You've been served." He shoved an envelope into my unsuspecting hand, and I stepped back, refusing to touch it. I knew what was inside that manila envelope, and I had no desire to accept it. Though, I'd been the one to ask for it in the first place, I wasn't ready for the finality. "Look, you've been served whether you take it or not. If you take it, I can go about my day and you can go take a shower or brush your teeth."

"Rude," I said and took the envelope. He offered a weak smile and turned to go before I could slam the door in his face. "Fucking perfect."

The envelope wasn't big. It didn't weigh much but it held so much more than just the papers that would officially end the best worst mistake of my life. No, mistake wasn't the right word. A mistake implies it was a simple oops. Not fourteen years of saying yes when I meant to say no. Not packing up in the middle of the night and leaving without so much as a goodbye. Not the single-word lie I brought with me. Those weren't simple mistakes. Those were conscious, calculated decisions, and for the most part, I accepted the consequences. Even if I didn't like them.

Jacob. His name buzzed around my head like a fly I couldn't swat. It hovered just out of reach, taunting and teasing me. I tossed the envelope on the counter and vowed to deal with it later. I'd sign the papers, I knew I would, I just needed a few more days to clear my head. It didn't matter that I was the one who left. I was the one who initiated all of this; I just wasn't ready to accept full responsibility or finality.

Niles worked his way in and out of the spot between my feet. He meowed and stared up at me. I bent down to pick him up and caught a whiff of myself. *Ugh*. The guy at the door wasn't wrong. I needed a shower. Badly. I picked up my phone and glanced at the date. It was Thursday. I hadn't bothered to look in a mirror or change my clothes since Monday. I'd only talked to my mother on the phone, no one else. I hadn't even left my condo. I wasn't even one-hundred percent sure the rest of the world even existed. I'd somehow managed to stay off social media; unless playing *Words with Friends* with random people counted as social media. (It didn't.) I'd sulked for three full days. It was time to rejoin the world. Maybe I could finally check out the bar that was on the first floor of my condo building. *Just one drink*, I vowed. *One.*

I slipped out of my clothes, cringing at the smell that wafted off of them, and tossed them onto the bathroom floor. Stepping over them, I reached into the shower and turned the water as hot as it would go. I'd need to boil the last few days off of me if I wanted a chance at a fresh start. Or, at least, a fresh scent. The start could wait until after I called my dad with the news that I'd ruined the shot he so generously gave me.

I reached my hand into the shower and yanked it back out. Flames rushed over my skin. The temperature was near perfect. Jacob would have hated it. I shuddered at the second reminder of him. There wasn't a trace of him inside this condo or in this town, but I still felt his presence. Inside my eyelids when I blinked. On my skin when the sun or rain kissed it. In between my fingers when I reached for a beer; the shape of the bottle reminding me of the feel of his hand in mine. He was nowhere but everywhere all at the same time.

I hated myself for thinking about him and romanticizing our brief marriage. A year ago, I'd never have considered that I might miss the doldrums of our routines. I also didn't assume I'd be living in a condo that my dad owned in downtown Nashville. A year ago, Jacob and Wishing, Missouri, were all I knew. Our relationship had survived high school, college, and our mid-twenties, but it couldn't survive our very different dreams. The dreams we'd once shared had shifted as we grew up and apart. His involved buns in the oven and mine involved guitars and lyrics. I'd once been convinced that they could live together and become a shared future. Jacob hadn't seen it that way. His home was, and always would be, in Missouri. I used to think mine was too; then one day it wasn't.

I'd always felt safe and content with him and in the hometown we shared. But contentment wasn't what I thought it would be. Safety wasn't love, and it certainly didn't inspire any life-changing songs. That came from leaving your high school sweetheart and packing up everything you owned into the back of a decade-old Toyota Camry and making the 500-mile drive to the city of music and begging your estranged father for a place to live and selling your soul for a paycheck.

Better than living and dying in the same small town I was born in. Just like all the small-town girls who came before me. Better than admitting my life was headed exactly where it started. Nowhere.

CHAPTER TWO

"Jack and Diet," I said and slid my ID and credit card across the freshly polished bar top. Climbing onto the tall barstool, I avoided eye contact with the man who stood on the other side. He'd shouted a hello to me when I walked in, but as ready as I was to rejoin the world, I wasn't quite ready for humanity.

"Anything to eat? Or just a liquid brunch?" the bartender asked and glanced down at my license. He gave me the once over. Either he didn't look too closely, or he ignored my still wet hair, red-rimmed eyes, and tattered old University of Missouri sweatshirt I'd thrown on over my leggings. As I slipped it over my head after my shower, I caught a faded whiff of Jacob's cologne and broke down in my closet. I lay on the floor, curled into a tight ball of salty tears and emptied the contents of my heart onto the cool, wood floor. I'd somehow managed to throw myself together enough to take the elevator down to the lobby and sulk into the bar.

I rolled my eyes and glanced at the clock. It was mid-afternoon, so this hardly qualified as brunch or an opportunity to judge my drinking habits. "Just the drink."

The Gulch Dive Bar was empty aside from the homeless man camped out in the corner near the front door. He, thankfully, kept to himself. I tapped my fingernails on the bar top and tried to ignore the chipped nail polish and damaged cuticles. Since moving to Nashville and leaving Jacob, I'd taken up my old childhood habits of living off generic Lucky Charms and biting my fingernails. My new unemployed status may reduce me to off-brand ramen.

"So, Missouri, what brings you into my pathetic bar this lovely Thursday?" He leaned forward and propped himself against the bar.

"Unemployment. Desperation. A self-awareness of my patheticness." The honesty poured out of me far more freely than I'd intended.

"The usual."

"Yup." I lifted the glass to my lips and tipped it back, finishing it in one quick chug. The cool liquid burned as it rolled down my throat. I hated the way it felt going down but craved the aftereffect. Jack Daniels had gotten me into this mess, and I knew I couldn't drink my way out of it, but I was willing to permit myself to drown my sorrows one last time.

"Will you judge me too harshly if I order another?" I asked, not caring if his answer was yes. I ignored the nagging voice inside my head that tried to remind me that I'd planned to only have one. *Shut up.*

"Nope, it gives me something to do and pays the bills. Assuming you can pay, Missouri."

"I can, and my name is Abby," I replied. I hadn't done any formal calculations, but I should be able to pay for at least one complete pity party without draining my non-existent savings. Hopefully, I wouldn't find myself homeless once my dad found out I'd screwed up everything.

"Nice to meet you, Abby. I'm Noah."

I glanced up at him and gave him a quick once-over. Dark hair, green eyes, a Chris Evans–worthy beard, and broad shoulders. He could be my type with the right amount of liquid courage, but he wasn't giving off one-night-stand vibes.

"So, Abby from Missouri, what do you do?" he asked as he slid my second glass across the table.

"Right now? Wallow and mope."

"Let's say it was Monday and you weren't unemployed, where would you be?"

"The job that pays is in marketing and advertising; the dream that doesn't pay the bills involves lyrics and a guitar I may be pawning soon. Jesus, I'm the worst possible Nashville cliché." I tossed the drink back and slammed the glass on the bar. I ignored the tears swelling in my eyes.

"Songwriter, eh?" I didn't detect even the slightest hint of sarcasm in his voice. He pointed at himself and said, "Drummer."

I smiled and nodded. "Of course. We're everywhere here, aren't we?"

"Just a couple of clichés tending bar and day drinking."

"Oh, and let's not forget the divorce papers I was just served," I said and sighed. "You know, until right this second, I didn't realize just how horrible all of this was."

"Sounds like you've got everything you need to write a hit song."

"Aside from motivation."

"Another?" he asked. He lifted the bottle of Jack Daniels and shook it. "On the house? I can't in good conscience charge you after that sob story."

"Um," I said, hedging. "I shouldn't. I'm already primed to make terrible decisions."

"Like go home with a stranger?"

I nodded as my cheeks flushed. For a split second, I let my mind wander off to a lovely daydream where I made out with Noah and he continued to pour free drinks.

He laughed and said, "Don't worry, I won't let that happen."

"You shouldn't make promises you can't keep."

"I can keep that one."

"Sure," I said with a nod and an eye roll.

"Look, I've got a fiancée and three little sisters. I'm pretty well versed in women."

Fiancée. I silently cried as my fantasies of an illicit affair with Noah drifted off into nothing.

"So, Abby from Missouri, have you ever waited tables?" he asked.

"Once or twice. I'm not very good at it."

"Sounds like the rest of my staff. You interested in a job?"

"I don't know," I said and laughed. "Not sure I trust a man who's giving out free liquor and offering waitressing jobs to self-admitted horrible waitresses."

He ignored my comment and said, "You know we have an open mic night every Wednesday, and when you work here, you get first dibs."

"Really?" I shifted in my seat as the butterflies returned to my stomach. These, though, came from the thought of standing on a stage again. My fingers tingled at the possibility. Did I remember how to play or sing or do anything other than work, sleep, or eat?

"Owner's rules."

"Guessing the owner is a songwriter, too?"

"I am. Well, my cousin more so than me."

My mouth fell open. I gave him another hard look. He couldn't be much older than me. "You own this place?" My gaze shifted away from him, and I took in the room around me. The bar itself wasn't anything fancy. The windows that lined the walls overlooked Twelfth Avenue. Light filtered in through the pale tint and danced through the dust particles in the air. Twenty or so two- and four-top tables dotted the empty dining area. Each one spotless. The small stage at the far right of the room held a microphone, a keyboard, and a smattering of lights and gear.

"Don't look so shocked," he said with a laugh. "My cousin, Derrick, and I both own it. I run it. He uses it to pick up girls."

"Ahh."

"My uncle owns the building." He explained further. His eyes drifted toward the ceiling for a moment. I caught the tiniest of flinches when his gaze made its way back down to me.

I coughed, choking in the ice I was chewing. "What?" The Gulch Dive Bar was located beneath the condo building I lived in. The very expensive and ornate condo building that still took my breath away every time I walked into the lobby. I barely believed I lived in it. Now looking at Noah, I tried to imagine what his life might be like.

"Heard of the Bale family?" I shook my head. "Well, after a few years in Nashville, you will. My grandfather was the governor. My father is a senator, and my Uncle Rob practically built half the high rises in the city."

"Wow," I replied, not even bothering to hide my amazement. Now that he'd mentioned it, I'd heard and seen the name before. Rob Bale's name was on a plaque in the lobby of our building. And, if memory served me, Noah's dad was Richard Bale. "Your dad is Richard, then?"

"So, you have heard of us?" He raised an eyebrow.

"Well, I do live in this building and have turned on the news a time or two."

"Hard to escape the notorious Bale boys," he said. He picked up a dish towel and wiped up the ring left by my glass. "But they want us to be humble, and neither Derrick nor I want anything to do with politics or real estate. So, we signed over our trust funds and opened this place."

"I don't think you can use the words *humble* and *trust fund* in the same sentence."

"You'd be surprised. So, what do you say? I haven't posted the job yet, but I need one more late-night waitress, and you could start this week."

"Can I think about it?" I asked. The Jack Daniels was working its way through my veins, warming me from the inside out. I didn't trust myself to make any life choices at the moment. And I still needed to talk to my dad.

"Sure, you know where to find me."

I thanked him for the offer and free drink. Then, I excused myself and promised to be in touch. As I walked out, I tried to picture myself in this tiny bar owned by a drummer and his cousin, whose fathers just so happened to be two of the most powerful men in Nashville. Dealing with my father's ego was bad enough, I couldn't imagine what it was like growing up under that level of scrutiny.

I had to admit that the possibility of finding a job before talking to my dad was promising. But what was more enticing about the whole thing was I'd be forcing myself into a situation where I could play again and get back into a writing groove. After all, that's why I uprooted and ruined my entire life.

I stopped just outside the bar and pulled my phone out of my purse and dialed the number I'd been avoiding. "Hey, Dad," I said when he answered. "Can we meet for coffee tomorrow? I have something I need to tell you and should probably do it in person."

"Abby," he said, his voice sounding as though it had been pulled taut, "I'm pretty busy tomorrow."

"Please, Dad? It's important. I can meet you early."

"Seven at Starbucks at Fifth and Church?"

"See you there." I hung up the phone before he could change his mind. Or before I could change mine.

"Excuse me, ma'am," a gruff voice said. I glanced up and was met with a captivating set of piercing gray eyes. When I didn't move, he nodded to the door behind me.

"Oh." I exhaled without breaking our eye contact. There was a twinkle of mischief in them. Those were the eyes of a bad decision waiting to happen.

CHAPTER THREE

Flopping onto the thrift store couch I'd bought with the last of my Missouri savings, I clenched my eyes closed and tried to thwart the onslaught of tears. The Jack and Diets were slowly working their magic, but my heart was resisting. My brain wanted to forget pretty much every minute of the past few months, but my heart refused to focus on anything other than that one night in December that I wanted to forget.

Christmas Eve.

What kind of woman leaves her husband and the man who has loved her unconditionally for more than half her life? Me. I am that kind of person. I'm the worst. Heartless. Cold. Bitch. All of those things. Yet, none of them are entirely accurate. Yes, I'd left. But if I were being honest with myself, I'd left Jacob long before that night. If I dug deep enough into my subconscious, I'd have to admit that I left him before I vowed to never leave him. He was the easiest part of my life. Consistent. Strong. Boring. At one point, I'd stopped seeing him as a partner and a lover and more as an anchor that tethered me exactly where I didn't want to be.

We had the kind of small-town fairytale that they write Hallmark movies about. We grew up together in our tiny, one-stoplight town. His mom and my mom were best friends; or they were before my dad left and my mom decided Jack (Daniels) and Jim (Beam) were her best friends. He played football, and I cheered on the sidelines. I detested cheerleading but did it for him. To be fair, I didn't start hating it until being forced to retell our story over and over again to a chorus of "oh, of course" anytime I mentioned our former roles. In high school, I loved dressing up in the tiny, pleated skirt and cropped tank top to wave glittered gold and purple pompoms for my team. *Go Wishing Bobcats!* We'd been crowned homecoming king and queen. Later, they voted us the cutest couple and most likely to breed like rabbits. Jacob Rhodes and Abby Monroe were the "it" couple of Wishing High.

When I said we fit into every perfectly molded cliché, I wasn't exaggerating.

I knew it wasn't a great idea, but I grabbed my phone and opened my text messages. There wasn't anything good hiding in them—no secret messages and certainly not the answers to whatever question I couldn't seem to ask. Since leaving Wishing, the only messages I'd gotten were from my mother, my sister, Jacob, and my best friend, Melissa. In the past few days, my phone had been more silent than midnight in Wishing. There weren't even crickets. Jacob stopped texting three months ago. My sister and mother were more constant. It probably helped that I actually replied to them. I didn't have words for Jacob's. What does one text to the man they left on Christmas Eve? I suppose I could've told him the truth or admitted that I'd lied to him, but I wasn't ready for that confession.

I tapped his name and reread the string of messages from him.

Where are you?

Abby, it's Christmas morning.

Are you okay?

I'm sorry. Let's talk.

Jesus Christ, where are you?

Just be okay.

Call me. Now.

Abby.

They'd started rolling in around six on Christmas morning. We were due at Jacob's parents' at ten. I was already camped outside my dad's house by the time he woke up. I called my mom just before eight and let her know I was fine but wasn't coming home. I knew she'd be asleep and that I'd be safe leaving a message. I asked her to do what I couldn't. He'd called exactly five minutes after I left Mom the voice-mail. I didn't answer the first, fifth, or thirteenth time he called. He got the hint and sent a text.

Your mom just called. What are you doing in Nashville? Abby, why won't you answer the phone? What is going on? The test was negative, just like you wanted.

I could almost hear the anger in my now estranged husband's voice as the day went on and his messages became more and more irate. Reading the messages now, I cringed at the collection of memories from that Christmas Day, including seeing my dad for the first time in nearly twenty years.

I'd sat in my car outside his house and watched for shadows in the windows and wondered if I'd recognize the man inside. At ten that morning, I finally got out of my car and took a deep, cleansing breath of the crisp winter air. I hadn't told anyone I was coming, not even my dad. I wasn't sure what he'd do when he saw me, the daughter he'd walked away from, standing outside his house. I don't remember how long I stood outside in the cold staring up at his McMansion, as my mother would've called it. Each breath hung in the air like a tiny heart-shaped cloud before floating away and breaking into tiny pieces of rain. When I finally made my way up to the door, he was already waiting for me.

His hair was a bit more salt-and-pepper than I recalled, but exactly like the photo I'd found of him on LinkedIn. I'd gotten his address from an envelope I found in my mom's dresser. The postmark on the letter was five years old. I couldn't be certain that he still lived there or whether he'd even want to see me. When I got in my car that morning, I'd convinced myself that, of course, he still lived there, but the longer I stayed in my car, the more unsure I became. I didn't have many memories of my dad, but the last one had been of him leaving, so in my mind, he was always on the move and never settled down.

I stopped at the edge of the porch and stared up at him. It took my breath away for a moment, seeing how familiar he felt. He had the same sad brown eyes as me. His nose was more like my sister Lindsey's than mine. He was lean and long, like both of us. He was the exact man they'd cast as my father if this were a movie.

"Abigail." His voice sounded as if it had skipped a beat as my name caught in his throat.

"Alan," I'd replied, forcing my nerves to take a backseat. I stood still as he studied my face, to allow him a moment or two to process before I dove into my pitch. I'd had nine hours of blackness outside my windshield to prepare for this moment. He hadn't.

"What are you doing here?" I knew that would be the question he'd ask. After two decades of radio silence, what else is there to ask?

"I need help, and I figure you owe me. Can I come inside?" I remember shivering and rubbing my hands together, whether from nerves or the chill in the air, I wasn't sure.

He glanced over his shoulder and that's when I saw her. *Jenny*. The name my mother had cursed every day since he left. She wasn't as young or as blonde as I was expecting. She appeared to be a few years younger than my mother. Her hair, pitch black, fell into loose curls around her face. She didn't look as though she did Pilates or yoga or whatever trendy workout my mother cursed upon her. *Pilates Polly,* she'd called her. She appeared normal and maybe even kind.

"Why don't we go get some breakfast and catch up."

"We may need more than a short stack and over-easy eggs to '*catch up,*'" I'd said. I was on the verge of losing control over the emotions I'd managed to suppress. Seeing him in the flesh was like a punch in the face. The knuckles hard and cold against my jaw caused me to stiffen. "You know what. This was a bad idea. I shouldn't have come here."

I turned and jogged back to my car. My heart pounded, sending blood rushing through me in loud, throbbing waves that were so loud, I could hear them.

"Wait, Abigail!" he called after me. I sensed him getting closer but didn't stop. "I'm sorry, wait."

"Why? I'm sorry. I shouldn't be here." I climbed into my car and pulled the door shut. He grabbed it and leaned inside.

"No, you shouldn't be here unannounced on Christmas morning, but that doesn't mean I'm not happy to see you. Please, let's go somewhere and talk."

I didn't hesitate long before agreeing. I let him buy me IHOP pancakes, just as he'd done so many Sundays growing up, and he listened to me whine about how stuck I'd been in Missouri. I told him about Jacob and our marriage—well, not everything. I showed him photos of Lindsey and the twins, Kelsey and Kasey. He didn't ask about Mom, and I didn't offer up any information. He sat across from me and studied my every word and move. His eyebrows furrowed and his forehead wrinkled in concern whenever my voice would waver and betray me. When I was done, he agreed to help. Jenny still owned her condo from her bachelorette days, and he had a buddy who owned a marketing agency; surely, he could pull a few strings.

"Does she know you're here?" he asked when I pulled back up to his house. "You should call her if you haven't."

"Mom?" He nodded. "I called her. She knows I'm here."

"You know I didn't leave because of you or Lindsey. Right, Abigail?" His question came out in one desperate breath, like he'd been holding it in for two decades.

"Abby," I said and swiped a runaway tear away from my eye. "No one calls me Abigail unless I'm in trouble."

I ignored his question, unwilling to consider an answer. That one sentence couldn't erase a lifetime of proof to the contrary. Besides, why he left wasn't the issue. His leaving was. No matter the reason, he chose to walk away. He couldn't undo that choice any more than I could undo mine. There was no going back. I was new to this whole leaving thing, but even I knew going back in time wouldn't change anything.

When he sensed that I wasn't ready to rehash our past, he left me, only to return a few minutes later with the keys to Jenny's old condo and his friend's business card; he'd written his own cell phone number on the back. I took both with a mumbled thank you and a promise to be in touch.

The next morning, I woke up in a twelfth-floor, one-bedroom condo in one of the most expensive buildings in Nashville. The space was unfurnished and likely worth more money than my mother or I could ever earn or dream of earning in our lifetimes. I opened my eyes to a bright Nashville sunrise and fifty-five missed calls from Jacob. I didn't bother reading the texts he'd sent or listening to the voicemails he'd left. I didn't call him back then. Or the next day or the next. I ignored him and the life I'd left behind. Now as I stared at the papers that would officially end our marriage, I cracked. I needed to hear his voice before I signed anything. I needed to know if I'd made the right decision. And, above all else, I owed him an explanation. I owed him the truth.

Busy?

I typed message quickly and hit send before I could change my mind. The bubbles indicating he was typing a message appeared, disappeared, and then reappeared. I watched his indecision dance across the screen and waited.

You got the papers? he asked.

Yes, can we talk?

No. You had your time to talk, and you ignored me. Sign the papers and send them back. You left, don't make this difficult.

Can we talk?

I asked one last time and then waited. He didn't respond, and I read and reread his message. A shiver ran through me each time I read the coldness in his words. I knew I didn't deserve more, but that didn't stop me from wanting more. My entire being itched and ached to run home. Knowing he was on the other end of that message holding his phone and staring at it made me want to erase every moment of time that had passed since I left.

No. I turned off my phone and shoved it under the couch cushion. No amount of Jack Daniels or regret could undo what I'd done in leaving.

Or what he'd done to try to force me to stay.

CHAPTER FOUR

I arrived at Starbucks at 6:45 a.m. I wasn't a morning person, but in the short time I'd gotten to know my dad, I learned that was not a trait we shared. He was always early, and I was perpetually late. I'd made an extra effort to show up early today, hoping in some small way it would soften the blow of the news I had to deliver. I even curled my hair and doused my face in makeup. No amount of concealer could hide the evidence of my sleepless week. I'd spent much of the previous night tossing and turning and dreaming about Jacob and Wishing.

The sounds of Nashville's early-morning hustle and bustle flowed in and out of the cafe. I sat at the back corner of the tiny space and watched as well-dressed men and women mingled with hungover tourists clad in blue jeans, hats, and cowboy boots. Nashville wasn't quite the country music mecca everyone thought it was. The music here was as wide and varied as the melting-pot population. I hadn't been here long, but even I knew the locals wouldn't dare dress like they'd just stepped of the Opry stage in 1989. It made it easy to pinpoint the partiers, vacationing families, and bachelorettes. I let the chorus they left in their wake lull me into a sense of contentment. There wasn't much peace to be found in this city, and I often found myself missing the rolling hills and silence I'd left behind. What I wouldn't give for a lazy day on the lake or an aimless drive down a long, winding dirt road with nothing but my music and my thoughts for miles and miles.

Right on cue, my father walked into the busy Starbucks at exactly 6:55 a.m. This was his preferred meeting spot, despite the fact that they had just two tiny tables and were always busy. It was located in the lobby of the Fifth Third building in downtown Nashville. His office was on the fifteenth floor, and I'd yet to be invited up. He never offered, and I never asked. Not that I wanted to. He was an accountant or banker or something equally boring. I should probably get around to asking him for more details about his life, rather than spending our weekly coffee dates staring out the window while we both awkwardly sipped our coffee.

"Abby," he greeted me. I stood and stepped into his timid embrace and quickly pulled myself back. "Have you ordered?"

I nodded. "Tall Americano for you."

"Over-sweetened, milked-down iced latte for you?" he replied. I returned his sheepish smirk and lifted my cup. "You are your mother's daughter."

I tried not to react to his comment and instead handed him his drink. Anytime my mother professed that I was my father's daughter, it was delivered as a back-handed compliment. I'd yet to learn what Alan Monroe meant when he said things like that.

"Sorry," he said, his voice dropping as he picked up on my trepidation, "I meant that as nothing more than an observation."

He was right, my mother drank coffee that was a shade darker than the cream she doused it in. I let the fact that he'd remembered such a tiny detail soothe my momentary irritation.

"So," I said and decided to dive right into my announcement, "I lost my job at Akerman and Carlisle."

"I'm aware." His voice took a sharp tone. Disappointment seethed through it.

I winced. Before I could respond, he took a quick sip of his coffee and then said, "Look, Abby, I knew the job was a bit of a stretch for you given your past experience. To go from selling ads for a small-town radio station to creating full marketing campaigns for regional and national brands was quite the leap, but at nearly twenty-nine years old, I expected you to have the level of maturity needed to not royally mess this up. Paul was furious when he called me on Monday. I put my reputation on the line, and you let me down." His words dripped with frustration. I felt he was holding more back than he was letting out.

"I know," I said. I didn't dare look up at him. The disappointment in his voice stung, but the realization that he hadn't believed in me from the start broke me in two. I'd disappointed my mother more times than I could count, but there was something in his words that dug deep. I'd been too naive when I believed we'd built any goodwill since my move here.

"Judging from those dark rings under your eyes, am I to assume you haven't yet learned your lesson?"

I didn't bother informing him that I'd learned that lesson more times than I could count. "I had trouble sleeping last night."

"Look, Abby, while I'm glad you're here, I can't have you endangering my business or personal life. I stuck my neck out for you with Paul, and this is how you thank me?"

"Alan," I said, refusing to refer to him as "Dad" after what he'd just said, "it's not like I did this on purpose. Yes, the job was a challenge for me, but I was making it work. I was a part of the team. What happened Monday was an unfortunate mistake. I shouldn't have gotten drunk on Sunday. I shouldn't have slept through my alarms. I should have prepared more for the presentation. I know all of this." I could have added that I was still trying to figure out how to cope and to process everything that had happened, but he knew what I'd been dealing better than anyone. Which made his reaction all the more brutal.

"Yet, here we are."

"Here we are." I sat back and folded my arms across my chest. When I glanced up, I found my father in the exact same pose. His lips curled into a deep frown, and his forehead creased in concentration.

"If you were me, what would you do?" he asked. Something in his tone sparked a fire that had been bubbling below the surface. I bit the inside of my cheek and begged my tears to remain at bay.

"For starters? I wouldn't have abandoned my wife and young daughters." As soon as the words exited my mouth, I regretted them. I'd dipped my toes into the subject before but never dove all the way in. This was supposed to remain an unspoken truth that lived between us. I just busted it wide open.

He sucked in a ragged breath and closed his eyes. A heavy silence fell between us. With that one sentence, I'd managed to undo any of the progress we'd made over the past few months. All those times that I'd bit my tongue before no longer mattered. I'd shown my hand. That truth had always been between us, but neither of us had verbalized it. My heart pounded in my chest. I opened my mouth to take it back, but he spoke before I could.

"I can't change the past. I'd hoped you of all people would understand why I did what I did."

"I left a husband. We didn't have kids." *Yet.* Despite this truth, his words stung. He was right. I was no better than him.

"Regardless. You saw a better life for yourself, and you decided to take it."

"And I admit it was selfish," I said, "but that doesn't change what you did."

"It doesn't, you're right. I can't expect you to understand why I left, but Abby, I never abandoned you."

"Really?" I laughed.

"I didn't."

"What do you call leaving your daughters alone with their mother without a dime of support? What do you call missed birthdays and holidays? You never called. You never wrote. You just left. You took the easy way out and fled to Nashville and a successful new life while your old life crumbled in on itself. Do you know what we had for dinner most nights? TV dinners if we were lucky, nothing if we weren't. New school clothes? Nope. I got Lindsey's hand-me-downs, which she got from the church's thrift store. So, don't even come at me like what I did was anything like that. Jacob is just fine without me."

Better probably. At least he didn't have to come home to a bitter, disappointed wife every night.

He sat up and leaned forward. His face went white. I didn't break my gaze. After a second or two he dropped his eyes and focused on the table. I watched as he struggled to find the words to respond. In the short time I'd known him, I'd never seen him unable to speak. Having the truth of what he'd done laid out so plainly must have been more than he could handle.

"I won't apologize for speaking the truth," I said when the silence became too much.

"No, I wouldn't ask you to."

"I will apologize for ruining the opportunity with the agency and with Paul. It was a juvenile mistake, and I own that."

"As long as you can start paying rent next month as originally planned, I'll consider us even."

"We won't even be close to even, but you'll get the rent."

"It's $1,200 a month, and I trust you realize what a bargain that is. The going rate for a one-bedroom condo in the RBX building is at least three times that."

"I appreciate your generosity." I didn't bother hiding the snark in my voice. "I've already had a job offer, so don't worry about me. Or, should I say, don't start worrying about me."

"I've always worried about you, Abby. I've got to get to work. I'll be in touch." He sounded tired and ready to be done with this conversation.

He stood and hovered beside me for a moment as though he were unsure how to end things. We'd met at least once a week since I'd moved here, but our greetings and partings remained awkward. Today was almost as painful as our first coffee date. *Almost.*

I glanced up at him, and our eyes met. There was a sadness in them I hadn't noticed before. Had it always been there, or was this new? When I didn't stand to offer my hand or a hug, he gave a soft exhale and gathered his coffee and briefcase. "I wish I could do it all again, Abby; I really do. But more than anything, I wish I could tell you everything."

I let the question of what he'd meant by that linger in my mind before shoving it aside. Whatever he had to say didn't matter, I reasoned. He'd left, plain and simple. I held my breath as I watched him walk away. The lump in my throat rose until it escaped my lips in the tiniest of sobs. I clenched my mouth and shut my eyes, not daring to allow anything else to escape. No tears. He didn't deserve any emotion from me.

The sweetness of my latte wasn't enough to drown the bitterness he'd left in me. I pulled out the notebook I used to write down ideas for songs or random notes on people watching. My sister called it my "burn book," but I called it my "ideas for humanity" book. I chewed the end of my pen for a moment before writing *I wish I could do it all again. I wish I could tell you everything.*

I traced my fingers over the tiny indentations left by the blue ink pen. I didn't know what he'd meant by those words and didn't care. He was right, he couldn't take any of it back. Not the hunger or ache I felt in his absence. Not the hole he left that I'd been trying to fill ever since.

I dropped my pen and notebook back into my purse and pulled out the paper I'd written Noah's number on. I didn't have enough to cover rent in the bank, and I was fairly certain Akerman & Carlisle had no intention of releasing my final paycheck. As much as I didn't want to spend my nights waiting tables and surrounding myself with other wannabe songwriters and musicians, I needed a paycheck more. Serving would put cash in my pocket, even if it stole my pride and will to live.

CHAPTER FIVE

NEITHER NOAH NOR THE GULCH DIVE BAR LOOKED MUCH DIFFERENT at eight in the morning than they had at two in the afternoon. As I walked into the empty restaurant, I wondered if he really needed a waitress or if he was just being nice when he offered. Either way, I had zero intention of turning him down. Dad had made it clear that he expected the rent money, and as much as I hated handing him a single dime, I didn't want to prove him right. I intended to take care of my financial obligations, even if he hadn't done the same. Besides, I may be a screw up, but I wasn't going to run back to Missouri with my tail tucked between my legs because my own father evicted me. Failure was always an option, but I was going to do whatever it took to make sure I never failed that hard.

It wasn't that they wouldn't welcome me with open arms, they would. Well, everyone but Jacob. I could easily come home and take up residence in the two-bedroom duplex my mom now shared with Grandma. I could work at the bar everyone worked at in Wishing, the one that had paid for college, until I was able to beg for my old job back at the radio station. I could help Mom in her makeshift garden and watch the twins for Lindsey. I could pack it all up right now and head straight back into a life of discontent with predictable routines.

The problem now, just like it had been then, was I no longer wanted any of that. I needed to be more than Jacob's wife or Sue Monroe's daughter. I wasn't the homecoming queen anymore. The watchful eyes of a small town weren't the loving gaze I was after. There was more to the world than closed minds and stereotypical expectations, and I had every intention of exploring every possibility in front of me.

Even if it meant becoming a stereotype in Nashville.

The door alarm chimed above me as I held the door open. I let it shut behind me and stood in the quiet stillness of the empty space. Looking around, I didn't see Noah. He'd assured me the door would be unlocked and he'd be waiting for me.

"Noah? It's Abby. We talked on the phone a few minutes ago?" I called into the empty space. I ignored the nagging racing of my heart and the voice that kept insisting I didn't need to wait tables to make it.

"In the back," he yelled back. I followed the sound of his voice and found him in the cooler, knee-deep in beer kegs. "Glad you called."

"Desperate times," I replied.

He laughed and said, "Let me wash up, and I'll meet you in the office." He pointed behind him and nodded. I left him to do whatever one does with beer kegs and made my way to the office. The kitchen, if you could even call it that, was a minimalist's dream. A single flat-top grill that looked like the ones I'd seen on *Diners, Drive-ins, and Dives* stood next to a two-basket fryer. A reach-in cooler was the only other piece of equipment in the kitchen. As I glanced around, I realized food was an afterthought. Gulch Dive Bar was all about the liquor. The bar out in the dining room had been well stocked but walking through the back of the house, it felt more like a liquor store than a restaurant. There was no way he needed a full wait staff.

"What do you think?" he asked as he sat down. His eyes beamed when they met mine. It was clear he was proud of the space he'd created at Gulch Dive Bar. I tried to hide my shock at how small an operation it truly was.

"Do you serve food?"

"We make our own chips and salsa," he said with a laugh, "and I can fry up a mean basket of chicken tenders and fries if anyone ever orders it."

"How many waitresses do you have?" I wasn't sure I wanted to know the answer.

"Three. My fiancée, Claire, works nights with Jessie or Leah usually working a mid-shift."

"And you need four?" He didn't even flinch at my incredulous tone.

"Yeah, especially heading into the weekend, and to cover for when someone needs a night off. I've been looking for a replacement for Shanna for two months now."

"Shanna?" I wished he'd stop dropping names I'd never remember.

He rolled his eyes and said, "Another one lost to the charms of One-Night-Stand Derrick." His voice dripped with disdain.

"Your cousin?" I asked, the name sounded somewhat familiar from our earlier conversation.

"The one and only, which leads to the one rule I have here."

"Don't drink on the shift?" He shook his head. "Don't steal?"

"One rule that isn't common sense," he clarified. He stared at me with a look of expectation as if he were waiting for me to fill in the answer to the question he hadn't asked. I had nothing. "Any guesses?"

I shook my head and glanced around the office. The silence between us grew louder and louder with each passing second. I wasn't in the mood for guessing games. I just wanted to get this interview over with. My knee bounced up and down, rocking my entire body. Why was I so nervous? I'd waited tables before. I could handle a few drink orders. This was nothing compared to leading client pitches or ad meetings. Noah and his bar were rattling me nonetheless.

"Don't fuck Derrick," he said after a long minute of silence. His tone startled me. My eyes grew wide as I waited for him to explain.

Don't fuck Derrick!? Why would I?

"Excuse me?" I asked. If my heart had been racing before, it damn near stopped now. My cheeks flushed. I wasn't a Puritan by any means, but I wasn't used to such direct, vulgar language coming from a potential boss. Especially not one that was issued as an order against fornicating with the co-owner of the very bar I was interviewing to work in.

"I'm serious, Abby. You may see yourself as above all this, but this one is important. I can't keep swapping waitresses in and out because he can't keep his hands to himself and girls can't seem to resist him."

"Um, sure, no problem." I stuttered and blinked at him; I was more than a little offended that he felt the need to say this to me. I was here for a job, not a good or bad lay.

"Okay with that out of the way, why don't you tell me about your waitressing experience?" He resumed his all-business pose. I took a deep breath and tried to recover from the shock of his rule announcement.

"Well, like I said the other day, I don't have much. I waited tables in high school at a pancake house in my hometown. Then in college, I worked at Lace & Grit, which is a bar, but they served a wider menu than yours."

"Anything recently?"

"Nope," I said. I forced a smile and swallowed my pride. Truth was, I needed this job just as much as he needed me. "I've mostly been in marketing and advertising since then. But I'm excited about getting back to my roots."

He laughed. I offered a half-smile that I hoped convinced him I was only being a little sarcastic.

"How quick can you learn a menu?"

"How big is the menu? I'm pretty sure I can handle chips and salsa and chicken fingers. See, already memorized."

"Drinks. We have a full wine, beer, liquor, and cocktail menu."

"I mean, I don't have a photographic memory, but I'm pretty sure I can remember names or whatever."

"Names, ingredients, shot ounces, and garnishes. You won't be making drinks, but you'll need to know every drink on the menu."

"Are you sure you want to hire someone without much experience?" I asked. It wasn't that I didn't want the job but more that I didn't want to screw up another one. Noah seemed like an okay guy who, perhaps, put a little too much faith into people he didn't know. I wasn't about to be another letdown for him.

"Look, Abby, I'll be honest, you wouldn't be my first choice, but I'm a sucker for a lost cause."

I bristled at the casual way he insulted me for a second time. Sitting back, I folded my arms across my chest and stared at him. Now, I wanted the job. I wanted it more than anything, and I wanted to smack that stupid, smug look off of his face.

"That came out wrong," he said and leaned forward, "what I mean is, I've seen a lot of people walk into my bar who were on the verge of giving up on their dreams. I don't know you or the songs you want to write, Abby, but I do believe that every dreamer should have a shot at actually chasing that dream. Based on what you said the other day, you haven't had that chance yet. Sure, waiting tables at a bar won't get you there, but the people you meet here might help."

I let his words roll over me and sink in. He wasn't wrong.

"Plus, I think you'll do well here. It won't be easy, and you'll go home dead tired every night, but you'll be surrounded by people just like you. People who left their small towns and lives in search of something bigger."

"How old are you?" The question leapt from my mouth before I could stop it. Noah looked to be about my age but spoke like someone on the other end of retirement.

"I'm thirty-six, why?"

"How do you have it so together?"

He laughed and said, "I'm a really good actor. But in all seriousness, growing up like I did and with the family I had, you don't really have a choice but to grow up and be responsible. Though, my dad would tell you that running a bar isn't the most respectable or responsible job to choose. But we hold our own."

"Noah," I said and took a deep breath, "I can't promise I won't disappoint you but if you're willing to take a chance on me, I'll do the best I can."

"Can you start today? I'll have you shadow Claire. Friday nights are a little crazy, but you'll get a good glimpse into what to expect."

"Sure, what time?"

"Two," he replied and handed me a menu. "Study this in the meantime."

I took the menu from him and thanked him. He rattled off a list of things I'd need to bring in in order for him to set me up on the payroll. I listened and made a mental checklist.

"Seriously, Noah, thank you for this. I'll see you in a few hours."

"Make sure you pull your hair up… closed-toed shoes, jeans, and a black tank top. Maybe something with a little less… cat hair on it."

I glanced down at my shirt and brushed away a stray piece of Niles's hair. "Got it. See you tonight."

CHAPTER SIX

THE HIGH OF LANDING A NEW JOB LASTED THE ENTIRE TWO-MINUTE
ride up to my condo. I hadn't had a long commute to the agency but
working just twelve floors down from home was going to be incredibly
convenient. I might even be able to sell my car if I needed to make up
the rent. The instant the word "rent" popped into my head, everything
came crashing down. The weight of it clung tightly to my neck and
shoulders. I closed my eyes and waited for it to pass. When it didn't, I
pushed open the door to my condo and inhaled the stale air.

I hadn't talked to Mom since Thursday morning. I was starting to
miss her voice. Between getting served with divorce papers, meeting
Noah, having coffee with Dad, and getting a new job, it seemed like
more than a day and a half had passed. A quick glance at the clock
confirmed I had less than four hours to set my head right and get
presentable for my first shift at Gulch Dive Bar. I pulled the menu
Noah had given me from my purse and grabbed a glass of water.

My balcony was my favorite space in my entire condo. It was tiny
and barely had enough room for me, a chair, and a small side table.
Niles loved to walk too close to the edge and terrify me. So, I'd
rearranged the furniture to block his access as much as possible
because he hated being stuck inside when I was outside. We hadn't

exactly reached a compromise on his daredevil antics, but we made it work. I tucked my feet beneath me as I sat down and pulled the menu to my chest. I needed to at least familiarize myself with the menu; I owed Noah as much after he took a big risk in hiring me.

The city I'd chosen as my home was alive and thriving just twelve floors down. Laughter and random voices filtered up through the symphony of cars and construction that seemed to the theme song of music city. From my balcony, I counted no less than ten cranes on any given day. Now I wondered how many were constructing the buildings Noah's uncle owned.

My family had never owned anything aside from hand-me-down cars and clothes. Not the trailer I grew up in, the land it was on, or the duplex my mom was in now. None of it was ours. I was used to being handed a rotten lemon and asked to make something of it. We were scrappy, as my grandmother liked to say. With this reminder, I opened the menu and started scanning for familiar items.

My four years with Rayna at Lace & Grit gave some basic under-standing of cocktails but her small-town bar menu was nothing compared to the five-page beer, wine, spirit, and cocktail menu Gulch Dive Bar offered. I ran my finger up and down each page and mumbled the names and ingredients to myself. On the wine page my finger stopped cold. *Barefoot Cabernet.* The name lingered in my mouth long enough for my memory to pull me away from my balcony in Nashville and back to Missouri.

"Are you sure you can order that?" Jacob had asked when I ordered a single glass of the cheapest cabernet Rayna had.

"I'm one day late, Jacob. I'm sure it's fine." I'd been short with him ever since I'd realized my always-dependable cycle wasn't making her expected appearance. "One day."

"I'm not comfortable with you drinking right now." He looked up from the table and narrowed his eyes. "You're never late, and we both know—"

"Know what?" I asked. "That you forgot to wear a fucking condom? That I missed two stupid pills?"

I was well aware of our recent birth control failures. We'd been arguing about them for two weeks now. It was all his fault. He knew that, and I knew it. I knew without a doubt that I'd packed my pills in my overnight bag. I've never forgotten them. Not once in the ten years I'd been on them. Not when he begged me to stop taking them. Not when I went away for weekend trips with my friends. Not when I went out of town for work. But most certainly not when I was going to spend a weekend babysitting my niece and nephew. My sister's twins were the best birth control reminder. I'd packed them. It wasn't even a question. Yet, when I went to pull them out before bed that night, they were gone.

He denied doing it, but I could always tell when he was lying. Jacob pulled them out of my bag and put them back into the medicine cabinet. There was no other explanation. Then, a week later, he conveniently poured me a bottle of wine and forgot to wrap it up when he seduced me.

No. It was too convenient. Too on-brand for my husband.

"Did you pick up the test?" His voice was barely above a whisper. Our hometown wasn't exactly keen on keeping secrets.

I nodded. "I'll take it tomorrow. Tonight, I'm drinking this wine."

"Would it be so bad?" he'd asked.

"Would what be so bad? Me drinking one measly glass of wine?"

"No," he'd said and sighed, "if the test were positive."

I sat back, exasperated. "Do you want to do this right now?"

"We're already fighting, so why not?" he spat back.

"Yes, Jacob, it would be '*that bad*.'"

"Why?"

"I don't want kids."

"You used to."

"That was a lifetime ago." He wasn't wrong. There was a time we used to daydream about a house full of kids. Then my dreams got bigger, that town got smaller, and I changed my mind. Though, I never really knew if the dream had ever been mine to begin with or if it had been his alone and I'd just absorbed it into my being.

"What about what I want?"

"I've told you what my compromise is."

"I'm not moving to Nashville," he'd said and laughed. "You need to let that one go, Abs. Our life is here in Wishing. *Our* life."

His life, I silently corrected him. I wasn't so sure my life was there anymore. Or, that my life was part of his.

"What about my dreams?" I'd asked. Heat rose into my cheeks as my entire body flushed.

"Of what? Being a songwriter? I can't believe you're still on that. Those ridiculous teenage dreams are just that, Abby. You're supposed to let go of them and move on. We're almost thirty; don't you think it's time to grow up?"

Grow up? I had grown up. I'd settled down. I'd put on the white dress and promised to grow old with him. I'd gone along and picked out the starter home. I'd slipped into my big girl pants and gotten a real job. I'd kept my dreams tame. But the longer I ignored the call, the louder it became. At night while my husband slept, I crawled out of bed and sat in our garage and scribbled out lyrics and fumbled over chords. My dreams had never died. They just faded a bit. I wasn't about to let him snuff out the embers that remained.

"You get that right? Your life is here. It's time to face reality." He reached across the table to take my hand into his. I pulled it back. I didn't want to face his reality because I refused to believe it was mine. "Jesus, what happened to us?"

I flinched and opened my mouth to fire back a retort, but I didn't have the fight anymore. I needed an answer to the question lingering between us. Rather than launch into another argument that would end in a stalemate, I placed my hand back into his. "It's Christmas Eve. I don't want to fight."

He hedged for a moment as he studied me. I felt the intensity of his gaze but didn't pull back like I normally did. "I'm sorry, you're right. I love you, you know that, right?"

I nodded, unable to say the words back. "You know what, I'll just take an iced tea and fried pickles," I said and gathered my purse. "I'll be right back."

He offered a weak smile and nodded. Inside my purse, the pregnancy test I'd bought early in the day felt as though it were a boulder pulling me down. I hadn't planned on buying one. My drive into Springfield, the largest town within an hour's drive of Wishing, was intended to be a last-minute Christmas shopping trip with Mom, but in true Sue Monroe fashion, she cancelled just as I pulled down her street. When I finished my shopping, I stopped into Walgreens and grabbed a single digital EPT. One test. That was all I needed.

Once in the safety and privacy of the bathroom, I removed the test from the packaging, careful to not drop it. I stared down at it and tried to force all of my bitterness into the thick plastic. I slid my jeans down to my ankles and positioned myself over the toilet.

"Don't let me down," I whispered to myself and prayed for a negative. I sat on the toilet and watched the screen. Three minutes.

One.

Two.

Three.

I could hear the music playing through the thin walls of the bathroom. My foot tapped along, and I sang softly to myself. Each note and word that passed through me brought me closer to the calm I needed. Music was my home. It always had been and always would be. When the results appeared, I let out the breath I'd been holding and dropped the test into the trash.

On my way back to the table, I ran into our waitress and said, "I'll take that glass of wine."

"Barefoot Cabernet?" she asked. I nodded and returned to Jacob.

"Everything okay?" he asked.

I plastered a fake smile over my face in an attempted peace offering. "Everything is fantastic."

"So?" he asked, reading me. He wasn't dumb. He'd watched me carry my purse into the bathroom. Like me, he'd probably counted down the minutes. He knew.

"Negative," I replied without hesitation.

The smile he'd plastered on faded. "Oh."

For a moment, I let his disappointment linger between us. I took it in and sifted it through my heart and mind and tried to find the balance between his dreams and mine. As he mourned the loss of the baby he'd been certain he'd given me, I relished the revelation I'd just had. It was then I knew that the *us* I'd been clinging to no longer existed. The Jacob I'd fallen in love with wasn't the same man that sat across from me. We'd sat together at that very table nearly every Friday night for fourteen years. We shared our first kiss in the parking lot of that bar. Our first drink as legal adults had been at that same table. We celebrated our engagement and wedding in that bar.

So, it was fitting that I decided to end us in that very spot. In hindsight, I should have told him goodbye. I should have told him the truth. I should have been strong enough to face our problems head on, but I wasn't. It was then that I finally understood what my father had done all those years ago. I didn't belong to Wishing any more than I belonged to Jacob. I wasn't the Abby he'd fallen in love with. We'd both changed. Our dreams changed. I was just the first one to find the strength to do something about it.

I blinked away the tear that had formed in the corner of my eye and turned my attention back to the menu in front of me. I shook my head and shoved my last memories of my marriage and my husband aside.

CHAPTER SEVEN

I TUGGED AT MY BLACK SHIRT AND SMOOTHED IT OVER MY STOMACH. When I'd scanned my closet earlier, I'd been disappointed to realize I didn't actually have a black tank top that fit. So, I'd had to make a last-minute run to a boutique down the block. I still couldn't believe I'd been forced to spend $25 for a tank top that would have cost $3 at Walmart. Just in case I needed another reminder that zero income was not conducive to the downtown Nashville life that I was hoping to continue.

"You must be Abby." A young woman with striking platinum hair greeted me. "I'm Jessie."

She held out her hand, and I took it. "I am." I tried to shut up the jealous voice that immediately started comparing my own dirty blonde hair and brown eyes to her long white, platinum hair and piercing blue eyes. I reminded myself that I was above petty girl rivalries. I was not, however, above the tiny girl crush I already felt forming as Jessie grabbed my arm.

"Oh, thank God. You look sane and normal. You are sane and normal, right?"

"Depends on the day," I said. She let out a loud laugh and pulled me back to the bar.

"You know Noah," she said, and Noah nodded a silent hello. "This is Leah and Claire."

I smiled and waited for the two brunettes to indicate who was who. When neither spoke up, I glanced at their hands. The girl with the pixie cut and high cheekbones had a massive diamond ring on her left hand. "Claire?" I guessed. I gave a quick glance to Noah who blushed slightly. Yes, the pixie-haired brunette was his fiancée. "You must be Leah."

She nodded and scowled. "I'm not training her, Noah. I suffered through the last stray you brought in. She looks like she's never even tasted whiskey."

"Be nice," Noah said, his voice taking on a fatherly warning tone. "And, I can assure you Abby here is familiar with whiskey."

"She's with me," Claire said and slipped off the barstool. She tossed Noah an unreadable look and then turned to me. "Look, my rent is due tomorrow, and I don't have the time or patience to apologize to people all night on your behalf. So, try to pay attention and just learn."

So much for a warm welcome. "I'll do my best."

"Alright, new girl, tell us, what's in the Lower Broad?" Jessie asked. She didn't look up from her perfectly manicured fingernails. They were a deep shade of blood red and filed into sharp points. I couldn't decide whether I wanted to be her friend or just become her. Either way, she intimidated me, and my mouth went dry.

"Um," I said and stuttered out my response, "one shot of Malibu, triple sec, and pineapple juice, and garnished with a cherry."

"Nashville Mule," Leah said. She was the most intimidating of the three, between her initial greeting and the chill in her voice, I hoped I wouldn't have to work too closely with her. But her soft face and perfectly curled hair told me she wasn't as hardened to the bar life as she seemed.

"Vodka, ginger beer, and lime juice."

"Garnish?" Claire asked.

My mind went blank, and I shrugged. The three women glanced at each other and then at Noah as if to say, "We told you so."

"Cut her some slack, she got the menu a few hours ago. Claire, can you give her a tour and run through the table assignments? Jessie and Leah, make sure the bar is stocked."

"Sure thing, boss," Jessie said and grabbed Leah's arm. I watched as they disappeared into the back.

"Don't worry, she won't bite," Claire said with a smirk, "hard."

I nodded and turned my attention to the bar. I tried to study it with a new set of eyes. I'd be spending a lot of time here, and I needed to memorize it.

"This is our section," she said and led me to a collection of eight tables near the front. "Tables 10 through 18." She pointed at each one and counted them off. "Leah has the high tops in the bar and Jessie mans the tables around the stage."

"Where will I be?" I wasn't quite sure where I'd fit into the mix once I finished training.

"We'll worry about that when you pass the trial."

"Got it," I said and followed her back to the bar. She pulled out a menu and opened it to the happy hour section.

"Happy hour is short on Fridays, from four to five. We'll have a few tables, mostly business assholes and moms taking the edge off before heading home to their screaming children and sexless marriages."

I snorted. "Sounds about right."

"You married?" she asked and looked down at my hand. I rubbed my finger over the deep tan line left by fourteen years of a promise ring, engagement ring, and wedding band.

"Separated," I said, swallowing back the lump that had lodged itself in my throat, "and soon to be divorced."

"Fun." I waited for her to ask more questions, but she didn't.

"So, how can I best help you tonight without getting in your way?"

"Listen to what I say, keep moving, and don't flirt with the customers."

"Easy enough." I stood beside her and rocked from one foot to the other. "When does the crowd hit?"

"After happy hour, we'll see a slow trickle of the pre-gaming crowd. These are mostly locals and people that live in the RBX. Noah mentioned you lived in the building."

I could tell by the deep judgment in her eyes that she assumed I was some spoiled rich kid. "Yeah. I'm renting."

"Cool."

If Claire was curious to know more about me or my story, she didn't let on. Instead, she launched into a monologue about Gulch Dive Bar and my future role as a waitress. She grilled me about the menu and how to greet customers. In the kitchen, she showed me how to fry up the chips and portion the salsa. It appeared this would be my primary duty tonight. She'd greet the customers and introduce me as her trainee, then I was to do exactly as she said.

Easy enough, I thought. As the crowd started pouring in, I wasn't surprised to see Claire's description of each wave and who to expect had been spot-on. We served up draft beers and glasses of cheap wine during happy hour and then shifted to cocktails and shots as the night progressed. I smiled as the three women interacted and their roles and personalities started to come through.

Jessie was brash and unapologetic. She flirted with every table and had a smile that could diffuse pretty much any situation. For her part, Leah was efficient and fast. She darted around the dining room like a woman on a mission. She smiled on demand and laughed at the stupid jokes her customers shared. Claire was an odd mixture of the two. She saved her flirting for Noah, and it was clear he worked overtime to avoid showing her any favoritism, but Jessie called him on it if he made Claire's drinks before hers.

As I trailed behind Claire and took in my new coworkers, I couldn't help but wonder where and how I'd fit in. I wasn't bold or assertive. I didn't want to laugh at lame jokes or swat away the roaming hands of drunk frat boys. When I moved here, I never imagined I'd lose five years of progress and go right back to making $2.13 an hour and begging for tips. Though, based on the wads of cash I'd watched the girls shove into their pockets, I had a feeling the tourists and residents of Nashville were a bit more generous than the townsfolk in Wishing.

"Abby!" Claire shouted across the dining room. I grabbed a basket of chips and rushed back to table 11. "I need you to grab the drinks for table 15."

My eyes grew wide. I was on chip duty tonight. I'd grown comfortable with dropping baskets into the fryer and dishing out two ounces of greasy, homemade goodness. I was not prepared to deliver drinks to a table of already drunk bachelorettes.

"Now!" she shouted and returned her attention to the table in front of her.

I wiped my hands over my apron and sucked in a deep breath. *You can do this, Abby; it's just drinks.* I made my way through the crowded space and let the low rumble of voices seep into my ears. The music blaring from the speakers thrummed a steady beat that calmed me. I didn't know why I was so nervous. I was more than capable of delivering cocktails. I'd done it hundreds of times at Lace & Grit, but this was different. I wanted to impress Claire and prove that I'd earned my job.

"Two margaritas, a Nashville Mule, and a Bridal Shower," Noah said as he slid the tray with filled-to-the-brim cocktails towards me. "Don't worry, Abby, they're just drinks; they won't bite."

"Do I look that nervous?" I asked with a laugh.

"A little. Just drop off the drinks and maybe Claire will upgrade you to ice duty."

"Funny." I slipped my left hand under the tray and used my right hand to steady it. The weight of the drinks felt safe in my hands. *Just like riding a bike.* I smiled at Noah. With the tray carefully balanced in my hand, I weaved through the crowd. Jessie stepped out of my way and made room for me and Leah to pass.

"You're a natural," Jessie said with a wink. I smirked and let her confidence in me fuel me.

I sighed with relief when I reached table 15. "Guessing the Bridal Shot is yours?" I asked the young, red-haired woman with a tiara encrusted with rhinestone penises. She offered a drunken nod and reached for the drink. The abrupt movement of her hand startled me, and I stepped back. My right heel caught on the chair and tangled. I tried to brace myself but lost the battle with gravity and tumbled backwards.

"No!" Claire's voice pierced through the air. I attempted to grip the tray and steady it, but it slipped off my hand and crashed onto the table. Tequila, lime, creme of coconut, vodka, and a menagerie of other fluids spewed from the cascading glasses. I flinched as the glass shattered and ricocheted off the floor.

Before I hit the ground, Jessie was at my side. She grabbed my arm and held me up. When the drinks finished falling, she pulled me upright. My shirt and jeans were drenched, both clung to me. When I dared to lift my eyes, I found Claire standing in front of me. Her face red, her nostrils flared, and her eyes wide with a mixture of rage and disappointment.

"Are you fucking kidding me?" Penis Tiara shouted. She flung her hands at her side. She'd taken most of the margaritas and had a lime wedge resting in her cleavage. The girls around the table sat stunned, mouths open. The girl to her right dropped her lower lip into a pout as the other two cracked wide smiles and burst into a fit of giggles.

Their laughter was the only sound in the dining room. I didn't dare move my gaze from Claire's face.

"Go," she growled through gritted teeth. "GO!"

Jessie tugged my arm and guided me to the back.

"I really fucked up. Shit. Shit. Shit." I shook my head.

"It's okay. It happens."

"To me, yeah. I bet you've never dropped a tray of drinks on Claire's table. She's going to hate me."

"Probably," Jessie said and handed me a towel, "but she'll get over it. Trust me, she's seen you hustling tonight. You're working hard like the rest of us."

"Yeah, frying chips and chasing after her, trying to learn."

"It's your first day, go easy on yourself."

"What the fuck was that?" Claire burst into the back room. She nudged Jessie out of the way. "I told you not to screw with my tips. Now I have to comp an entire table."

"I'm sorry," I said and dropped my gaze. "I'll cover it."

"Not necessary," Noah said. He placed his hand on Claire's shoulder and nodded at her. "Abby, why don't you head home, clean up, and come back tomorrow."

Claire shook her head and said, "I'm not training her again."

"She'll be with me," Jessie offered. Claire seethed beside her. "Okay? You saw her busting her ass. It's not like none of us have never done that. Besides, that girl tried to grab the drinks off the tray. So, it wasn't like Abby klutzed out or did it on purpose."

"Fine," Claire said and left us alone.

"At least let me go clean up the mess," I said.

"No, we've got it. If you don't get out of those clothes soon, you'll be a sticky nightmare. We've got it, Abby, go home."

"I'm sorry, Noah."

"Don't worry about it.

"You sure?" I asked.

"Yes, see you tomorrow at two."

I waited for a beat or three and tried to get a read on him, but he just kept smiling. Finally, I nodded and thanked him and Jessie. When I passed Claire in the dining room, she didn't even look at me. Leah scowled as she knelt on the floor and wiped up the mess I'd left.

Perfect, Abby, way to stay on-brand.

CHAPTER EIGHT

I survived the weekend and spent my days off on Monday and Tuesday moping and ignoring my mother's calls. I couldn't bear to face the disapproval in her voice when she learned I'd taken a job at a bar after snubbing my nose at her suggestion of coming back and working for Rayna. Another thing I avoided all weekend? The manila envelope with my divorce papers. They sat on the counter and stared at me. I hadn't even opened the envelope. I knew there was nothing but a steaming pile of shit inside them.

On Tuesday, I remembered that Wednesday was the open mic night at the bar. I pulled my guitar out of the closet where I'd sent it to think about all the tunes it hadn't played and reflect on its decision to remain silent. The fact that I was the one responsible for playing it wasn't the point. I was more than willing to place all the blame on this ancient, inanimate object. I, Abby Monroe Rhodes, have no shame.

It was with the complete lack of shame that I sauntered into the bar on Wednesday night fully prepared to grovel for Claire's forgiveness. She'd given me the cold shoulder all Saturday and Sunday while I trailed behind Jessie and managed to somehow keep all the drinks in their glasses. When I came through the doors, I found Jessie, Noah, and Claire huddled together at the bar.

"Hey," I said. The first word I'd spoken out loud in two days caught in my throat.

"Ready for open mic?" Jessie asked with a tinge of sarcasm. "We're just looking over the lineup and taking bets on who pukes, chokes, or sucks ass. Want to join us?"

Claire snorted and turned to me. I tensed and retreated under her gaze. When she saw my reaction, she softened long enough for me to utter yet another apology.

"It's okay," she said after a pause, "I made my rent. And, I gotta give you props for showing up after that disaster."

I didn't really have much choice in the matter, but I'd spent Saturday morning weighing my non-existent options.

"So, we're good?"

"Sure, we're good."

I sighed and turned to Noah. "Am I on my own tonight?" I wasn't certain I was ready to field my own section, but I knew Leah was off, and I was getting sick of eating off-brand canned spaghetti for dinner. I needed the tips.

"You'll be in section three, tables 5 through 10." Jessie gestured behind her. "It's a shit section tonight because that's where all the *'artists'* sit." She threw air quotes around the word "artists" and rolled her eyes.

"Oh," I said and glanced around her to try and place which tables were where.

"They'll be needy, thirsty, and broke. So be prepared to pour a shit ton of ice water, stroke a few dozen fragile egos, and go home with pennies."

"They aren't that bad," Noah said.

"No, they're worse. Almost as bad as the church crowd on Sunday," Leah said.

I shuddered. In my days at Lace & Grit, I'd begged Rayna to let me wear a button or shirt that said "Jesus would tip 20%." But she never caved, and I went home every Sunday broker than I'd started the day and with a little less faith in humanity.

"Can I see the list?" I asked. Not that I'd know any of the names, but I was curious. Jessie handed me the clipboard.

"So, the way we do it," Noah said as I read, "is we take sign-ups through Friday. They can sign up on our website or in person. In-person gets preference. If we hit the max, we roll to the next week. We aren't the Bluebird, but we get a decent turnout."

I scanned down the list. The only names I recognized were Leah's and Derrick Bale, Noah's cousin, whom I'd been forbidden from fornicating with.

"Looking for your name?" Claire asked. I glanced up at her startled. "What? Noah mentioned you were a songwriter, too."

"Oh, I mean, yeah, I guess," I stuttered. Flames rushed through me and flushed my skin.

"Ready?" Jessie asked and pulled me over to my tables. She ran down how the night would go and went through the names on the list, described them, and shared their usual drink order. "Normally, this is Leah's section but since you're here, she took the night off to prep for her song tonight."

"Is everyone here a songwriter or musician?" I asked.

"Sort of. I dabble but just for fun. Claire and Noah both used to play, but I don't know the story there. Noah's cousin and Leah are two of our more regular participants."

"Derrick?" I asked. His was the last name on the list.

"Oh, yeah, Derrick." She rolled her eyes.

"Why does everyone say his name like that?"

"Like what?"

"Like you hate and love him all at the same time and in two slow, painful breaths."

"I'll let you figure that one out on your own. He always comes in last and closes out the night. Then, he sticks around and harasses Noah while pretending to sweep the floor. It's his one and only contribution as a co-owner."

I nodded and pretended to understand. In reality, I had no idea what to expect tonight or with Derrick.

Around six, the real crowds started flowing in. This wasn't the usual happy hour crowd. Bachelorette party after bachelorette party filed through the doors. They brought a loud roar of giggles and curse words with them. Noah and Jessie had warned me about this. I served far too many novelty drinks and answered questions about who I'd seen wandering downtown (no one). A few asked if I was a songwriter, and I stuttered through my own answer. Most just wanted to know who was singing that night and if they'd get to see the next Taylor Swift. I'd just shrug, take their drink order, and smile.

Open mic started at eight, and the girls hadn't been wrong. My tables soon filled with nervous, eager, and sensitive musicians who ordered water by the pitcher and fretted over scribbled lyrics. By the time the first person graced the stage, I'd barely managed to pocket $30 in tips.

It was going to be a long night.

"How's your first solo night going?" Leah asked. I hadn't noticed her come in.

"Okay, so far."

"I see they left you with the shit section tonight."

I shrugged. Sure, I wasn't making money, but it was kind of nice to not have to deal with bachelorettes and drunken assholes. I could stroke egos and reassure the stage-frightened musicians.

"You're up next?" I asked.

"Yeah," she said with a shy smile. "I do this every week, and every single week, the butterflies overtake my stomach."

"I'm sure you're going to be great," I said for the fifteen time that night. In the short time that I'd known Leah, I'd never once seen her nervous or unsure of herself. It was jarring.

"Oh, I know I will."

I smiled and turned my attention to my remaining tables and the nervous guy in overalls who was trying his best to remember the lyrics to the song I was certain he'd just penned about Jessie. I caught her eye and laughed when she winked back. She flipped her long platinum hair over her shoulder and blew a kiss to the guy. I bit back a giggle when he stuttered and forgot the words again.

By the time he was finished, Leah was already standing at the side of the stage. Her black guitar hung loosely across her chest. I watched as she closed her eyes and mumbled something to herself. If she was anything like me, she was probably running through her song. It had been at least a year since I sang in front of a crowd, and it hadn't even been one of my own. I flinched at the memory.

It had been Jacob and my fourteenth anniversary, our fifth as husband and wife. His parents and my mom threw us a surprise party and plied me with champagne before asking me to sing the song I'd sung to him during our ceremony. My husband tried to stop them, insisting he didn't want to embarrass me. He'd told them I didn't sing anymore. As he argued in my *defense*, I'd retrieved my old guitar from the bedroom and returned to belt out the song we'd once danced and made love to. I'll never be able to forget the look of disgust on his face. In his mind, my guitar was the one thing that stood in the way of his dreams of fatherhood.

Leah took a deep breath and strummed the first chord. Jessie came up beside me and bumped her hip into mine.

"She's amazing," she whispered into my ear.

When I turned to smile at her, the front door opened, and my breath caught in my chest. I glanced around the room to see if anyone else had noticed but every set of eyes was locked on Leah. Her voice and her acoustic guitar had the entire room captivated; everyone but me. My attention was locked on the door and the majestic specimen of the male species that was sauntering through it.

I let my gaze wander down his black T-shirt, tight over his tattooed biceps, and down to his ripped jeans. He held a black guitar case at his side, and by the way he walked in as if he owned the place, I knew instantly that this black-haired, gray-eyed man was Derrick. The captivating stranger I'd bumped into the first time I'd been to Gulch Dive Bar. He caught my stare and held my eyes in his for a moment. A slow half-smirk teased at his lips. My stomach flip-flopped. He recognized me, too. I watched as he waved at Noah at the bar and then nodded to Jessie.

"Need a mop?" she asked, whispering into my ear.

"Huh?" I blinked and broke my gaze. When I looked at her, she laughed.

"For all that drool." I snapped my mouth shut and swiped at it. "He's something else."

I didn't respond. For once in my life, I didn't have the words or wit to reply. Suddenly, Noah's rule made sense, and I could definitely see myself trying to break it.

Leah finished her song, and the room erupted into applause. I joined the chorus and made a quick round of table check-ins, desperate for anything that might pull my mind away from Derrick.

"How y'all doing tonight?" a deep voice boomed over the speakers. I didn't dare turn around. "Welcome to Gulch Dive Bar, I'm Derrick Bale."

He said his name as if he were confident that everyone already knew who he was. Judging by the eruption of cheers and applause, he wasn't wrong. If I'd thought they loved Leah, they were infatuated with Derrick.

"I'm going to sing a song called 'In Her Eyes' for y'all tonight," he said and winked in my direction. I stepped back and bumped into the bar. "You just may be hearing it later tonight when Beau Grant takes the stage at the Ryman."

My mouth fell open. Beau Grant was the biggest thing to hit country music since Luke Bryan. If Derrick had a cut on his new album, he was right to be overly cocky.

He strummed the first note and leaned in toward the microphone and sang the first line. "*In her eyes, I can't do wrong. In her eyes, I'm her only one.*"

Derrick Bale's deep baritone voice rolled through my ears and snaked its way through my veins, circling my heart and gripping on tight. I forgot the drinks I was waiting for and the customers waiting on them. I was transfixed by his presence. My mouth moved along with his as he sang. I didn't think I'd ever heard the song, but somehow, I already knew the words.

"*In her eyes, I'm the man I want to be,*" he sang the last line and stepped back from the microphone. His smile overtook his face as the crowd leaped to their feet and shouted their approval.

I could feel his eyes on me as he walked off the stage. Blushing, I turned my attention to Noah and the drinks he'd set up for me. I reached for the tray, but a hand landed on mine, stopping me. My skin tingled under his touch.

"You must be the new girl," Derrick said.

"Abby," I replied, not trusting myself with more words. His hand lingered over mine, and my body stiffened.

"I'll run these out," he said. "Table 6, right?"

Dumbfounded, I nodded and let him grab the tray. He smiled down at me and said, "Relax, Abby, I won't bite."

CHAPTER NINE

"Hey," Jessie said as she flopped into the chair across from me. "We're all headed down to Lower Broad to mingle with the tourists and bachelorettes, want to join us?"

I stifled a yawn and dropped the last roll of silverware into the bucket. "Who all is going?" I asked. I tried to keep my eyes down and not search the dining room for Derrick.

"All of us. Claire, Noah, me, Leah." She smirked and added, "Derrick."

I tried to ignore the tingle that ran through me at the mention of his name and said, "Oh, I don't know. I'm pretty exhausted after tonight." I wasn't great at playing coy, but I was going to give it my best shot. She'd seen the way I watched him. Everyone had. Including him.

"Alright. I won't force you, then." She stood to leave.

"Wait, do I have time to run upstairs and change?"

"Sure, meet us down here in ten? I'll get all this put up."

I thanked her and hunted down Noah so I could cash out. I found him in the office arguing with Derrick. Their voices boomed through the metal door. I lifted my hand to knock but stopped myself.

"Are you fucking kidding me?" Derrick shouted. I dropped my hand and stepped closer to the door. "Every week, man."

"Well, get your shit together, and we won't have to have this argument."

The door flung open, and I fell forward, landing right in Derrick's unsuspecting arms. "Sorry," I said, mumbling. "Noah, can I cash out?"

"Sure." He held out his hand. I dropped my cash and receipts into it. He did a quick scan of the receipt and then counted the bills. I didn't look at him or Derrick, choosing to wait in silence rather than insert myself into their fight any more than I already had. "You're good."

"Thanks." I took my tips and shoved them into my pocket.

"You are coming out with us, Missouri?" Derrick asked.

I shrugged and didn't commit to an answer. As he spoke, I felt Noah's body tense up beside me. Before they could start their argument again, I excused myself and raced out the door and up to my condo.

I couldn't explain the reaction I'd had to Derrick. Everything about him screamed "don't touch me" and "touch me, touch me, touch me," all at the same time. It was like the warmth of a bonfire on an autumn night. Your body craved the warmth and pulled you closer and closer until your brain screamed at you to stop. Except, no part of me was telling me to stop. I'd never touched fire before. I had a feeling Derrick was going to tempt me in ways I wasn't prepared for.

Once upstairs, I dove into my closet to find a clean pair of jeans and a bright, light-weight tank top. Summers in Nashville were even more humid and brutal than the ones in Missouri. Despite it being near midnight, the air outside was still heavy with stickiness. I grabbed a lacy, floral top and threw it over a pink cami. Paired with skinny jeans and my one pair of decent flats, it looked sweet and innocent. I wasn't sure that was the aesthetic I was going for, but it's what I landed on. I gave myself one final look in the mirror and pulled my hair free from its ponytail. It cascaded down around my shoulders in loose waves. I'd sweated through most of my makeup, but I didn't have time to reapply. I was already late.

I found Jessie and Derrick waiting for me in the lobby.

"The others got tired of waiting," she said.

"Are we walking or catching an Uber?" Derrick asked.

As soon as we walked outside, the thick, Southern air gripped me and drenched me in a layer of sweat. "Uber," I said.

"I need a cigarette, so I'll walk," Jessie said. "You two can Uber. We'll meet down at Legends?"

"Sure," Derrick said. He pulled out his phone to order the car. Panic seized me. I wasn't prepared to be alone with Derrick. Sure, I'd agreed to this night solely because he'd be there, but I hadn't considered this a possibility.

I opened my mouth to ask Jessie to wait but closed it just as quickly. As awkward as a solo ride with Derrick would be, the promise of air conditioning outweighed my anxiety.

"Tell me about yourself, Abby," Derrick asked me as he leaned over and bumped his shoulder into mine. Despite the stifling heat, a shiver ran through me.

"Sounds like you already know all about me. What did Noah tell you?"

"Not much, just that you're new to town, from Missouri, and a songwriter."

"That about sums me up."

"Oh, come on," he said. He turned to face me and placed his hand under my chin, lifting my face to his. He scanned my face as if he were trying to confirm my identity. "I can see there's more behind those brown eyes."

If I'd had chills before, goosebumps overtook my skin as his fingers lingered. "Not really," I whispered. "I'm your average small-town girl chasing clichés in Nashville."

"Married?" he asked and took my left hand into his. He ran his thumb over the tan line left by my ring. *Stop touching me... Don't stop touching me.* Was it possible to crave something you've never tried before?

"Divorced," I said, lying. He didn't need to know all the complicated details.

"How long?"

"A few months."

He lifted my hand to his lips and kissed it. I pulled my hand free and took a step back. Noah's words echoed through me. Derrick was a playboy. I'm sure he had more moves and tricks up his sleeve than any boy I'd ever seen. He looked at girls like me like we were his prey. He was dangerous.

My heart raced and thudded inside my chest.

"Our ride is here," he said and gestured for me to move forward.

The Uber ride was, thankfully, quick. Derrick made small talk with the Uber driver, and I stared at my phone. Jacob still hadn't texted me back or called or anything. I had no right to be hurt by this, but I was. I'd ghosted him first, but now he'd served me with divorce papers, and he couldn't even be bothered to call or check in. I know I didn't deserve either, but I couldn't help but want to hear from him. At least now I knew how he'd felt.

Noah, Claire, Leah, and Jessie were waiting for us outside Legends.

"Can we be total tourists and head over to Brewhouse for Bush-whackers?" Claire asked. She was intertwined in Noah's arms with a look of pure bliss on her face. I'd rarely seen her smile at work, but seeing her now with him, I noticed a raw, natural beauty about her. Noah seemed to be a calming force for her.

"Yes!" Jessie shouted and threw her arm in the air. "I think my buddy is working, so he can slip us some extra Bacardi."

"Ugh," I groaned. "I may stick to beer and water. Last time I got drunk on Bacardi, I ended up engaged and trapped in a small town."

The group looked at me for a second before Leah said, "Don't worry, none of us plan to propose to you tonight."

"I don't know," Jessie said with a laugh, "you're looking pretty cute in that little floral top."

Derrick slipped his arm around my waist and pulled me close. "I'll drink beers with you, Missouri."

"Thanks, I think." I tried to sound cool, casual, and unaffected, but inside I was shaking like a dog whose human just came home after a weekend trip.

I let him lead me across the street and into the bar. As soon as we walked in, Jessie transformed into a show woman. She waved at and hugged nearly everyone we saw. Claire and Noah slinked into a booth at the back of the restaurant and proceeded to get lost in each other. Leah followed Jessie to the bar.

Derrick slid into the booth across from his cousin and patted the seat next to him. I hesitated and caught Noah's eyes. They narrowed for a moment. He shook his head as if to remind me of his one and only rule. My body ignored every warning, and I gave in to Derrick's invite.

"Thanks," I said to Jessie when she slid two beers onto the table.

"Cheers to new friends," Derrick said. I lifted my glass to his and smiled.

"I'll drink to that," I said and looked at Noah. "To new *friends*."

I put the extra emphasis on "friends" for Noah. If my new boss heard me, he ignored me. His attention was back on Claire, and he didn't seem interested in what Derrick and I were talking about or doing.

"What kind of songs do you write?" Derrick asked after taking a long, slow sip of his beer.

"Lately? Silence." I laughed to show I was joking but flinched at the admission.

"Not inspired?" His gray eyes twinkled in the dim lighting. He shifted in his seat so he was facing me and leaned back into the wall.

"Let's just say my first few months in Nashville haven't been what I thought they'd be."

"What were you expecting?"

"Well, when I made the move, I was expecting a fresh start. But a few years ago, I thought I'd find my voice in Nashville and that this would be the place I was finally able to be myself."

"So, what's keeping you from being yourself?"

"Let's just say that my decision to move to Nashville was a bit spur-of-the-moment." Memories bubbled up inside of me, but I shoved them aside. As comfortable as I felt with this relative stranger, I wasn't ready to bear my soul to Derrick Bale.

"The divorce?" he asked.

I flinched and nodded. "Starting over was harder than I thought."

"Starting over isn't supposed to be easy. You have to hurt a bit to be reborn."

"Are you always like this, Mr. Miyagi?" I asked and nudged him with my leg.

"What? You think a tattooed musician can't be insightful and wise?" The intensity in his eyes sent a rush through me. I wasn't quite sure how to read him.

"That's not what I said." I let my gaze hold his for a split second before asking, "What about you, Mr. Bale? What's your story?"

"Me?" he asked and shifted slightly. "I'm just a guy with a guitar."

"And a trust fund?"

This time he flinched. He pulled away from me and lifted his beer to his lips. It took every ounce of me to not picture my lips replacing the glass.

"It's complicated."

Picking up on his discomfort, I changed the subject. "Married? Divorced? Playing the single scene?"

"No," he said. His body relaxed.

"So, the rumors aren't true?"

"Noah," Derrick said and turned to his cousin, "what have you been telling her?"

Noah shrugged but didn't look away from Claire. "The truth."

"Whose version? Yours or mine?"

Noah didn't answer. He dove right back into his conversation with Claire, ignoring us.

"What else do you want to know?" he asked.

"What will you answer? You seem to enjoy avoiding the questions."

"You've asked me two."

"And you haven't really answered either."

"You want the truth, Missouri?" he asked and leaned towards me. I nodded. "What you see isn't always what you get. There's more to people than the stories told about them."

I sensed I wasn't getting any more out of him, so I excused myself and got us both another round. When I came back, he was waiting for me. He took my hand and guided me into the booth.

"Thanks," he said and rested his hand on my knee. I tensed. This touch was different from the causal ones before. This was a soft, tender gesture. He slipped his hand away, and my body cooled from the absence of him.

Get it together, Abby.

"My music," he said, "it usually does all the speaking for me. There's a safety in the guitar. I guess it's my shield."

To anyone else, that comment would have been random, but it made sense to me. If he couldn't answer my questions with words, he'd have a melody and lyrics to share.

I slid closer to him. He kept his hands to himself, but my leg brushed against his. I wanted to give in to the pull of him. My positive to his negative. But I could feel the weight of Noah's judgement firing from across the table.

I yawned and checked my phone. It was nearing two. "I should be getting home. I have to work tomorrow, and it was a long day."

"I'll close us out and get us an Uber."

"I can get it," I argued, but he shook his head.

We rode back to my condo much the way we rode downtown. Derrick had an easy presence that seemed to invite strangers in. He was open and talked freely with everyone. This was a trait I didn't possess —not that I wanted to. Small talk was torture for me.

The car pulled up to the RBX building, and I reached for the door. Derrick jumped out and raced around the car to open it for me.

"You live here, right?" he asked. "Noah mentioned it earlier."

"Yeah, my stepmom owns the condo," I said. I'd never referred to Jenny as my stepmother before, but it was easier than sharing the messy truth. "Your dad built an incredible building."

"Yeah, I guess so," he said with an air of disgust.

There was a lot to unpack in that, and I wasn't anywhere near drunk enough to dive into it. "Did you know that I avoided the Gulch Dive Bar for my first few months here? I thought it would be too dangerous to frequent a bar within walking distance of my bed." My face flushed at the mention of my bed.

"Seems smart. I'm glad you eventually made your way in," he said as we walked into the elevator. The doors shut, and he watched for a second. "What floor?'

"Oh, twelve, sorry." I reached for the button at the same time he did. Our fingers touched. Neither one of us moved. My skin burned beneath his, and everything inside me vibrated as the elevator rose.

It stopped on my floor, and the doors opened. I cleared my throat and reached into my purse for my keys. He followed me to my door. We stood together outside it for what felt like an eternity. Neither of us spoke. My breath quickened as he reached for my hand. He slipped the keys free and used them to open the door. I stepped forward but he remained still. I turned back to face him.

"This is you," he said. His tone had a new gentleness to it. My eyes locked on his lips as he spoke. They looked soft and inviting. I'd never kissed anyone other than Jacob. He'd been the only man I'd ever been interested in. As I watched Derrick and wondered what he was thinking, I tried to imagine what his mouth would feel like against mine. Would his hands roam my body? Or would they lock around my waist and hold me close? "I enjoyed meeting you, Abby."

"Same." I was surprised that I managed to get a word out.

"I don't have your number," he said and handed me his phone. "Maybe we can meet up tomorrow before work and see if we can help you find your music again?"

I took his phone and put my number in it. "Sure."

"Great, I'll text you in the morning."

"Okay." Apparently, I'd lost my vocabulary. I couldn't seem to find more than one-word answers.

"See you tomorrow, Abby."

I smiled and leaned against the door and watched as he walked down the hallway. I wasn't sure if he'd intended to invite himself in.

I wasn't entirely sure if I'd have stopped him if he did.

CHAPTER TEN

Niles rubbed his cold, wet nose against my cheek.

"One more minute," I said and pulled the covers over my face. Niles didn't give up; he meowed and nudged his face below the blanket. "Fine, but your bowl better be empty."

I threw the covers off of me and flinched as the bright sunlight assaulted my eyes. I glanced at the clock and was shocked to see it was almost ten. I rarely slept past eight; Niles wouldn't allow it. I rubbed my hands over my face and silently thanked my past self for not going overboard on the liquor the night before. I'd been tempted to let myself give in to the call of bad decisions and liquid courage, but my common sense prevailed.

Sitting up, I grabbed my phone and did my morning check of social media, emails, and text messages. No matter how much I tried to deny it, all I wanted to find was a message from Jacob. He'd unfriended and unfollowed me sometime around Valentine's Day, so there'd be no likes or comments, that much I knew, but a tiny part of me held on to hope. I don't know why. I hadn't had it when we were still in the same bed.

It wasn't even that I wanted him back—at least, I didn't think I did —it was more that I wanted him to want me back. *I'm a selfish bitch*, I thought as I set my phone back on the nightstand and lifted myself out of bed. Just as it blinked off, it lit up again with a text.

It's Derrick. Open your door.

What? Shit. I looked down at my old T-shirt and laundry-day panties. You know the ones. Old, holey, some ugly-ass grandma pattern.

What? Now?

I fired off the reply and raced into the closet, just in case I'd read his message correctly. I vaguely remember agreeing to touch base with him about meeting up to write, but as far as I knew, I hadn't committed to a time. Niles rubbed against my leg and meowed louder. He sensed my panic had nothing to do with refilling his food bowl.

Yes. Open your door.

I grabbed the first pair of leggings I could find and ripped the faded purple Wishing High School Bobcats T-shirt off my body and threw on a cleaner, less Missouri-y shirt. I reached down to scratch Niles and said, "I'll get the door and then food. Promise."

My heart leaped into my throat when I reached for the doorknob. I closed my eyes and sucked in a deep, ragged breath before pulling it open.

"Hey," I said as casually as possible given that I was out of breath and completely flushed.

"Did I wake you up?" he asked with a smirk as he handed me a coffee. "Didn't know how you took it, so just had them make it black."

Niles mewed in response. "No, this guy did. I need to grab him some food. Come in, make yourself at home," I said and took the coffee from his outstretched hand. "Thanks."

"Sure." He knelt down and lifted Niles into his arms.

"Careful, he hates dudes," I said. In truth, he hated my dad. No other men had been in the house, but he'd made his opinion on the male species known when he scratched a gash into my dad's freshly pressed gabardine slacks.

Niles nuzzled his head under Derrick's bearded chin. "I think he likes me just fine."

"Hmm," I mumbled in response. I poured some food into his bowl and topped off his water. Normally, Niles was all over me the instant he heard the *clink clank* of his food hitting the bowl but now he nestled himself deep into Derrick's embrace. *Am I jealous of my cat? I think I'm jealous of my cat.*

Derrick set him on the ground and said, "Breakfast time, bud." Niles gave him one last look and trotted off to his food dish without even acknowledging me. I was definitely envious of him. Derrick flopped down on the couch and crossed his arms behind his head. "So, I know I said I'd call later to set up a time, but I kind of did some internet stalking of you last night and couldn't wait."

"You did what?" My eyes grew wide as I scanned every nook and cranny of my memory for what might be out on the internet that would make him need to rush over first thing in the morning.

"I stalked you. Found videos of you singing on Instagram and hoped I'd find you in those pigtails."

"Oh. My. God." I gasped and shook my head. "You didn't."

A mental image of me in my denim overalls and white tank top popped into my head. The county fair. I'd let Rayna talk me into signing up to perform and had done a few covers of some Shania Twain songs from the '90s and had finished the show with a cheesy song I'd written for Jacob. I cringed as I recalled the caption I'd posted for that one. *This song is dedicated to my high school sweetheart and life mate.* That felt like a lifetime ago.

"I did, and I have to say, Abby, you've got a great voice. That song was a few years old, though, and I'd love to hear something you've written recently."

"I told you, I haven't written so much as a lyric or a chord since I've been here."

"Where's your guitar?" When I didn't immediately answer, he got up and made his way toward my bedroom.

"I'll get it," I said and rushed past him. I was fairly certain I'd left my grandma panties on the floor in the closet. I grabbed it and carried it into the living room. "Where is yours?"

"Didn't bring it," he said with a shrug. "I'm here to get you back into a groove."

"And how do you propose we do that."

"You're going to play something for me."

"Play what?"

"Anything."

"I don't have anything."

"You wouldn't be sitting here in Nashville if that were true. You have something; you just need to find it again." I sighed and stared at him. He sat back down on the couch and stretched his legs out in front of him. I took a seat on the floor in front of him. "I've got all day."

"I have to work at three."

"Okay, we've got until three."

"So, what, you're going to stare at me for five hours?"

"If I have to, yes."

"Surely, you have something better to do with your time."

"Naw," he said and smiled. "I could stare at you all day, and it wouldn't be a waste of time."

This made me blush. I giggled and waited for the punch line, but there wasn't one. He was serious. *Oh, Jesus. He's serious.* Normally, I'd fire back a smart-ass response to ease the tension, but he didn't deserve that. So, I picked up my guitar and positioned it on my lap. My fingers trembled against the strings as I started to tune it. Sitting in the closet for half a year hadn't done my ancient instrument any favors. Derrick sat patiently as I went through the motions.

"It's like riding a bike, huh?"

"I guess so. I forgot how good this felt in my arms."

"Almost as good as sex." He smirked. I coughed and forced my gaze to stay on my guitar. He fell silent as he watched me shift from tuning to strumming. I closed my eyes and tried to focus my attention on the music and words I'd written just before making the drive to Nashville.

"*Fourteen years,*" I sang. My voice cracked at first, so I started over. *"Fourteen years. I gave you half my life and twice as many tears."*

With the first line out, the rest of the words flowed out of me as if I'd never stopped singing them. When I finished, I sat back and held my breath. The song was my most vulnerable and one of the few I'd never played for anyone. When I'd written it, I'd intended to keep it for myself.

"Wow," he said as he exhaled softly, "is that about him?"

I glanced down at my left hand and nodded. "Jacob. We were high school sweethearts. Married for seven years."

"What happened?" he asked.

"It's complicated."

"The song isn't. I mean that in a good way. It has a lot of potential if you want to work on it with me," he said. Hope danced in his voice. "Your voice matters, Missouri, and so do your words."

I shifted and placed my guitar flat on my lap. "Maybe we could start something else? I'm not sure if I'm ready to unpack all of that just yet."

"Yeah, sure," he said, sounding disappointed. "Have anything in mind?"

"I think so, let me grab something." I didn't wait for him to respond. I got up and pulled my purse off the kitchen counter and retrieved my notebook. I flipped to the page where'd I'd recorded my dad's words. Back on the floor, I patted the spot next to me for Niles to join me, but he refused and jumped onto Derrick's lap. "Traitor."

"Your cat may dislike men, but he likes me."

"I can see that."

He rubbed the top of Niles's head. As I watched him, I felt more of my defenses melt away. I'd already felt at ease with Derrick, but seeing him with my cat softened the parts of me I thought would always remain hardened. I glanced down at the page and read my dad's words again and then looked back up at Derrick. I tried to say them, but they wouldn't come out, so I flipped to another page.

"How about something fun," I said as I skimmed through the notes and words I'd jotted down. Derrick nodded but didn't look up from my cat. My fingers stopped over one phrase, and I tapped the page. "Tonight's about drinking, dancing, and doing the things I shouldn't."

I'd overheard a former co-worker utter those words in the bathroom stall one Friday afternoon.

"I like it," he said and reached for my guitar. I handed it over. He placed his fingers over the strings and tapped his foot. I watched, mesmerized, as he bobbed his head, strummed, and tapped out a new beat. I closed my eyes and let the rhythm sink deep into me.

"*Hey, hey, hey,*" I sang and tried to follow his lead, "*it's lookin' like a good night to do what I shouldn't.*"

"*I'm gonna chase my whiskey with a double shot of trouble,*" Derrick added the next line without skipping a beat.

"*'Cause I'm not your girl tonight. I'm not yours anymore.*" The words started coming to me as quickly as he was playing. He nodded along and added in a line or two as we bounced the lyrics between us.

"*Tonight's about dancin'. And drinkin'. And doin' what I shouldn't.*" I finished out the last lyric of the chorus.

"Whew, girl," he said and leaned over the guitar. "I think we might have a song. Let's go back and write this down. But, first, I'm signing you up for Wednesday's open mic."

I laughed. "How about we finish a few songs first?"

"Nope. Whatever is happening right now, it's magic. I'll play and sing harmony, but your voice owns this one. I won't take no for an answer, Missouri."

I felt the "no" bubbling up inside of me. Jacob's voice mingling with my own. I shoved it back and said, "Alright, then, let's finish this."

CHAPTER ELEVEN

I yawned and stretched my back over the stiff metal chair. My eyes were heavy with the sleep I'd missed out on. Aside from working the closing shift at the bar, Derrick and I had been meeting up after work every night to write. It was exhilarating and exhausting at the same time. I wasn't sure if the butterflies in my stomach were from the thrill of writing or the promise of seeing Derrick each night.

The cynic in me was certain it was nothing more than a renewed passion for music. The woman in me that hadn't been kissed or touched in more than half a year was hoping it was more than that.

This morning, I'd splurged on a quad venti latte with the slim belief that four shots of espresso would get me through my coffee date with Dad. The scowl on his face when he walked in left me wishing I'd brought something stronger than espresso.

"Good morning," he said as he sat down. "Thank you for the Americano."

"You're welcome," I said and passed it across the table to him.

"You look dead to the world."

"Thanks." I rolled my eyes.

"What I mean is, are you getting enough sleep? If you're out looking for a job, you need to be on top of your game, Abby."

"I see we're diving straight into the business portion of this meeting. You'll be happy to know that I've already found a job." I reached into my pocket and pulled out the check I'd written before passing out last night. "Here's next month's rent."

He glanced down at the check and then back up at me. "It's not due until the first."

"Two weeks early," I said, "I thought you'd be proud of me for being on top of my game."

"You know we don't have to make these coffee dates so painful, Abby. I get it, you resent me for leaving. I missed out on most of your life, and I do deserve some coldness from you, but I'd hoped you coming here and asking for my help would at least allow us to start to build a bridge."

I clamped my mouth shut to keep from saying something I couldn't take back. He was the one who'd sat across from me two weeks ago and shared his deep disappointment in me. He'd been the one to demand I pay him rent.

He was the one who left.

"I'm sorry I don't know how to be your dad, but if you'd let me in even a little, I think we could start to at least be friends."

"Sure," I said. It was the only word I could muster.

"Why don't you tell me about your new job?"

I took a long, slow sip of my latte and once again wished it were something stronger. "It's at the Gulch Dive Bar."

"The bar at the RBX?" he asked. I nodded. "Are you doing social media or marketing for them?"

My mouth went dry at his optimism. This was not going to be the conversation he was hoping for. "No, waiting tables."

"Oh," he said, and I could tell he was trying to hide his true reaction. "So, it's going well?"

I smiled, and I don't really know what came over me, but the words started spilling out of me in rapid fire. "It is. I really do love it. I mean, it's way harder than sitting at a desk all day. I'm always tired, but I have today and tomorrow off. I've even started writing again, which is amazing. Derrick Bale, he's the co-owner of the bar and a singer-song-writer, and I have been working on a fun new song. I think we're going to sing it at open mic night on Wednesday. Oh! You should come."

I felt like nine-year-old me coming home to tell my dad I'd gotten the lead in our third-grade production of *Annie*. I remember walking into the house with that ridiculous curly, red wig. I didn't know how to tap dance, but my legs just started moving. Mom had started laughing and rolled her eyes at me, but Dad scooped me up into his arms and whispered, "Way to go, my little star!" He'd been so proud of me that day.

Now, I couldn't read his reaction. Silence settled between us like an uncomfortable, smothering blanket.

"You're waiting tables?" he finally asked.

"Out of all that I just said, that's what you heard?"

"I'm sorry, but you're better than that."

"Better than honest hard work that just paid my entire month's rent in under two weeks and allowed me to buy groceries and new guitar strings? Really?"

"You have a degree." He sat back and crossed his arms over his chest. The disappointment in his eyes stung.

"Yes, I'm aware of that useless piece of paper sitting in a box in my closet. Maybe I'm not cut out for the nine-to-five world, *Dad*."

"So after one bad job, you're just giving up?"

"No!" I shouted and slid my chair back. "I'm not *giving up*; I'm finally doing what I want."

"You want to wait tables?"

"No, I want to write songs. I want to sing at open mic nights. I want to embrace my dream and not be afraid of what everyone else thinks. Not you. Not Jacob. No one."

A hush fell over the busy Starbucks lobby, and every set of eyes was on us. My cheeks flushed, and my entire body shook. I didn't come here to fight. I also hadn't planned to invite him to the open mic night, but here we were.

"Please sit down, Abby," he said, "and lower your voice."

"Why? So, you can tell me what a disappointment I am? Well, you don't get to do that anymore. You lost that right when you left."

"You're not a disappointment." Tears brimmed at the edge of his eyes as he silently pleaded with me to sit down. "I just want more for you."

"You don't get a say in any of it."

"I understand that."

I sat back in my seat and sucked down the rest of my latte. We were at an impasse. "Well, great seeing you this morning. The offer still stands. If you aren't too ashamed of me, open mic night is Wednesday at eight."

"Abby, please," he said and swiped at his eye, "I am not ashamed of you."

"Then when do I get to meet Jenny and the boys? I mean, I don't even know their names. Do they know about me and Lindsey?"

"They do," he said. He reached across the table and placed his hand over mine. I twitched and started to pull away, but his skin was just as warm as I remembered. "It's complicated; I'm sure you understand that. My past isn't something I'm proud of."

I yanked my hand away from his. "You're not ashamed of me, but you're not proud of your first family? How the fuck am I supposed to take that?"

"That is not what I meant. I'm sorry, I'm not like you or your mother; words aren't my strong suit. What I meant is that I am not proud of how I left things with Sue and you girls. I can't erase the past, and I want more for my boys. I want them to be the man I couldn't be."

"Oh," I said and exhaled. I didn't have anything to say to that. In our short time together, he'd never been this open or honest. He'd never admitted to being the bad guy.

"Your mother and you girls were my entire world; everything I'd ever wanted or dreamed of. When I met Jenny, something changed. It wasn't anything to do with you or your sister. Maybe not even Sue. But more to do with the man Jenny made me want to be. I don't know if I can explain it, but it was as if all of a sudden the life I had didn't make sense, and I knew there was more."

Hearing his confession should have hurt. It should have made me angry, but it didn't. Those were the same thoughts I'd had about Jacob. There hadn't been another man but there had been something else that I wanted more than him and more than us. My dreams had faded when I was with him, but they didn't die. They smoldered below the surface waiting for me to feel the fire again.

"It was like you were meant for more than what you'd laid out for yourself," I said.

"Yes, exactly."

"Maybe we aren't so different."

Our gazes met, and there was something different there. A smile. A common ground.

"I'll think about how I can introduce you to Jenny and the boys," he said with a soft smile. "Their names are Adam and Eric."

"Adam after Uncle Adam?" I asked, shocked. Adam was Mom's older brother who'd died when he was sixteen.

Dad nodded and said, "Adam and I were best friends in high school. I met your mom because of him. I was in the car with him the night of the crash."

"I didn't know that." Mom had told me about the car accident so many times but mostly as a warning for my own terrible driving skills. Not once did she mention that my dad was in the car. She never even said Dad's name in the same sentence as Adam's, but it was clear they were close. He'd named his son with his new wife after him.

"There's a lot about my past you don't know."

"I'd like to know," I said, my voice barely above a whisper. "Can we start this over?"

"What?"

"This," I said and waved my hand in front of me. "Everything. I showed up here bitter and angry and ready to hate you, but I also needed you. And I didn't think you'd show up for me, but you did, and I didn't know how to handle any of it."

The confession tasted bittersweet on my tongue. As much as I'd once hated him, I couldn't deny all that he'd done for me when I'd showed up.

"I'd like that."

"Hey, Dad," I said and smiled. "How's your Monday going?"

"Better now."

CHAPTER TWELVE

"Okay, so, I kind of invited my dad to open mic on Wednesday,"
I said to Derrick as soon as he walked in. Nervous energy had been
bubbling inside of me ever since I left Dad earlier. "So, maybe we can
go through the song a million more times so it's perfect and he doesn't
think I'm a fool?"

"Slow down, Missouri," he said with his smooth voice and
smirked. "The song is pretty fucking perfect, and you're not a fool."

I shrugged off his compliments and stepped aside to let him in. I
paused long enough to admire his ripped jeans and black concert T-
shirt.

"What's that?" I asked and pointed at his hand. He held up a brown
bag with a tiny bow.

"Cupcakes."

"Why?"

"To celebrate finishing our first song, and because last night you
mentioned wanting a white cupcake with a big-ass pile of frosting."

"You were listening to me?"

"I'm always listening to you." He stood quietly beside me, and I
sensed he wanted to say something else, but the words never came.

Blushing, I took the cupcakes from him and he followed me into the kitchen. I was acutely aware of how close to me he was. In all our writing sessions, he'd not made a single move other than a casual touch here or there. I'd even tried to flirt a few times to no avail. I was beginning to wonder if he was the player everyone claimed him to be.

"I was thinking we could tighten up the bridge a little," I said and handed him a plate. "Wine?"

"Do you have milk?"

"Yeah," I said and reached up for a glass.

He bumped his hip against mine and reached over me. I closed my eyes for a moment and tried to ignore the thoughts that kept racing through my mind. His hips. My hips. *Stop*.

"I'll get it," he offered.

"Milk is in the fridge," I said and then immediately gave myself a mental slap. Of course, the milk was in the fridge. I'd spent every night for almost a week with him, and now, suddenly, I was turning into a lovesick moron.

Nope, I scolded myself. Not love. Not sick. Definitely a moron, though.

He looked down at me and smiled. "Are you having wine?"

"Actually, milk sounds great."

"Here, you take the cupcakes into the living room, and I'll get us milk from the fridge."

I took the cupcakes and plates and made my way into the living room. My heart was racing. There was something different in his eyes tonight. He'd brought cupcakes and rejected booze. He didn't walk in and immediately start talking about the song or some new chord progression he wanted to try.

Taking my usual seat on the floor in front of the couch, I set the cupcakes on the plates beside me. I leaned back and watched him walk into the living room. His smile was wide, but shy. He handed me the milk and then stood beside the couch.

"Why do you always sit on the floor?" he asked.

"It's easier to play," I said with a shrug.

He sat on the couch and rubbed his hand over the empty cushion beside him. "Sit by me?"

"Um, okay," I said. He leaned forward and offered me his hand. I took it, and he lifted me off the floor and guided me to the seat next to him. As soon as I sat down, he slid closer. Every nerve ending in my body went on high alert.

He kept my hand in his and interlaced his fingers between mine. Tingles ran through my skin. He inched his body closer and closer to mine until we were touching. His leg nudged mine. Shivers of anticipation shot through me. My mind ran away from me as I pictured touching more than legs. Lips. Bodies. I'd admired Derrick dozens of times since that first night. The way his lips moved when he sang. The way he closed his eyes with every deep, important line. The way he listened to me and gave my dreams credence.

I wanted him. The realization slapped me hard, startling me. I'd toyed with the daydream of kissing him, but now under his gaze, I realized it wasn't just a daydream. I wanted Derrick Bale, and I didn't know what to do with that want. With Jacob, it happened naturally. We were young, stupid, and naive enough to believe we knew what we were doing. Now, I was smart enough to know that I didn't have a fucking clue.

"So, cupcakes?" I asked and jumped up. He laughed and bent down to pick up a cupcake and handed it to me. "Look at all that frosting!"

"You did say 'a big-ass pile of frosting.'"

"Frosting is the best part," I said as I sat back down a few inches further away from him than I'd been.

"Eh, I'm a cake man." I watched in horror as he scraped the frosting off the top of the cupcake and dropped it onto his plate. "Frosting is too sweet."

"No! You can't waste all that goodness." I took my fork and pushed it from his plate to mine.

"Take it all," he said with a laugh. He dipped his finger into the frosting and held it up. I didn't move an inch. He brushed his finger against my lips leaving a trail of frosting. I ran my tongue over my lips to clear it off. I swear his gaze followed my tongue as it moved from one side of my mouth to the other. I took my time cleaning off the frosting. "Good?"

"Very," I said, my voice lower than I'd intended. I don't know what came over me. Between the way he was watching me and the way my body was reacting, I lost all sense of control. Then, I did something completely out of character and unexpected. I dipped my finger into the frosting and wiped it over his lips before leaning in to kiss him. I pressed my lips against his and then ran my tongue over his lips.

"Oh, shit," I said, gasping as I pulled away. "I'm so sorry, I don't know what came over me. I haven't—" I stopped myself before I could admit that I'd never kissed anyone other than my now ex-husband.

"It's okay," he said with a sly smile, "I've been wanting to do that for the last week."

His confession jolted me back to life. That one sentence emboldened a side of me I didn't recognize. I wasn't some naive small-town girl anymore. I wasn't the girl who'd only ever made love to one man. I became someone else entirely, and I embraced this new me.

"Oh, then can I do it again? You still have a little bit of frosting right," I said and brushed my lips against his, "there."

Derrick laced his fingers through my hair. I could practically taste his hunger. The sweetness of the frosting mixed with the salty taste of his tongue. Despite the urgency between us, he kept his touch soft and light. I pulled myself up to get closer to him, needing to feel all of him. He wrapped his free arm around my waist and brought me closer to him. I positioned myself over him and slid down into his lap without breaking my hold on his lips.

His breath, hot against my face, quickened. It matched the pace of my heart beating in my chest.

"Wow," he said and pulled back. I sighed at the loss of contact. When I leaned in for another round, he held up his hand. "Let me catch my breath. I don't trust myself to hold back with you."

"Then don't."

"Abby." The way he said my name split me in two. "I know you've heard all about me and whatever it is Noah and Jessie think I am. But I like you. A lot."

A lot. He liked me *a lot.* I tried not to read too much into that and said, "I like you, too, and I don't care what they say. I'm capable of making my own decisions."

"I know. It's just that—"

"Just what?"

"You're hurting, and I don't want to add to that."

"You won't. I want this. I swear I do." And I did. I wanted him more than I'd ever wanted anything. Right now, he was the big-ass pile of frosting I was craving.

"You say that now."

"I'll say it tomorrow, too. I'm not saying I want a relationship or commitment, but that kiss right there might have been the best of my life."

"How many men have you kissed?" he asked with a laugh.

"Two, counting you," I admitted without a hint of shame. I was who I was and lying wouldn't change the truth. I was done pretending to be who I thought men wanted me to be.

"Two?" His mouth fell open in shock.

"What? I met my ex-husband in high school." His hands rested on my hips. They held me closer while also putting distance between us. I placed my hands over his and pulled them up to my waist, pushing my shirt up. Heat radiated from him.

"I'm no good for you," he said and swallowed hard. Desire rose in his eyes, and he held his gaze on me. I didn't break eye contact either; I wanted him to know that I didn't believe a word he'd said. He was exactly what I wanted and needed right now. "I'm not the marry-your-high-school-sweetheart kind of guy."

"I'm not asking you to be that." I slid his hands further up my side. He shivered slightly as his fingers grazed the bottom of my breast. I closed my eyes and bit my lip. "Do you want to kiss me again?" I asked without opening my eyes.

He didn't answer. The only sound was each of our inhales and exhales. Rapid, in-sync gasps for air. Then, I felt the full length of him push against my leg. His lips landed on mine and pulled me to him. I parted my lips and invited him in. His kiss deepened, and I dropped my full weight into his lap. He groaned and slipped his thumb beneath my bra. Whether intentional or a subconscious move, I'd chosen the one and only black lace bra I owned today. He ran his thumb over my nipple, and my body trembled in response.

"Do you—" I started to ask, but he nibbled my bottom lip silencing me.

"Bed?" he asked. I nodded, and he stood. I wrapped my legs around his waist. I kept my lips locked to his.

"A condom?" I asked. I felt his head bob up and down.

"Pocket," he growled.

He carried me into the bedroom, kicked the door shut behind him, and laid me on the bed. I sat up on the edge and admired him for a moment. He stood between my legs and ran his hand through his hair.

"How'd you know where the bedroom was?" I asked.

"It's a one-bedroom condo, it wasn't hard to figure out."

"Touché," I said with a giggle. I reached my hand into his pocket and pulled out the condom. I held it up and asked, "Need help with this?"

Before he could answer, my fingers were looped through his belt buckles. I pulled him toward me and flipped the button of his jeans open. I tugged at his waistband, but he placed his hands over mine and stopped me.

"You first," he said with a grin and pushed my body back onto the bed before kneeling in front of me. I started to argue, but he already had me half-naked and his mouth on me before I got a word out. His lips and tongue moved with the precision and expertise of a surgeon. I closed my eyes and gripped the back of his head, pulling him closer until I couldn't hold myself back, and then I let go. The release rushed through me in pulsating waves that I couldn't have stopped even if I'd wanted to.

"Condom, now," I ordered and sat up. I pulled my shirt over my head and reached for his jeans again. This time, I had them down before he could stop me.

"Yes, ma'am," Derrick replied. He traced the length of my stomach with soft, slow kisses. He slipped his hands behind my back and released my bra. It slid down my arms, and he gently removed it and tossed it on the floor.

"Look, as much as I enjoy the feeling of your lips on my skin, I need you to move things along." I yanked his shirt over his head and ran my fingers over his chest. He smiled and pushed me back onto the bed. His lips met mine again as I guided my hips towards his. I reached between us and took hold of him and guided him right where I wanted him. He gasped as he slid in, taking his time. "Please stop teasing me and fuck me."

I didn't know who this Abby Monroe Rhodes was, but I liked her.

CHAPTER THIRTEEN

When I awoke the next morning, my body sore in places I hadn't used in far too long, I was acutely aware of the naked body beside me. I ignored the morning sun and closed my eyes as I curled against him. The scent of us lingered on him. I drank it in with each lazy breath.

One-Night-Stand Derrick. Noah's words of warning flashed through my mind. One night. One morning. However long I had with him was enough. What I was feeling with him was more than a rushed, lust-filled night. I knew that, but the warning lingered. The sirens blared in my ears, but I shut them out.

"Good morning," he whispered. He wrapped his arms around me and held me against him. His skin, still sticky with our sweat from last night, cooled against me. I let myself sink further into him.

He felt safe.

He's anything but safe, my heart reminded me. My bed wasn't the first bed he'd woken up naked in. And it wouldn't be the last.

Niles jumped up onto the bed and nudged his way under the blankets. He nestled himself between my stomach and Derrick's. I giggled as his wet nose brushed my skin.

"I thought you closed the door," I mumbled into Derrick's chest.

"I did, but he kept crying at the door, so I let him in at some point. Little furball slept on my face most of the night." His chest rose with his yawn.

"I think he likes you."

"I hate to admit it," he joked, "but the feeling just might be mutual."

"I'm starving," I said and sat up. Niles mewed, and Derrick groaned in agreement.

"Don't you dare get out of this bed," he said and grabbed my waist. He tickled my side, and I screamed and lurched towards the edge of the bed. I didn't fight him too hard and let him drag me back to him. I gently pushed Niles out of the way. He mewed in protest but acquiesced. I waited until I couldn't hear his paws padding across the hardwood floor.

I lay on my side, facing Derrick. He shifted forward and took my face in his hands. I studied his face as he studied mine, both of us looking for answers to questions we weren't asking. I traced my finger over his eyebrow and noted a tiny indention just above his right eye. A small scar whose story I might never know. I ran my finger over it again, and he flinched. I traced down the edge of his jawline and neck. I lingered over his neck, pressing my finger against his pulse. The buzz of it tickled my skin. Derrick sat patient and still, my head still cradled in his hands. A slow smile crept over his lips, and he leaned in for another kiss.

This kiss was far more tender than the urgent, needy ones we shared the night before. He lingered at my lips, teasing them apart with his tongue. He tasted as good as I remembered. I was aware of the world waking up outside this room, but I wanted nothing to do with it. All I wanted was to feel wanted by him. I slid closer to him and wrapped my legs around his, nudging him.

"You are insatiable," he whispered. His beard tickled my ear, sending a shiver through me. Heat radiated from my center, igniting a fire only he could extinguish. I ran my fingernails down his back and pulled him to me. There wasn't an inch of air between us, and he still wasn't close enough. He reached over my shoulder and grabbed a condom off my nightstand. I took it from him and ripped the foil package open before removing it and sliding it over him. He made the same low sigh when he entered me that he had the night before.

Like with his kiss earlier, he took his time. The morning sun beamed in on us. We kept our eyes opened and focused on each other. When our lips found their way back together, there was a new intimacy between us. We knew each other now. He knew how my body felt, how it reacted, and what it needed. I understood his silent cues and could sing harmony without thinking about it. We moved in sync as our breaths hitched at the same time.

There in the sunlit room, I saw another side of Derrick. The soft, tender side. This was the man I'd seen pour his heart into every word he sang or wrote. The man who saw something in me that no one else did. He drank me in as if I were the last drop of water lingering in a dried-up well, and I wanted to be enough to quench his thirst.

The slow release built inside of me, but each time I came close, he slowed his pace and brought me back down.

"Please," I whispered between gasps for air when I couldn't hold it back any longer. He heard my plea and a look of determination crossed his face. When the release came, it came in waves. Long, intoxicating waves crashed between us. He collapsed on top of me and kissed my shoulder.

"I'm starving," he said with a small laugh.

"We could make breakfast and then come back to bed?" I teased.

"I wish I could, but I do need to get going."

"Breakfast first?" I asked. He sat up and looked at his phone.

"I do make a mean pancake."

"You may have to settle for generic Cheerios because this girl doesn't have flour or eggs."

"That does pose a problem. Generic Cheerios it is."

I looked back at him and admired his bare chest as the sun peeked through the windows and danced across his tanned body. He wasn't chiseled, and he certainly wasn't competing for six-pack abs of the year, but his body was the perfect balance of hard and soft. Last night, I had tried not to notice how I fit perfectly into the curve of him, or how his legs intertwined with mine in this magically seamless way that made it impossible to know where I ended and he began. But it was all I could think about this morning.

He joined me in the kitchen, stepping behind me and leaning his body against mine. He draped his arms over my shoulders like a shawl. I closed my eyes and drifted back against him. *Danger, Will Rogers, danger*, my brain screamed at me. *One more kiss, one more touch*, my body begged. My heart seemed to be playing the part of Switzerland. She'd gone quiet somewhere around midnight as I laid beneath a moonlit Derrick and decided I didn't really care if he was just here for one night. One night was all I needed at that exact moment, but in the harsh reality of the morning sun, I couldn't be entirely sure where I stood on the issue. While I was okay with last night and this morning being our one moment, a bigger part of me knew it wouldn't be enough.

Derrick Bale was worth more than one night even if I knew that's all I'd been promised.

We stood like that, two bodies still buzzing from a night of bad (or good) decisions, neither of us willing to move. It was if we were both waiting for the other to confirm that what had happened had actually happened. It wasn't a dream. We hadn't been drunk. We'd been two clear-headed adults who willingly gave in to the chemistry combusting between us.

"I feel like I've known you forever," he said, breaking the silence and the connection between our bodies.

"It's been less than three weeks," I said. I ignored the nagging feeling that I'd somehow betrayed myself and my life by having mind-blowing sex with this man I'd just met. We'd shared our souls through music, I reasoned. This wasn't happening too fast. Besides, I was allowed to have fun, and that's what this was. Fun. "A *good* three weeks."

"Hmmm," he hummed as I handed him a bowl of cereal. "Milk's in the fridge?"

"Unless you left it on the counter last night." I pointed to the jug behind him.

"Whoops." He offered a sheepish grin as an apology, and I forgave him. "I was a little distracted."

"About that," I said and cleared my throat, "I had fun. I mean, I think we both did, but I want you to know I don't expect anything. Like you said, you're not the marry-your-high school-sweetheart kind, and I'm okay with that. I really am."

"Oh." He shoved a handful of dry cereal into his mouth. "So, I should cancel the 'thanks for having sex with me' roses I just ordered?"

My entire body flushed. "I mean, I'm not expecting them, but I'd never say no to flowers."

He nodded and chewed another bite. I picked up one piece and popped it into my mouth. The taste of him still lingered on my tongue and mixed with the unsweetened dryness of the cereal. I grabbed two glasses from the cabinets and went to the fridge. Thankfully, I still had some orange juice and poured us both a glass.

"I'm thinking we should practice the song one more time," I said, "I mentioned I invited my dad, right? Well, I need him to see that what I'm doing at the bar and with you is worth it, you know? No one but you seems to think I'm cut out for any of this."

"That can't be true. I recognized your talent immediately."

Not one to take a compliment well, I said, "My talent or my boobs?"

He frowned and rinsed his glass in the sink. "I hope you know the answer to that one without me having to spell it out."

I'd meant it as a joke but seeing how his face fell when I said, I realized he hadn't found it funny. I'd just done to him what everyone else had done. I assumed he was who I'd been warned he was.

"I'm sorry. I didn't mean it like that."

"It's okay, Abby. I've got to get going. I'll call you tonight, and we can meet up to practice a few more times."

"We could practice now," I said, my voice timid. I realized I didn't want him to leave.

"I have to go meet Noah to go through the books. Tuesday is our accounting day."

"Oh, sure," I said and bit my lip. "Hey, Derrick, can I ask a favor?"

"Don't worry, I know all about Noah's stupid rule. I won't tell him what happened last night."

"Thank you." My stomach dropped. Sadness radiated from him in waves of frustration. When he looked at me, the desire and heat that had been in his eyes the night before was gone. "Last night was amazing, you know that, right?"

"I was there both times," he replied.

"Three times," I said with a smile. "Four if you count this morning."

"I do." He turned to go. I followed him to the door, my heart raced, and my mouth burned to kiss him again.

"Derrick?"

"Abby?"

"Things won't be weird between us now, will they? I meant what I said last night, I like you, too, and I've very much like to do *that* with you again."

"What exactly do you want?" He turned back to me and placed his fingers under my chin, lifting my face to his.

I swallowed hard and blinked. Words escaped me as he bent his face closer to mine.

"What do you want, Abby Rhodes?"

"You," I whispered. "To kiss you again and to write more songs and to—" He didn't let me finish. He brushed his lips over mine, teasing me.

"I'll call you," he said and opened the door. "Hey."

"Hey," I said back.

"Abby." This voice was different. It wasn't Derrick who had said my name, but I knew the voice. I knew it far too well.

"Jacob?" I shook my head and peeked around Derrick. I pressed my hand against his back, and he tensed. I willed him to understand what I was asking him to do. *Don't move. Don't leave. Stay.*

"Well, I should be going," he said, ignoring my unspoken pleas. He turned back and kissed my forehead. "I'll call you later."

My mouth went dry, and I couldn't speak, so I just offered a small nod. When my eyes met his, I tried to beg him to stay one last time. He just shrugged and turned to go.

"Don't worry, man," he said to Jacob. "I took *real* good care of her."

My mouth fell open. *Did he just tell my husband that he'd taken care of me?* A heat wave rushed through me. I didn't have to look at Jacob's face to know what I'd see. Anger. Disappointment. Disgust.

"Hey, Jacob," I said and looked up at the man I'd left on Christmas Eve.

CHAPTER FOURTEEN

"You look different," he said as his eyes scanned my body. I tugged at the T-shirt I'd thrown on and tried in vain to cover myself.

"You look the same." He grinned and shoved past me. The sight of him inside my condo sent a thrill of terror through me. I'd never pictured him here in Nashville or inside my new home. It was very apparent that he didn't fit here. His unwrinkled khakis and tucked-in pastel polo felt as stuffy and out of place here as they did in Wishing; the only difference was that *he* fit in Wishing. It was his home. Always had been and always would be.

"Geez, this place is tiny." Niles hissed at him and sat in front of me as though he were protecting me. "Nice cat."

"It's enough for me."

"Good for it."

"What are you doing here, Jacob?"

"You haven't signed the papers." He picked up the manila envelope off the counter and said, "Have you even opened them?"

I shook my head. I'd been avoiding them like he'd been avoiding me. "You never called me back. I wanted to talk to you before I opened them."

"You've had several months to talk to me, Abby. You don't get to make the rules now. You left, not me. You."

"I'm well aware of that."

"Who was that?"

"Who?" I asked coyly. I knew who he meant.

"Cut the shit."

"That was Derrick." My face turned crimson at the mere mention of his name. As soon as I said it, I noticed the hole his absence left.

"Are you sleeping with him?"

"I'm not sure that's any of your business."

"If you'd have signed the papers, maybe not. But seeing how we're still married, I think I have a right to know who my wife is fucking."

"We're writing together," I said, offering half of the truth.

"Cute." He rolled his eyes. "I can tell by that hickey on your neck and beard burn on your lips that you're doing more than writing."

I rubbed my hand over my neck and then my lips. My lips and the skin around them were tender and swollen.

"That's what I thought."

"I'm going to go get dressed. Make yourself at home, but don't get too comfortable."

"I see you still suck at keeping a house clean," he said as he walked into the living room. He bent down and picked up the cupcakes Derrick and I hadn't finished. "Disgusting."

I ignored him and rushed into the bedroom and slammed the door behind me. I dug my phone out of my purse and checked for missed calls or messages. Nothing. I sent my mom and sister a text to ask why they hadn't warned me.

Jacob is here. In Nashville.

Well, you're not here. My sister replied within seconds.
What do you expect him to do?

Not ambush me. Did you know? Why didn't you give me a heads up?

Mom chimed in next. *This is your mess, Abby, not mine. It's time to face the music.*

"Ugh!" I groaned and threw my phone onto the nightstand. My eyes drifted to the disheveled sheets and discarded condom wrappers. The evidence of my night with Derrick laid bare in front of me. I touched my lips again and smiled. He'd been in my bed with me. He'd kissed these lips. He'd touched every inch of me.

What I wouldn't give to be back in that bed with Derrick right now.

In the bathroom, I stripped off what little clothing I had on and turned on the shower. I slipped inside and let the water rush over me and wash away whatever remained of Derrick. I wanted to scoop it all back and pour it over me. I wanted to still smell and taste him.

Get a grip, I scolded myself. One night. We'd had one night. No matter how amazing it had been to be the one under the spotlight of his gaze, it had been one single night.

The man I'd spent countless nights with was standing in my living room cleaning up the cupcakes that had been foreplay with the man I'd just cheated with. *Fuck.* I cheated. I mean, technically, I'd cheated. Jacob and I hadn't been together in months. We were over. I knew that and he knew that, but it didn't change the truth.

Jacob and I were still married, and I was feeling something for Derrick.

I bit back a surge of emotion and swallowed my tears. I couldn't show Jacob even an ounce of regret or weakness. I had to own what I'd done. It was time to put the past where it belonged.

I shut off the water and grabbed a towel. Running it over my body, images of Derrick's roaming hands flashed over my eyes. I shivered; whether from the chill or the memory of him, I wasn't sure. I slipped on my underwear and decided to put on a bra, despite my strict rule of not wearing one on my day off. My girls hated being stuffed inside boob prison. In the closet, I grabbed a pair of jeans and a T-shirt.

I didn't bother with my hair or makeup. I cared less and less about making myself what someone else expected the longer I was in Nashville. I stopped by the mirror to see if I could see the evidence Jacob had pointed out. There wasn't a hickey, but my lips and chin were red.

I shook off the shame I'd felt earlier and decided I wouldn't be embarrassed about what had happened last night. I would let it empower me and remind me of the life and love I wanted.

Not that I loved Derrick.

I didn't.

At least, I didn't think I did.

"Nice," Jacob said and smirked at my outfit when I finally emerged from the bedroom, "I see you've fully let yourself go."

"Or, maybe, I'm finally myself."

"No, I know you, Abby, and this isn't you." He was baiting me. I knew it. He knew it.

"What isn't me?" I took the bait.

"This." He waved his arm around the condo and then towards me. "Dirty. No makeup. Fucking wannabe musicians. Leaving milk out on the counter. At least you have a decent job, I guess."

"Naw. I lost that. I'm waiting tables in a bar now."

"Perfect."

"It is."

"What happened to us, Abs," he said, his voice softening as he called me by the name he used to.

"We changed."

"We've changed before, and we always made it work. This time was different. I just don't understand."

The room grew stuffy, and the walls started closing in around me. I'd never felt suffocated in my tiny condo, but with Jacob in the room, all of the air seemed to evaporate.

"Why don't we go for a walk? Get some fresh air?"

"Sure, whatever," he said. I slipped on a pair of flip flops and grabbed my keys. He followed me out the door and into the elevator. We didn't look at each other or speak, but I could feel the resentment flowing off of him.

"How did you find me?" I asked as the elevator doors closed.

"Your mom gave me your address." Of course she did.

We rode in silence the rest of the way down. When we entered the lobby, I forced my eyes to stay forward and not look toward the bar.

But I still caught a glimpse of Derrick as we passed. I felt his eyes on me, and I broke a little knowing that I couldn't return his gaze.

Out on the street, the sounds of Nashville buzzing around us filled my ears and flowed through me like the melody of my favorite song. People talked around us. Cars honked and sped past. Cranes clanked and dropped concrete beams onto the new high rises, and I wondered how many were being built by Derrick's dad.

Derrick was everywhere in this city.

"I called the police on Christmas morning," Jacob said as we headed down Twelfth Avenue. He matched his pace to mine. At 5'3", I was always shorter and slower than everyone. Jacob used to love reminding me of my short legs and would make a show of walking slowly to keep pace with me. "When I woke up and noticed the bed was empty, I thought you'd gotten up early to make coffee or load the presents into the car. Then I came out, and your car was gone. Most of your clothes were still in the dresser, so I assumed you'd be back. You'd just gone to run an errand. I made us breakfast. Cinnamon rolls, bacon, and scrambled eggs. I brewed us coffee and poured it. I checked my phone. I called you, and you didn't answer."

My chest tightened, and I struggled to catch my breath as he spoke. I'd never forget the overwhelming freedom I'd felt as I'd watched our house grow smaller in my rearview mirror or the rush I'd felt as I crossed the state line. While I knew he'd be upset, I hadn't known he wouldn't realize that I was gone.

"There was no note. No explanation. Nothing. Your mom didn't even know where you were. I wanted to call the police and file a missing person report, but she insisted you'd show up. None of us believed you'd actually leave us."

"I—"

"No, Abby, it's my turn to talk," he said, silencing me. "But you did leave. Then you refused to answer my calls or texts. Then when I finally accept the end of us, you keep me hanging."

We reached an intersection, and he hesitated. I pointed to the right, and he took my hand and led me across the intersection. His hand was cold and limp as it held mine. When we reached the other side, he dropped it.

"I think I always knew Wishing wasn't enough to keep you, but I thought I was." He paused for a moment and took a deep, ragged breath. "Goddammit, Abby, I gave you everything. I worked my ass off to buy your dream house. I sat and listened to you sing your songs and go on and on about a dream that I knew would crush you. And all I wanted in return was you."

"You wanted more than that," I said.

"Yes, Abby, I wanted to have a family with you."

I stopped walking and sat down on a bus bench. I closed my eyes and leaned forward. An image of me sitting in the bathroom stall at Lace & Grit while clutching the pregnancy test came to me. I squeezed my eyes shut and forced the image away. Before it disappeared entirely, the results of the test flashed in front of me in a single word. POSITIVE.

A lump rose in my throat, and tears welled in my eyes. I squeezed them tighter. I held my breath and counted to ten, waiting for the moment to pass. As hard as I'd tried to forget that one single word, I couldn't. It and what it had meant had followed me all the way to Nashville.

"I thought you wanted that too, Abby." He sat beside me and rested his hand on my back. He rubbed it back and forth, warming the skin beneath it. "We used to talk about our future kids and what their names would be."

Everett Grant. Ava Grace. In our daydreams, they had his blue eyes and my dirty blonde hair and full lips. Their cheeks would be round and rosy like his had been when he was a baby. Chubby legs and arms and rolls for days. We'd spend hours lying in bed, our bodies sealed together, picturing what a baby we'd made would look like.

"I thought I wanted that, too," I finally whispered. "I really believed it. But the more I thought about it and the closer it came to becoming a reality, the less I wanted it. Music is important to me; my words and voice matter." I echoed what Derrick had said the first time we wrote together.

"Your family matters more. When are you going to realize that it's not about you? Everything isn't about you."

"No, but my life is," I countered. "Our life together was slowly killing me, Jacob. Your dreams and mine, they didn't mesh."

"Dreams are bullshit. You really think you're going to become something here?"

"Maybe, maybe not. But if I don't try, I never will."

"So, that's it, huh? You'd rather live in this tiny condo in this loud, crowded city and wait tables than live in a gorgeous house in our hometown with me."

"Yes," I answered. "I'm happy here."

"Great," he said and stood up. "Then let's go sign those papers and get this over with."

CHAPTER FIFTEEN

I didn't sign the papers. When we got back upstairs, he left to make a phone call. I stood alone in the silence of my apartment. I could still feel Derrick's energy in the space. I closed my eyes and tried to pull his energy and confidence into me.

Something about Jacob being here was rocking me to my core. On one hand, it reinforced my decision to leave. On the other, I couldn't help but noticed the familiarity of him and us. Even in our hateful words and cold stares, there was still a comfort in him. We still fit together.

My phone buzzed in my pocket and pulled me out of the trance I'd been in. It was a text from Derrick.

You okay?

I smiled as I read the words. Knowing he was not only thinking about me but also concerned made me happier than it should have.

Yes. No. I don't know.

I didn't feel like I had to lie or pretend with him. The truth was I didn't know how I felt about Jacob being here. Or how I felt about whatever was going on with me and Derrick.

Want me to come up? I can have security keep the ex out.

As tempting as the offer was, I knew it was only asking for trouble.

Yes, but I'm not sure that's a good idea.

I didn't want to send the message, but I knew it was the responsible thing to do. I had to resolve things with Jacob. I owed him that much.

We used to be able to talk to each other, like really talk. Even as teenagers, we had this way of communicating that was open, honest, and vulnerable. I used to trust him with everything. He was the only person who knew the truth about my dad. He knew about Jenny and Dad's new family. He knew how devastated and broken it had left me, and he'd been the only one who'd ever been able to fill that gaping wound.

The night he proposed, we had just left a friend's barn party. We were walking through the clearing that stood between his house and the trailer we'd moved to after Dad left. We were eighteen and on the cusp of everything. We'd both been accepted to college in Springfield and had plans to rent a tiny apartment off campus. We had our whole lives planned.

"Do you know what my two favorite things are?" I'd asked as I bumped my shoulder against his. He draped an arm over me and leaned into me.

"My lips and my d—" he said, and I slapped his stomach before he could answer.

"No, perv." He laughed and kissed my cheek. We'd been together for four years but had known each other for most of our lives. Yet, each time he kissed me; it was if a family of hummingbirds had taken up residence in my stomach. My body raced and hummed under his touch.

"Are you going to make me keep guessing?" he asked after a long pause. I stopped walking and slipped out from his arm. I sank to the ground and lay down in the wet grass. I ignored the dampness as it seeped through my thin summer dress. He dropped to the ground beside me and slid his arm beneath my back and shimmied closer. It was well after midnight. Both of our curfews had come and gone. But his mom and my mom had been best friends who'd dreamt of our wedding day and their grandbabies since we were toddlers stealing each other's pacifiers. Rules didn't exist when I was with Jacob. That was truly my favorite thing about us.

"No," I said as I stared up at the clouded, starless sky. "You and the way you look at me when I'm singing."

"How do I look at you?" he asked.

"Like no one else exists. Like no one has ever spoken or sung those words before. Like I'm all there is." I leaned into him and sighed as his fingers teased at the cotton dress over my breast.

"You are," he whispered. His breath tingled against my ear. "You are all there is."

"I wish we could stay right here in this moment forever. Young and unafraid."

"Maybe we can." A gentle breeze picked up and rustled the trees. My dress fluttered along with it, teasing my skin. He sat up suddenly and looked down at me. "Marry me, Abs."

"What?" I sat up and stared at him. As many times as we'd talked about our future wedding and children, he'd never said those words. I studied his face and searched for the punch line. Something that showed he wasn't serious. But he locked his gaze on mine and held it. He didn't blink.

"Are you serious?"

"As I'll ever be, Abs. I want us forever. I don't want to wait to make you mine."

"I'm already yours."

"Officially, I want to make you mine in front of God and everyone. I want to stand in front of our families and hear you say those words. I want to marry you."

"Yes," I answered, intoxicated by the romance of it all. "Yes."

He climbed over me and braced himself on his arms and knees. I lay beneath him shivering from the chill of the spring air and wet grass. When he leaned down to kiss me, our entire life flashed before me. The white dress. The chapel. Our wedding bed. His hand in mine. Our future was clear, and at that moment, there was nothing I wanted more.

And I had wanted it all with him. Then, one day I woke up and everything had changed. I don't remember the exact moment, but it arrived with such crushing force that it knocked the wind out of me. We weren't those two kids anymore. We'd thought we were so mature and so ready to take on the world. We'd been so stupidly in love that we forgot about the big stuff. Neither of us knew how to breathe without the other, and when we stopped inhaling and exhaling together, we drowned under the weight of our own expectations.

When he finally returned from his mysterious phone call, Jacob found me sitting on the couch holding a glass of wine.

"It's not even five," he said. His voice startled me. I glanced up at him and didn't bother to hide my red-brimmed eyes or shiny, tear-stained face.

"Which means you still have time to make it halfway back to Missouri before the sun sets." Niles curled up in my lap, and I scratched his ears.

"Oh, I'm not leaving until you sign those papers." I leaned back into the couch and raised the glass to my lips. It wasn't that I didn't want to sign the papers. I just wasn't ready.

"I hope you either booked a hotel room or brought a pillow and blanket. The couch is somewhat comfortable."

"What are you waiting for?" he asked.

"I'll sign them when I'm ready."

"You've got to be kidding me, Abby."

"Goodnight, Jacob." I grabbed my wine glass and the bottle of wine off the floor. Niles hissed at Jacob and followed me into my room. I retreated to my bedroom and left him to his own devices. He was a grown man; he could take care of himself.

I slipped my phone out of my pocket and sent Derrick a text.

I won't be able to come practice tonight. Maybe we could FaceTime.

Within seconds, my phone was lighting up with an incoming Face-Time request from Derrick. I took my phone into the bathroom and shut the door.

"Hey," I answered, out of breath.

"Are you in the bathroom?" he asked. As soon as I saw his smile, the tension I didn't realize I'd been carrying seemed to melt away.

"Hiding," I said. My walk-in closet was tucked away in the corner of the bathroom. I held the phone in front of my face while I walked into it and pulled the door closed.

"Is he still there?" Something in Derrick's voice changed. I detected a hint of jealousy in his tone.

"Yeah," I said. I could have told him about the divorce papers or the million other complications, but I didn't. "I left him with Niles. He hates him."

"Good," Derrick said with a laugh. "You look beautiful in that fluorescent light. What did you do with your hair?"

I ran my fingers through my humidity-tainted, air-dried locks. Normally, my hair fell loose and flat around my face. At the bar, I'd been leaving it braided or in a ponytail. Now, it was wild and had a mind of its own.

"Nothing."

"I like it," he said.

I bit my lip to keep from asking him if he'd spent the day thinking about me and last night. I wanted to know that images of us had teased and tormented him all day, too.

"Do you want to talk about, um, Jacob?" I could tell he didn't want to say his name.

"No," I said and propped my phone up on a stack of boxes in my closet. I sat down in front of it and pulled my guitar onto my lap. "Can we just play?"

"Of course." I leaned back against the wall and waited as Derrick got ready. "You know, it's okay to not be okay, right?"

Tears pricked at my eyes, and I wrinkled my nose to stop them. "I know."

He opened his mouth to say something else but stopped. He thumped his hand against the body of his guitar and counted us in. We strummed the first few chords together, and he nodded at me to start singing.

There on the floor of my closet with my soon-to-be-ex-husband in the other room, I allowed myself to give in to the music. Derrick's voice and guitar weren't as clear over the phone as they were in person, but I felt every note and every word as we sang together. At first, my voice was timid, and I worried that Jacob would overhear, but as I watched Derrick get lost in the song we'd written together, I stopped thinking about anything other than us and the music.

Normally, I close my eyes when I sing. I let the music flow through me and consume all of my senses, but I wanted to see Derrick's face as I sang. I selfishly wondered if he looked at me the same way Jacob used to. Through the shaky video on my phone, I felt his eyes on me. A slow smile spread across his face as I sang. He drank me in. Every inch of me.

"I wish you were here," I whispered when we finished playing.

"What was that?" he asked and picked his phone back up. His smiling face filled my screen.

"Nothing," I said.

A pounding on the bathroom door pulled my attention away from Derrick.

"Abby, I need the bathroom!" Jacob shouted.

"Sorry," I said to Derrick.

"I'll let you go," he replied. I wanted to beg him not to and ask him to stay on the line with me all night just so I could hear him breathe. Of course, I didn't say anything. I let him hang up.

I opened the door and let Jacob in. He glanced down at my guitar and scowled. When his gaze made its way back up to my face, I couldn't see a trace of the teenage boy who'd stolen my heart. I was no longer his everything. In fact, I wasn't anything to him now.

CHAPTER SIXTEEN

THE NEXT MORNING, I AWOKE TO THE SWEET SMELL OF COFFEE brewing and bacon cooking. I opened my eyes and sat up. I surveyed the room to make sure Jacob hadn't kidnapped me and taken me back to Missouri while I slept.

Nope, still in Nashville. Still in my bed. I shook the covers off of me and climbed out of bed. I found Jacob in the kitchen.

"You really need to go to the grocery store more often."

"Where did you get bacon?"

"The grocery store." He rolled his eyes. "I went this morning."

"Why?"

"Because no self-respecting adult eats dry Tasty-Os for breakfast."

Derrick didn't complain, I thought to myself but didn't dare say the words out loud. I pulled Niles's food out of the cabinet and fixed his bowl. When I placed it on the ground for him, he gave Jacob a stern look before diving into his breakfast.

"You could grab something on your way out of town."

"Are you planning to sign the papers?"

"Yes, I will. I can mail them to you."

"I'm not leaving without them."

"Then don't bitch about my food." I slid up onto the barstool, and he handed me a cup of coffee.

"Cream and sugar," he said. "You know we don't have to make this painful, right?"

"Then what's the rush? I told you I'd sign them when I was ready. Why do you need them now?"

I had my answer before he spoke. He shifted from one leg to the other and chewed his lip. This was his tell. He was hiding something he didn't want me to know about.

"Who is she?" I asked. An uncomfortable jealousy rose inside me.

"Does it matter? You've clearly moved on with random music dude."

"You know his name."

He shrugged. "So?"

"I think I deserve to know that much."

"Melissa," he said after a beat.

"Melissa Hanson? My best friend Melissa?" The one who'd been texting me non-stop to check in. The one who was so concerned about me?

He just nodded. He slid a plate of bacon and scrambled eggs across the counter. I pushed it back. "You're hooking up with my best friend?"

He narrowed his eyes at me. "Really, Abby?"

"What? How long has this been going on?"

"Since February. *After* you left."

That made me feel a little less betrayed. "Four months and you're just now telling me?"

"You haven't exactly been answering my calls or hers."

He had a point, but I wasn't about to concede that to him. "Out of all the girls, you had to pick her?"

"Look, Abby, you don't get to be mad or jealous about this. You left me, remember? You took the chickenshit way out and left in the middle of the fucking night. Now, you're here," he said and threw his arms up in the air, "drinking wine at noon and screwing guys with beards and tattoos."

"At least it wasn't your best friend."

"Fuck you, Abby. Sign the papers. Let me live my life, and you can live yours."

"I have to go to work," I lied and swallowed down the rest of the coffee. It tasted exactly like it always did. He knew me; I hated to admit it, but he did.

"We'll talk tonight, and I'll sign the papers. I need to process this." I left him standing slack-jawed in my kitchen while I got ready for work. I took my time getting ready since I didn't have to be there for another four hours. When I finished, I grabbed my guitar and snuck out before he could see me.

My stomach twisted into a knot when the elevator doors opened. *What am I doing?* Why couldn't I just sign the papers? I wanted this divorce. He wanted it, too.

I walked into the elevator and closed my eyes. The pregnancy test popped into my head again. *Positive. Positive. Positive.*

The truth that stood between me and Jacob. The truth I knew. The truth I owed him. The one thing that would fully break him. I held that image in my mind and fought back the tears.

He's never going to forgive me.

When I saw that one word pop onto the display of the test, I knew what I was going to do. I had my answer, and I had my plan. There were two undeniable truths in that one positive test. I wasn't ready to be a mother, and I wasn't sure I ever would be; and I knew I couldn't tell Jacob. He could never know the results.

When I dropped the test into the trash, I'd whispered a silent apology to the baby that would never be and then I thanked her for setting me free. Guilt swarmed inside those words and festered inside of me as I drove the five-hundred miles between Wishing and Nashville. I had to stop every hour to pull over and wipe the tears from my eyes.

Parked in front of my dad's house that Christmas morning, I thought about the child inside my womb and the child I'd been when my father left. I'd been broken and unable to separate who I was from what he'd done. He was my father, and his one job on this planet was to keep me safe, and he had failed. I was his daughter, and his failures were sure to be mine. This baby didn't stand a chance. My father had wanted me at some point, but I'd never wanted her, and that wasn't fair. Not to her. Not to me. Not to Jacob.

I didn't tell Dad about the pregnancy, and I didn't ask for his help. As soon as I'd settled into the condo, I made an appointment. January 10. I spent the next week convincing myself I was making the right decision. I cried. I changed my mind. I picked up the phone to call Jacob a dozen times. I hated myself for what I'd done and what I was about to do.

The cramping started on January 7, but I ignored it. Everything I'd read said cramping was normal. Spotting was normal. Despite knowing that I had no intention of keeping the baby, I went through the motions. I got prenatal vitamins. I decided she was a girl for no reason other than the fact that Jacob and I had decided our first would be a girl. I read article after article on what to expect in the early weeks. I knew based on my cycle that I was around eight weeks and she was the size of a raspberry. Jacob loved raspberries; I'd recalled with a pang of loneliness as the first wave of morning sickness left me doubled over the toilet.

The next morning, the cramping and spotting had intensified, but still, I ignored it. Just like I tried to pretend the lower back pain was normal. I'd agreed to meet Dad for coffee, the first of our new tradition, and I wasn't about to let him down. He knew something was wrong the instant he walked into the Starbucks.

"Are you okay?" His eyebrows pinched together as he tried to read the face of the daughter he'd only recently met again.

"Just tired," I lied. I clutched my arms over my stomach. He offered to get me a latte, but the mere thought of coffee made my stomach churn. I excused myself to find a bathroom. When I did, I noticed the pad I'd stuck in was soaked through. A chill grabbed hold of me, and I knew then that she was gone. I could barely stand upright, but I managed to make my way back to Starbucks.

Dad took one look at me and said, "I'm taking you to the hospital."

I tried to protest and failed. The pain grew stronger with every breath and every step. In the car, he kept one eye on me and one on the road. He didn't utter a single word or ask another question.

At the hospital, he parked the car and helped me walk into the ER. I don't remember much from that day, aside from the fear that wrapped itself around my abdomen and held tight. I'd never wanted this baby, but losing her by accident dealt a deeper blow than I'd anticipated.

Dad held my elbow and guided me to the nurses station. He cleared his throat and said, "My daughter is having a miscarriage."

"What?" I asked as a gasp escaped my lips. How had he known? Was he just guessing? Before he could answer, a nurse brought a wheelchair around and started asking hundreds of questions. Dad followed me back to the exam room and waited in the hallway. The nurse took a blood sample while a doctor wheeled in an ultrasound cart.

"How far along are you?" she'd asked.

"Eight weeks, I think," I replied.

"Who is your OB?"

"I didn't have one yet." I couldn't find the words to admit that I'd intended on terminating the pregnancy and that had been the only appointment I'd made.

From there, I zoned out and pulled myself somewhere far away. I pictured myself on the stage at the Bluebird Cafe, which I'd visited for the first time the night before. I curled my fingers around the neck of my guitar and imagined myself strumming and singing. This was my happy place, and I was grateful for the retreat.

I pretended the tears streaming down my face were from the overwhelming relief I was supposed to be feeling. She'd known she wasn't wanted and had made her exit on her own, sparing me from having to follow through with the abortion I'd only recently started to doubt. Not that I would ever admit that I was having second thoughts. Or that I could imagine a life where I raised Jacob's baby alone any more than I could imagine a life where I raised her with him. Neither option was even something to consider. I'd made up my mind, and there was no going back.

"I'm so sorry, Mrs. Rhodes," the doctor said and laid her hand on my shoulder. "It looks like you are experiencing a miscarriage." She went on to explain that my body was doing much of the work for me, and I wouldn't need a D&C. She prescribed a painkiller and urged me to get lots of rest.

I nodded and closed my eyes. The image of the little blue-eyed, blonde baby with chubby cheeks and rolls for days vanished from my memories. *Goodbye*.

Dad found me curled in a ball on the floor beside the bed. He sat down beside me and cradled me. I leaned into him and let him absorb the hurt I refused to admit I was feeling. Despite the sobs that erupted each time I took a breath, I was in denial. I couldn't grieve what I'd already committed to death. I'd chosen her fate first. But the guilt didn't see it that way. In my heart, I knew I was responsible for her death. I'd wished her away, and being inside me, she heard those wishes. She'd answered them for me. Just as she'd done in the bathroom at Lace & Grit, she set me free again.

"Jenny and I," Dad said after my tears subsided, "we had a hard time getting pregnant, and we lost two babies before our first son was born."

He took a deep breath and pulled me deeper into his embrace. "You may think I don't know you Abby, but you are still my daughter. I knew the moment you showed up at my door that you were pregnant. Your mother had the same glow with you."

CHAPTER SEVENTEEN

"ABBY," NOAH GREETED ME WITHOUT SO MUCH AS A HALF-SMILE, "MY office."

Shit. He knows. Of course, he knows. I followed him to the back of the bar and avoided the curious stares Leah, Jessie, and Claire gave me as I passed.

"I saw your name with Derrick's on the open mic sign up," he said as he shut the door behind me.

"Yeah, we wrote a song together." I tried in vain to talk my cheeks out of turning beet red and failed. Heat rushed through me, and I kept my eyes locked on the floor.

"Do you remember what my one rule is?" I nodded. "I'm not going to ask you if you broke it or not but if you did, don't bring that drama here. I like you, Abby, and you're a great waitress, but I won't hesitate to fire you if the shit hits the fan."

"Understood."

"Leah has agreed to cover your tables while you're up." He smiled and dismissed me with a wave.

"Thank you," I said and left. I closed the door behind me and went out to join the girls.

They were deep in conversation and speaking in hushed tones when I found them. I didn't want to intrude, so I headed toward my section to get it ready for the night. My mind was all over the place. I hadn't thought about the baby or miscarriage in weeks. It was always there, though, in the back of my mind and hovering in my fingers each time I thought about calling or texting Jacob. I knew he needed to know and that this was the one reason I hadn't yet signed the papers. He may believe I'd made a clean break, but it had been anything but. I'd made a mess and had intended to clean it up myself, but I was realizing that was impossible.

I had to tell him. I would tell him—if I could find the words.

I ran my rag over the table and brushed away imaginary crumbs. Menus were placed on each table along with a lineup of the night's performers. Each time I placed one down, I got a thrill from seeing my name.

Abby Rhodes & Derrick Bale. It had a nice ring to it even if I was on the verge of signing away the Rhodes part of my name. Monroe sounded just as good, I tried to reason.

"Hey." This whispered greeting tickled my ear and brought an immediate smile to my face. This was just the distraction that I needed. "Do you have a minute?"

Derrick placed his hands on my hips, but I shoved them away. "Are you trying to get me fired?" I hissed.

"No, come with me," he said and took my hand. I stumbled as he pulled me towards the door. I glanced back and caught Claire watching us. Her face, as usual, was unreadable. But the furrow in her brow appeared to be more from concern rather than anger. I just wasn't sure who the concern was meant for: me or Derrick.

"What is so important?" I asked once we were out on the street and away from the eyes and ears of the bar.

"Are you excited for tonight? Ready?"

"Yes and no."

He took my face into his hands and tilted it towards him. My body warmed under his touch, and when his eyes met mine, my heart jumped into my throat. *Easy girl.*

"You are going to be amazing tonight, you know that, right? Your dad will be proud of you."

"Shit, I forgot he was coming." Nerves and anxiety replaced the butterflies Derrick's touch had given me.

"Don't think about it. Just go back in there and do your job, get distracted by customers and gossip with the girls. Then, get your fine ass on stage with me and sing your heart out. It will come naturally once you're up there with me. And I'll be right there with you if anything goes wrong. I won't leave you hanging."

"Promise?" I asked, the question catching in my throat. I knew he'd meant he wouldn't leave me alone on the stage but a tiny (teeny, tiny, minuscule) part of me read a bit more into that than I cared to admit.

"Always," he replied. He didn't release his hold on me, and I didn't dare move. When he leaned in closer, my eyes fluttered closed all on their own. A surge of relief and calm filled me when his lips pressed against mine. Each kiss after our first had become more and more gentle. Noah had called him One-Night-Stand Derrick, but this kiss didn't feel like a one-night-stand kiss. The kisses yesterday morning hadn't felt that way either.

When he pulled away, I sighed. I didn't want to feel what I was feeling, but it was happening with or without my permission.

"See you in a few hours." He kissed my forehead and nodded towards the bar.

"See you," I said. I waited for a moment to see if there was another kiss or touch I could steal and keep with me as the night drug on, but he stood still as if he were waiting for the same.

"Abby," Jessie said as she leaned out the front door, "you've got a table. Super-hot old guy at table ten."

"Go get 'em," Derrick said and touched my arm. I closed my eyes to savor the feeling of his skin on mine one last time.

Back inside, I found the super-hot old guy at table ten was none other than one Alan Monroe. I had to laugh and gag a little at Jessie's description of my father and couldn't wait to tell her the truth.

"Abby," he said with a smile as he stood to hug me.

"You're early."

"I figured it would be easier to camp out here rather than go home and drive back. If I get bored, I can just head up to the condo for a few."

"Um," I said and swallowed back the bile that rose from my stomach, "I don't think that's a good idea."

"Why? I still have a key; I can just let myself in, so you don't have to miss any of your shift."

"No, it's not that. It's just that, um, well, Jacob showed up yesterday morning."

His eyes grew wide. He shook his head and whispered, "Are you okay? Is everything okay?"

I was touched by his concern. "Yeah, I think so. He wants me to sign the papers."

"You haven't?"

"No, I need to tell him about—" I couldn't finish the sentence. The words hung somewhere between my heart and my lips, and they refused to budge, but he knew. He nodded in understanding.

"Then, I'll be here all night. What do you have in the way of food?"

I laughed. "I hope you like chips and salsa or chicken tenders and fries."

He smiled and ordered a Yazoo draft and the chips and salsa.

I found Jessie huddled in the kitchen with Claire. When I told her who the super-hot old guy was, she laughed and asked if he was married, then proceeded to pout when I told her he was. I enjoyed the easy banter Jessie and I had and had hoped Claire would join in, but she kept quiet.

"What's her deal?" I asked Jessie when Claire excused herself.

"I really shouldn't say anything," she said with a sigh, "but I will say that she is very protective of Derrick."

"Why?"

"That's something only she can answer." With that, Jessie handed me a basket of chips and salsa and walked away.

The rest of the afternoon passed slowly. Aside from Dad, I didn't get many other tables until just before open mic started. The tips were equally depressing. Normally, I wouldn't have cared, but I didn't want him to notice or think I wouldn't be able to pay him rent. That wasn't why he was here, but I couldn't help but worry.

Derrick and I were up last. He had a thing about being the one to close out the night. For me, that meant I had to listen to one amazing song after another and convince myself that I wouldn't measure up. By the time it was our turn, my stomach had twisted itself so many different ways, I thought I was going to pass out. I'd been watching the door all night waiting for him to walk in. Each time I glanced that way, I'd catch Claire's eye. It was as if she knew what I was doing and was aware that my looking for Derrick had nothing to do with our song. I mean, it did and it didn't.

At ten until nine, I was starting to get worried. We were scheduled to go on at 9:15, and I hadn't seen Derrick yet. I stood at the bar chewing my thumbnail and staring at the door.

"He'll show," Claire said.

"What?" I asked.

"Derrick. He'll be here. He is dependable."

"That's not what Noah or anyone else thinks."

"Some people like to assume the worst, but I know Derrick, and I see how he looks at you. He won't let you down."

I turned to her to ask another question, but she was gone before I got it out. I didn't know how to take Claire on a normal night, and tonight she was anything but normal.

Rather than dwell on what she'd said, I checked on Dad and brought him another beer. He'd been pacing himself all night and had only ordered three. He'd stepped out once or twice to make a call but other than that, he stuck around and made small talk with me and Jessie.

As the minute hand ticked closer and closer to our time slot, my knees grew weaker. At 9:10, I sat down in the chair next to Dad. He put his hand on my shoulder. He could sense my nervous energy, and I was certain he knew his being there was part of it.

My eyes never left the door. So, when Derrick strolled in at 9:12, I was hit with a wave of relief and then complete and utter terror.

"No, no, no." I shook my head, and my body trembled. "This isn't happening."

Derrick found his way to me and started to ask if I was ready when he saw the look on my face. He turned and followed my gaze. The recognition hit him in an instant. "Do you want me to ask him to leave?"

I started to say yes but shook my head. "No, let's do this." There was no way Jacob had known he'd find me here. Judging by the shocked look in his eyes when he saw me in my Gulch Dive Bar tank top, he was just as surprised to see me as I was to see him.

I followed Derrick to the stage, and Jessie brought me my guitar that I'd stashed behind the bar. As we stepped onto the slightly elevated stage, Derrick took my hand and whispered into my ear. "He's a fucking fool."

I giggled and nodded. He was a fucking fool, and I was about to show him that the dreams he'd mocked weren't childish or ridiculous.

"How is everyone doing tonight?" Derrick asked into the microphone just like he did every week. "Tonight, I've got a very talented and beautiful guest with me. Please give a warm welcome to my new writing partner, Abby Monroe!"

I blinked and stared at him.

"What? His last name doesn't deserve credit for any of this," he whispered to me as he turned away from the microphone. I smiled and mouthed a thank you. I climbed up onto the stool next to Derrick and positioned my guitar on my lap. He counted us in and played the first chord just as we'd practiced.

"*Tonight's about dancin' and drinkin' and doin' what I shouldn't,*" I sang into the microphone. I scanned the crowd for Jacob so I could watch his face as the room reacted to the song Derrick and I had written. By the time I made it through the intro chorus, his face was red with rage. I looked right into his eyes as I sang the first verse. "*Hey, hey, hey. It's lookin' like a good night to do what I shouldn't. I'm gonna chase my whiskey with a double shot of trouble. 'Cause I'm not your girl tonight. I'm not yours anymore. I ain't followin' your rules. Tonight's about me. Tonight, I'm free.*"

He glared at me, shook his head, and stomped out of the bar. The door slammed behind him, and a tiny wave of victory and pride ran through me. Guilt followed and crashed my high. I managed to make it through to the end of the song but not without feeling like a complete and utter asshole.

Derrick took my hand, and we stood and bowed for the crowd. He didn't let go until we exited the stage. Before I realized what was happening, his lips were on mine, and the entire room was shouting around us. He released me and said, "Don't worry about him. You killed it, Abby. You were perfection."

I smiled and tried to respond with words but was overwhelmed. The rush of the stage, that intoxicating kiss, the anger on Jacob's face. It was all too much.

"Abby," Dad said and pulled me into a hug. If he'd seen Derrick's kiss, he didn't react. "Wow, that was incredible."

"Thanks."

He took my hand and placed a piece of paper in it. "I don't deserve this, and I don't need it. Take it and buy a new guitar or invest in studio time. I believe in you, Abby, I do, and I know it's too late to start supporting you and your dreams, but I'd like to if you'll let me."

I looked down at my hand and found the rent check. "Dad? No, I can't take this back; I agreed to pay rent."

"Then, I'm going back on our agreement. I meant what I said the other day, things are better with you here, and if I get a second chance at being your dad, I'm taking it."

I tried to argue again, but he pulled me into one last hug and said he had to get home. He promised to be there every week to see me perform. "Promise me, you will keep at it, Abby."

The room spun around me, and my eyes refused to focus. My stomach wouldn't stop turning. I needed air. I grabbed Derrick's arm and pulled him away from a group of adoring fans. "Can you get me out of here, please?" I asked, not caring about my tables or finishing my shift.

CHAPTER EIGHTEEN

Derrick pushed the door open and said, "This is me."

I stepped through the red doorframe and blinked as I took in the spotless living room. A brown leather couch and loveseat sat in the middle of the room on top of a brightly colored rug. We'd driven to his house in East Nashville in silence. He'd held my hand the entire drive and rubbed his thumb in tiny circles over my skin. By the time we pulled into the back driveway, my heart had slowed to a normal pace and my eyes were brimming with tears but clearer than they had been.

I sat down on the couch, and Derrick brought me a glass of water.

"Damn, Abby, what did he do to you?" he asked as he sat next to me and pulled me into his arms. I nestled back into his shoulder and let the rhythm of his breathing help me find the words.

"It's more about what I did."

"Do you want to talk about it?"

I shook my head but started telling him anyway. "I lied to him. Not just a little lie but a big one. The biggest lie possible and he has no idea."

"Was there someone else?" His voice softened and took on a raw emotion I'd never heard from him. It was strained and full of something I could only describe as pain.

"No, never." I drew in a deep breath, held it and then let it out slowly. "Jacob wanted to start a family. It was all he wanted. When we were younger and had just gotten married, we talked about it all the time. We'd have a boy and a girl. We gave them names and shared which feature we'd each pass on to them. It was always more his dream than mine but all I wanted back then was to make him happy."

He rubbed my back, encouraging me to continue.

"You'd think I'd have wanted it too, but I grew up with a fucked-up family. My dad left when I was ten. He met someone new and moved to Nashville. We never heard from him. My mom struggled after that. She couldn't keep a job or a boyfriend, and my sister and I were passed around from relative to relative while she tried to scrape together enough money for food and rent. I didn't have much of a childhood, you know, and I never wanted to put a kid through that. My mother tried her best, I know she did, but I didn't exactly have the best example growing up."

She tried so hard she nearly drank herself to death. It was Lindsey's and my job to make sure she fell asleep on her side and without a cigarette in her hand. When I was fifteen, just after I started dating Jacob, she finally got her shit together and got a job answering phones at a local insurance office. Things steadied out from there, but I was always waiting for the other shoe to drop.

Derrick kissed the top of my head. "That couldn't have been easy for you."

"We survived. I thought Jacob was my answer to everything. The way he used to look at me made my knees weak. God, I'd have done anything for him."

"What happened?"

"I'd always found peace in music and started writing when Dad left. It started with little rhymes about family to record my memories of him. Mom scraped together enough money to buy me a guitar for my tenth birthday, and I started teaching myself to play. With my guitar and pen, I started to find a way out."

"Music had the same effect on me, though I had less to escape."

"Growing up with money doesn't always make things easier."

"We all have our own demons to fight."

I let my body sink further into his. I ignored the nagging reminder that Derrick and I were just writing partners who happened to sleep together a few times. Nothing more. It didn't matter how I felt inside his arms or how tender his touch was. It didn't change anything. I couldn't let myself get too comfortable.

"When we first got married, Jacob encouraged my writing. He listened to me play and work out lyrics. After a while, I think he realized my hobby was more than a hobby and he started discouraging it. He'd accidentally throw away my lyric notes or forget to pick up new guitar strings when I asked. It was subtle, and I didn't even notice at first. He packed up my guitar and started talking about painting the spare room pale yellow."

"That's not very subtle."

"No, but I missed it all. One day, I was in the attic and found my guitar. I brought it down and started playing again. I lost track of time, and when Jacob came home and found me playing, he made some snide comment about me never letting go of my ridiculous dreams. That's when everything clicked. I started playing more and writing every night. I'd come to bed late."

At first, he tolerated my rediscovery of my passion. He never listened to me sing. Instead, he'd find an excuse to leave the room or leave the house. We started fighting more and more.

"I don't remember when I told him I wanted to move to Nashville and try to make something of it, but it became an ongoing fight. I even offered a compromise that we could start talking about babies again if he agreed to move, but he'd never leave Missouri or his family. He made that perfectly clear."

I closed my eyes and waited for the lump in my throat to subside. Derrick's chest rose and fell beneath my face. He didn't say a word as he waited for me to start up again. Swiping a tear from my eye, I sat up and looked at him. His eyes were intently focused on me.

"I don't know how to tell the rest of the story," I said.

He took my hands into his and squeezed them. "Tell it however you want to."

"We had a pregnancy scare around Christmas," I said and decided the leave out the part about Jacob sabotaging my birth control, "Well, for me it was a scare. He knew I was late and was practically bursting at the seams with excitement. We were out on Christmas Eve and fighting, as per our usual. I had a test in my purse but was terrified to take it. After he scolded me for ordering wine, I went to take it. When I did, it—"

A sob choked me as I tried to finish the sentence. I'd never spoken these words out loud to anyone. Not even to my dad, who was the only other person who knew the truth. We'd never talked about it after that day.

I couldn't stop the tears even if I'd wanted to. When they started flowing down my cheeks, Derrick took me back into his arms and rocked me gently until they slowed. I didn't have to tell him the rest. He knew. I could tell in the way his hand drifted over my stomach.

"I left Missouri that night and drove all way to Nashville. I made an appointment for early January but never made it. I lost the baby a few days before."

My body trembled as the truth gutted me. Admitting this to Derrick put the whole ugly truth out into the universe. It wasn't just my secret now. He carried part of it too. I hated that I'd unloaded it on him, but he seemed unphased.

"Abby," he whispered, "he doesn't know any of this?"

I shook my head. "I lied and told him the test was negative."

He let out a deep sigh but didn't break his hold on me. "That's a lot to carry by yourself."

"I know I have to tell him before I sign the papers. It won't change anything, and it will hurt him, but he deserves to know."

Derrick's arms tightened around me. I burrowed myself deeper into him and wondered if I could crawl inside his skin and be someone else for a while. Someone who had their shit together and wasn't burdened with life's hard truths, but I knew he wasn't either of those things. I pressed my hand to his chest and pushed myself up.

"Thank you," I said. "I know that you didn't want to hear any of that or deal with all of this, but I appreciate that you did."

"I want to know everything about you, even the hard stuff."

The sentiment was sweet, but I also knew the truth. One-Night-Stand Derrick was just that. He wasn't here for the long haul or to help me clean up my mess, but he could help me forget it. Now that I'd unleashed all of it on him, I wanted to forget all about it.

I slid one hand under his shirt and inched the other towards the waist of his jeans. He grabbed my wrist to stop me. I looked up at him and pouted.

"We don't have to do this." His voice was thick. I pulled my hand free and slipped inside his jeans to show him that while we didn't have to do anything, I wanted to. "Abby."

"What?" I asked. I held perfectly still. When I found his eyes studying me, a fresh wave of tears rose inside me. He shook his head. My tears changed from sadness to anger. "What? You don't want me now that you know the truth?"

He furrowed his eyebrows and frowned. "No, that's not it. Abby, you're too emotionally vulnerable right now; I don't want to take advantage of that or you."

"You aren't." My nose burned as I fought the tears back. "I want you."

"Abby," he whispered.

"Stop saying my name like that. Like I'm some fragile piece of glass," I cried. I pulled his face to mine and pushed my lips against his. He didn't kiss me back at first. "Please." I mumbled the word into his mouth.

He sighed and shifted below me and put his hands on my hips, pulling me deeper onto his lap. "Abby, I—" Whatever he had to say could wait. His lips found mine with a renewed sense of urgency.

There were no more words to be had. Instead, we spoke through long, desperate kisses and lingering touches. Each one erasing more and more of the memory of Jacob. I leaned into the burning pain that had never really left me and let it drive me further into Derrick's arms. He pulled my shirt over my head and removed my bra in two swift movements. I tugged the belt from his jeans and tossed it aside. His mouth found my breast, and he ran his tongue over my nipple. His hunger for me felt just as strong as mine for him. I didn't know the source of his pain, but I felt it in each desperate kiss. I took it and buried it alongside mine. Two lost, broken souls finding their way out of the darkness.

My back arched, pushing me further into his mouth. He lifted his hips. I slid my fingers through his belt loops and shimmied his jeans down his legs. He stopped me long enough to remove a condom from his pocket. I smiled down at him and silently thanked him for being prepared. I watched eagerly as he slid it down. By the time he was done, my jeans and underwear joined his on the floor. I guided him into place and then sank down. He groaned as I took control. I pressed forward and found his lips, pulling his lower lip into my mouth, I gave it a gentle nibble.

The salt of my tears dripped onto my tongue. He slowed for a moment to swipe his thumb over my cheek and clear away any that remained.

"Abby," he whispered my name into the dark room as if he were searching for something he'd lost and then suddenly found.

I tried to say his name, but my voice refused to cooperate. I rested my forehead against his and hoped my touch was enough to show him the words I couldn't find. I gasped for air and then hungrily pressed my lips against his and pulled him deeper into me.

The release I'd so desperately needed reverberated through me in an uncontrollable, melodic wave, and I collapsed onto him. He'd taken my heartbreak in as his own. He couldn't carry the burden for me, but he'd done what he could to lessen the weight.

Derrick raked his fingers through my hair and pulled me into his chest. I closed my eyes and listened to his heart racing in his chest.

CHAPTER NINETEEN

Armed with a goodbye kiss from Derrick and a latte, I pushed open the door of my condo, ready to confess everything to Jacob. The sun was just coming up and peeking through my living room windows. I hadn't intended on falling asleep in Derrick's couch, but when I woke up in his arms an hour ago, I didn't regret it for a second.

"I fed your ungrateful cat," Jacob said. I startled. I hadn't expected him to be awake just yet. I'd hoped for at least three minutes of peace on my balcony before confronting him.

"Thanks." I dropped my purse and keys on the kitchen counter.

"Little shit about took my hand off."

Niles rubbed up against my leg and mewed his confirmation that Jacob wasn't exaggerating.

"Where were you?" he asked.

"Do you want me to answer that?" He shook his head as I handed him the coffee, I'd picked up for him. "We need to talk, and I need you to promise you'll listen."

"If it ends with you signing the papers, then I'll listen."

"It will," I said and nodded towards the balcony. "Let's go out there and talk. I could use the fresh air."

I wasn't sure being out on my balcony when I confessed the truth to Jacob was a good idea, given that he definitely had the upper-body strength to throw me off of it if he wanted to, but I did need the air and the song of the city to help me through this.

I let him sit in the one chair I had. Pacing in front of him, I bit my thumbnail as I considered my words. Telling Derrick was one thing. He didn't have any skin in the game. My past was just that to him. Jacob was something else entirely. I was about to tell him that I'd lost a piece of him. Not just that but also that I'd lied to him and had planned to never tell him the truth.

"Do you remember Christmas Eve?" I started. He rolled his eyes and nodded.

"Pretty sure that's a night that I'll never forget."

"Fair enough. You know I took the pregnancy test in the bathroom, right?" My voice shook as I spoke. I tried to steady and calm myself by focusing on the rush of the cars below. This time, they didn't work. Nothing would calm me.

"Yes, I remember the look of pure joy on your face when you told me it was negative."

I closed my eyes and took a deep breath before blurting the beginning out. "It wasn't," I said.

"I'm sorry?" He shook his head and sat up straight. He'd heard me loud and clear; I was certain of it. Now he wanted me to spell it out.

"The test," I said as a wave of nausea passed through me, as if I needed any more reminders of my brief pregnancy. "It was positive."

I watched him closely as the truth sank in. His face went white as he took in my words and compared them with the lack of roundness in my belly. He leaned forward and wrapped his hands behind his head. His shoulders rose and fell with each slow breath he took. When he sat back up there was a coldness in his eyes.

"You were pregnant? *We* were pregnant?" he snapped and rose to his feet. "What did you do?"

I shook my head and took a step back. He took one forward, closing the distance between us. He stopped just in front of me and locked his eyes on mine. I shrank back, fearing the intensity buried in the ocean-blue eyes I used to love getting lost in. He stood quiet and still, then whispered, "What did you do?"

I flinched and looked away. I couldn't process or handle the desperation pouring out of him. My entire body shook. I'd seen Jacob angry before, but this was new. His anger mixed with the sadness. He looked as lost as I felt. His skin flashed with splotches of blood red, and his eyes were wide. With every ragged breath, his nostrils flared wide. The negative energy buzzed off of him.

"Jacob," I said his name as calmly as I could and held up my hands. A truck horn honked on the street below and pulled his attention away from me long enough for me to move back towards the sliding door that led back into my condo. I stood with my back to it and waited.

"I need a minute." He dropped back into the chair and let his head loll over the back. I waited a few seconds before continuing.

I spoke as slowly as I could in order to keep my own emotions under control. He was already angry; he didn't need my tears any more than I needed his. Not that he would cry. Jacob Rhodes never cried. "I was scared, and I panicked. I didn't plan any of this; I need you to know that. I wasn't planning to leave, but as soon as I saw that test, I knew I had to. I felt nothing but terror when I read the word. It was a cowardly thing to do, but I don't know that I'd change it if I could go back. I needed this, Jacob. I wasn't happy. We weren't happy. You and I both knew it."

"That was my baby." I could hear the unspoken question in his voice. The words he couldn't force himself to say.

"This is the part I need you to hear. Can you just listen?" He gave a slow nod that wasn't at all convincing. Cotton filled my mouth, and my chest tightened. *You can do this.* I closed my eyes and breathed in as deeply as I could. My lungs expanded and stretched until they ran out of room. I exhaled and said, "I did intend to terminate. I had an appointment set. But I … I lost the baby."

"Lost it?" He spoke slowly and with intention. He was trying to control the emotion that I could see brewing back up in his eyes.

"I had a miscarriage. The doctor said it was spontaneous and that it isn't that uncommon." I dropped my head forward, unable to look at him any longer. I wrapped my arms over my stomach and held myself.

"But you were going to abort my baby without so much as a phone call? You lied to me, Abby. You denied me the chance to have a say in any of this."

"I know." I couldn't argue with him even if I'd wanted to. He was right. What I'd done was far worse than anything he'd ever done. He'd tried to kill my dreams. I'd tried to terminate the life he'd planted inside of me.

A lifetime passed between us out on that balcony. Neither of us spoke or made a move to console or react to the other. In the silence, I struggled to find the peace I had hoped this moment would bring. I'd had some naive notion that the truth was what had been weighing me down. In a way, it was, but not in the words I'd needed to say. The weight came from the loss and having gone through it alone and without the one person who might have understood the pain and grief. I'd denied both of us of that. I'd been too selfish to see it then, but now it was clear as the sky. I'd needed him even if I hadn't wanted him.

He stood up and pushed past me to get into the condo. "Sign the fucking papers, Abby. I never want to see you again. Once you sign this," he said and shoved the papers in my face, "you no longer exist. I gave you fourteen years of my life and *this* is how you repay me? By lying to me and planning to kill the only thing I ever wanted from you? I was never the perfect husband, but I never lied to you. Not once. I know you think I sabotaged you and took those pills out of your suitcase, but I didn't. I didn't intentionally forget to grab a condom. I got caught up in the moment with my *wife*. I loved you, Abby. You seemed to have forgotten that in all of this. I would never do anything to you without your consent. I may have hated your stance on starting a family, but I would never force it on you."

I stood in front of him with my mouth hanging open. I didn't know what to say to that. If he was telling the truth, I'd misread everything. It didn't undo what had happened, and it wouldn't have if I'd have known. I probably wouldn't have listened to him if he'd tried to argue with me when I'd accused him of trying to impregnate me without my permission. My mind had been made up, and there was no changing it. I wouldn't have wanted the baby either way.

I took the papers and pen from his hand and carried them to the kitchen. I placed them on the counter as he stood behind me and pointed to each spot that need a signature or an initial. My hand trembled as I signed. He ignored the tears that dripped from my cheeks and left stains beside each signature.

"I am sorry," I said as I handed him the signed papers.

"Fuck you."

He ripped the papers out of my hand and pushed them into the envelope. He gave me one last look and was gone. The door slammed shut behind him. I slid to the floor and crumpled into a ball, tucking my legs into my chest. I rocked myself back and forth, just as I'd done so many mornings after I lost the baby. The tears would eventually stop, I reminded myself; they always did.

When they did, I picked myself up off the floor and called the one last person I needed to confess to.

"Mom," I said through my sniffles when she answered, "I need to tell you something."

CHAPTER TWENTY

I floated through the rest of the week by ignoring calls from Derrick and my mother. Mom hung up on me when I called her Thursday morning, and I was sure I wouldn't hear from her again. She'd never come out and said it, but I knew she'd been patiently waiting for grandbabies from Jacob and me. She was also strongly anti-abortion, which was the one reason I'd never told her. I hated keeping things from her, but at the time, I couldn't handle her judgment.

Derrick, for his part, had called several times a day. On Sunday, he showed up at the bar and sat in my section while I avoided him. I felt bad giving him the cold shoulder after our night together, but if I couldn't even stand the sight of myself, how could I expect him to? Not after all I'd confessed. Not after the things Jacob had said to me. I didn't deserve anyone's time, much less his. I missed him, though. His absence left a hole in my bed and in me. I tried to pretend the ache wasn't related to him, and maybe he wasn't fully to blame, but there was a sliver of emptiness that belonged to him. And that was a truth I wasn't yet ready to confront.

Sleep had eluded me, but when I did find it, I tossed and turned through dream after dream of the same towheaded baby girl with

Jacob's blue eyes. The dream always started with me alone in a dark room. The desperate cries of a needy infant would fill the room. My dream self would stumble toward the crib and reach for her. I'd stretch my arms as far as they would go as her cries grew louder and louder. My own tears joined hers as I realized I couldn't reach her. Our fingers would touch for a moment, only for her to slip further and further away. I'd pull myself over the railing and force my body to morph into Stretch Armstrong, but she was always out of reach. Eventually, her blood-curdling screams would pull me into the darkness with her, and I'd fall into the crib. I'd awake in my own dark, lonely room drenched in sweat and tears.

By Monday, I was dead to the world. But I dragged myself out of bed and slapped on tinted moisturizer before grabbing a T-shirt and jeans from the floor of my closet. I didn't bother with my hair. Dad had seen me looking way worse, and besides, it's not like he would say anything. Rather than calling an Uber, I decided to walk to Starbucks because I needed fresh air.

As if I hadn't learned my lesson the two other times over the last week that I decided I needed "fresh air." Because both of those had gone so well when I'd stepped outside with Jacob.

I regretted my decision the instant I stepped out into the thick, humid summer air, but I stuck it out, and by the time I made it to Starbucks, I was five minutes late, and my hair was as big as Reba's in the '80s.

I found Dad sitting at our usual table. He twisted in his seat when he heard me panting behind him.

"Jesus, Abby, did you walk?"

I held up my finger as I tried to catch my breath. "Yes."

"Is your car broken? Do you need money for an Uber?"

"No, I thought I needed fresh air," I said and eagerly sipped the latte he handed me. After the past few days, you'd think I'd have learned my lesson about fresh air. Apparently, fresh air wasn't actually good for me. Or, more specifically, me and Jacob. I cringed at his name. I felt the weight of Dad's stare and averted my eyes.

"What?"

"I told Jacob about everything."

"Everything?" It was then I remembered that Dad and I hadn't talked about the *incident* since it happened. I never brought it up, and if he'd tried, I never noticed. I'm sure there were underlying questions in all of his "Are you okay, Abby?" greetings, but he never pressed the issue.

I sank into the chair across from him and nodded. "The baby and the miscarriage. All of it."

"Wait, he didn't know?" Dad's nose wrinkled in concern. A week ago, I might have read that as disgust, but today I knew it meant something different. If there were a way to travel back in time and relive the last few months with this newfound knowledge, I'd do it in a heartbeat. I'd never given Dad a chance.

"Um, no." I might as well embrace my full assholeness. "I lied and told him the test was negative, and then I left in the middle of the night. I guess we have a lot more in common than I led you to believe."

"You're not me, Abby. It took me twenty years to own my mistake and to try to make things right with you."

"Jacob will never forgive me," I said. I had no right to expect him to. I dropped my gaze down to the table and ran my finger through the condensation that dripped from my cup. I drew circles and hearts and stars as a comfortable silence fell between us. It was nice to not feel like I had to fill the space with awkward small talk.

"I think you need to work on forgiving yourself first," Dad said.

"That may take longer than twenty years." I could live three lifetimes and I doubt I would ever be able to forgive myself, much less forget it.

"I'm really glad you invited me on Wednesday. I wish I could have stayed longer, but it was getting late, and I'm an old man."

I laughed. "How did you know that Jenny was worth leaving everything for?" I asked, and then realized I owed him at least one acknowledgment of his attendance before diving into hyper-personal questions. "I mean, thank you for coming. It meant a lot to me to have you there, and I promise I'm okay paying rent."

"Well, speaking of Jenny, when I told her about our conversation, she scolded me and said I had no right to charge rent on her condo."

"I'd like to know her, Dad, if you'll let me." I looked at him and waited for his answer.

He sighed and said, "I think maybe it's time. Let me talk to her, and we'll find a time, okay?"

"I'd love that." I did love the idea of it, and I was ready to meet his family, but the thought of being in his new house with the family he chose over us sent my insides spiraling. There was enough hesitation in his voice to make me consider changing my mind, but he reached across the table to put his hand on mine. My fingers, still wet from playing in the puddles on the table, slipped away from his.

"They do know about you," he said with a hint of sadness. I studied his face as he spoke. "Adam and Eric know I have two daughters that live in Missouri. They know Mommy wasn't my first wife, and they know that you live here now. I'm pretty sure they've watched the video of you singing a dozen or more times since I came home that night."

"You recorded it?" I asked. Pride beamed through my words. Just like that, I was transported back to third grade and seeing half of Dad's face poking out from the side of the camcorder as I sang "Tomorrow" during *Annie*. After he left, I watched that video over and over so I could watch myself through his eyes and try to find the reason he left.

"Of course, I did. Do you remember when you played Annie?"

I smiled as tears pricked my eyes. "I do."

"Before I left, I made a copy of the video and would watch it on nights I couldn't sleep. I remember showing Jenny the footage and telling her, 'My girl is a star.'"

"Dad." His name caught in my throat as a tear rushed from my eyes and rolled down my nose. "Why did you leave us? Me?"

"You asked me earlier how I knew Jenny was worth leaving everything behind, and the answer is, I didn't. I had no idea of the consequences. Your mom and I married young. I mean, we were seventeen when Lindsey was born and barely twenty when you came along. We didn't know what we were doing with each other, much less the two perfect, loud, needy humans we created together. I'd spent my entire life in Wishing and didn't have a clue what lay outside. When I met Jenny, all of those possibilities opened. If I could go back and do it over, I'd do it differently, but I'd still leave because I know now that I wasn't who I needed to be there."

I heard so much of myself in his answer. It hurt. I'd been left in the wake of his self-discovery, and we'd all paid a price for his happiness, but now I could understand it. At ten, there was no way to know or comprehend what happened. My mother was angry and bitter for years after, and she filled my head with horror stories of my father. Every birthday he missed was another reminder that there was someone more important to him than me. She didn't sugar coat anything, and I'd come here expecting to find a selfish, angry man who'd turn me out on the streets.

But he hadn't been any of those things.

Okay, maybe a little selfish but so was I. I'd taken so much from Jacob, and he'd never have a chance at getting any of that back. I regretted hurting him but not leaving. Leaving was the right thing to do. I wasn't who I needed to be in Wishing. I wasn't so sure I was who I needed to be now, but I was getting closer.

I wiped my eyes clear and smiled up at him. "We're starting over, right?" I asked.

"I'd like to, yes." This time, I reached for his hand and took it into mine.

"Me, too. I need you to know something, though, Dad. I don't remember a man who didn't know how to be a dad. I have so many memories of you lifting me high into the air and helping me fly. You were always in the front row. That's the dad I remember."

His chin twitched as he pulled his lower lip into his mouth and nodded. "Thank you for that, Abby."

CHAPTER TWENTY-ONE

I dropped back against the back wall of the elevator, grateful for both the silence and the air conditioning. Dad had offered to drive me home, but he'd been glancing at the time for much of our coffee date, and I assumed he had more important things to do. Turns out, the sun is way worse at nine in the morning than it is at six.

When my tiny, metal icebox reached the twelfth floor, I meandered down the hall with whatever energy I could muster. My eyes fought to stay open. The long work weekend combined with insomnia and nightmares had worked a number on me. I had every intention of collapsing straight into bed and not waking up until my shift on Wednesday.

My plans for a nap/coma were dashed when I saw the tall, bearded, tattooed man standing at my door. When he heard my shuffling down the hall, he turned around. My heart skipped a beat at the sight of him. He had a large brown bag in one hand and a single purple iris in the other. His guitar was propped against the door.

"I thought you weren't the type to bring a girl flowers?"

"I didn't bring flowers. I brought a flower." He smirked. The adorable half-smile dropped from his face as he took me in. I tried not to flinch or read too much into the way his eyes dimmed. "Have you slept?"

His question unleashed everything I'd managed to ignore during my time with Dad. The exhaustion, fear, and shame swelled to the surface, and I couldn't fight it anymore. I fell against him and burrowed my face into his shirt. His aftershave mingled with the smell of him, the familiar scent tickled my nose and comforted me all at once. With his hands full, he couldn't hold me the way I needed him to, so I slipped back and silently dug my keys from my pocket.

"I'm sorry I haven't answered the phone." I yawned and pushed the door open. He reached around me and held it open. I took the iris from him and lifted it to my nose. Any other man would have gone the easy route and bought a dozen roses, but not Derrick. I knew this iris was from the tiny garden in front of his house. I'd admired it when I was leaving his house before dawn. He'd been listening.

"You've been through a lot this week."

"That smells like cheap takeout Chinese."

"Your nose is wise, Missouri." He hadn't called me Missouri in at least a week. Until he said it just then, I didn't realize how much I'd missed it. He dropped the food on the counter and held his arms open. "Come here."

I didn't hesitate. I was in his arms in less than two steps. I breathed him in again and wrapped my arms around his back; his arms pulled me in. He stroked the top of my head with one hand and my back with the other. *This is what I needed*, I thought. Strong silence. A firm embrace. A sense that nothing could penetrate the calmness and bring reality crashing back in. With Derrick, everything hard melted away. The rough edges smoothed and whatever threats existed before were banished.

Fear bubbled below that calmness, though. The fear that he would eventually live up to his reputation and leave me without my dragon or moat to protect the glass castle we'd built in our short time together. *One-Night-Stand Derrick*. I'd tried so hard to be in the moment with him and focus only on the proof in front of me and not the warnings sounded by others, but they always managed to sneak in through the tiny cracks and fester.

I slipped from his hold and reached for the bag of food. "How did you get Chinese food at nine in the morning?"

"I know a guy," he said.

"And how did you know that Kung Pao chicken was exactly what I wanted for my second breakfast?"

"Because I know you."

"Yeah?" I smiled as he slid by me and went straight to the cabinet with the plates. I leaned against the counter and admired the ease with which he navigated my kitchen. "When do I get to learn about you?"

"You know all the important things."

"I don't." I took a plate of Kung Pao from him and stole an egg roll out of the bag. He kept his back to me and continued on as if I hadn't said anything.

"Coffee doesn't pair well with Chinese, and it's far too early for wine," he said as he peered into my fridge, "is this sweet tea or Midwest tea?"

"Midwest tea?"

"Dry, nasty, unsweetened."

"Then, it's Midwestern." He gagged and pulled a face. "I have sugar you can add."

"Not the same, Missouri." He settled for a glass of ice water and poured one for me too. We stood at the counter and took our first bites.

"Okay, so I know you prefer sweet tea. You'll order the local draft beer over wine or a cocktail, but you like to sip red wine while we write."

"Sounds about right." A piece of rice flew out of his mouth and landed on my arm.

"Gross," I said and plucked it off and dropped it back on to his plate.

"What else do have you figured out about me?"

I pressed my fingers into the soft spot between his ribs and his hip bone. He jerked away from me. His fork clattered onto the floor. "That," I said with a slight note of victory, "is your one and only ticklish spot."

He bent down to pick up his fork. He lingered on the ground for a minute and then rose slowly. His beard, lips, and the tip of his nose brushed over my arm. He paused at my breast and ran his thumb over my shirt. I sighed and closed my eyes.

"I know all your spots too," he whispered into my ear. I shook off the warming sensation rising inside of me that threatened to weaken my resolve.

"Your dad built this building," I said. We'd established more than once that we knew what made each other tick. I wanted more. I'd spilled my life to him the other night, and I didn't even know his middle name.

"I'm not my dad."

"I didn't say you were. I'm just trying to get to know you."

"You won't get to know me through him."

I sighed and shoved a bite of chicken into my mouth right as Niles jumped onto the counter.

"Hey, buddy." Derrick scratched under his neck. "Do you like rice?"

"Don't feed Niles rice and stop changing the subject."

"I don't want to talk about my dad," he said. I started at the sharpness in his tone.

"Fine." I exhaled and grabbed Niles. I carried him to the couch and sat down. Derrick followed me.

"What is going on?"

Taking a deep breath to steady myself, I chose my words carefully. I didn't want my own emotional state to taint them. "I told you things about myself that I've never told anyone. I opened up to you. The least you could do is tell me something about you."

"My favorite color is green." He laughed and tickled my elbow. I yanked it away from him. I wasn't amused. "Abby."

"No, don't 'Abby' me." I drew my word sword from its sheath and plunged it into him. "I get that this is just sex for you but I—" The words caught in my throat. I couldn't finish. I didn't have any fight left. Every fiber of me was screaming at me to let it go, but I couldn't bear to utter the words. If I spoke them fully into the universe, then they'd be real, and he'd be forced to admit the truth. I wasn't ready for the unfiltered truth.

"Why do you keep saying that?" He rested his hand on my arm and waited for a second, as if he were afraid I'd pull away again. I almost did, but there was something in his touch that stopped me. When my eyes met his, I could see I'd hurt him. My words had proven to be the sword I'd intended them to be. The sadness in his gray eyes gutted me. "Have I done something to make you think that's all I want from you?"

"No," I admitted. He'd never said anything either way. Sure, he'd shown up for me in ways no one else had. He'd done nothing to prove my suspicions right, but still I clung to them like protective armor. If I believed it was all true, it couldn't hurt me when he showed his true colors. "But you said you weren't good for me, One-Night-Stand Derrick."

He winced at the name. "So, you've already made your mind up about me, then?"

"No! I'm trying to get to know you, but you won't let me in."

"By bringing up my dad and rehashing the rumors people have told you?" I didn't respond. He sighed and scooted closer to me. "I want you to know me, too."

"Then talk to me like I've been talking to you."

He scratched his beard and shrugged. "I'm not sure I know how."

"Can I ask you questions, then?"

"If you avoid mentioning my dad, yes."

"When is your birthday?" I decided to start with the basics.

"April 15th."

"Tax Day, huh? That's exciting."

"It was until I opened a bar with my cousin. You'd be surprised how much free shit people give away on Tax Day."

"Why did you open the bar?"

"That is a long story," he said with a sigh. "Did you know Noah and I used to be in a band? Claire, too."

"Oh, can I ask about that?"

He hedged for a moment and closed his eyes. "Not yet." Something in the way he said those two little words told me there was definitely more there that I needed to unpack.

"So, the three of you were in a band." I nudged him to continue.

"Yup. Our parents decided that playing music and having a record deal wasn't living up to the Bale name and insisted we invest our money in a business. So, after we lost the record deal, Noah and I pooled our money and opened the bar. By the time we opened, it was too late for our parents to remind us that a bar wasn't much classier than a guitar."

I wanted to know more and dig deeper, but was afraid asking more questions would scare him back into silence, so I stuck with simple questions.

"One small question about your dad." I wrinkled my nose and pressed my hands together in prayer. "Please?"

"I'll allow it since you're adorable when you beg."

"How did you manage to open a bar in the building your dad owns without him knowing what you were doing."

His lips unfurled into a mischievous grin. "At the time, I was running the leasing for him. So, I approved our lease without him knowing."

"I bet he was pissed."

"I allowed one question about him; that's all you're getting."

"Fair enough." I paused to think of another question. "What's your middle name?"

"Robert."

"Derrick Robert Bale." I liked the way his full name felt on my tongue. I yawned and laid back against the couch. "I want to keep asking questions, but I'm exhausted."

He stood up and then leaned over me. He slipped his arms under me and hoisted me off the couch.

"What are you doing?" I glanced up at his face. He gave me a slow, half-smile. Tenderness filled his eyes.

"I can't, in good conscience, let you sleep on the couch again. I'm taking you to bed."

"As tempting as that sounds, I don't think I have the energy to do that."

He shook his head and set me down beside my bed and pulled back the covers. "In you go." I obliged his request and climbed into my warm, welcoming bed. I adjusted and shifted into position as he pulled the covers up. He bent down and kissed my forehead.

I grabbed his arm and said, "Don't leave. Can you just lay with me?"

He answered by sliding into the bed behind me and wrapping his body over mine. I closed my eyes and let sleep take over for the first time since Jacob left. This time, I was met with a sweet, deep, and dreamless sleep.

CHAPTER TWENTY-TWO

"WHERE ARE WE GOING?" I ASKED AS I CLICKED MY SEATBELT INTO place. Derrick smiled at me and winked.

"It's a surprise."

I debated telling him how much I disliked surprises, but the excitement in his eyes proved to be a good silencer. He reached across the Jeep and grabbed my hand. I squeezed his hand and said, "Can't wait."

I rested my head back against the seat. Almost a month had passed since Jacob's surprise visit. I'd spent much of it tangled up in Derrick's sheets and arms. We didn't do a lot of talking, but we wrote and kissed and did all the other things that left me blushing and filled with warmth.

"How much of Nashville have you seen?" he asked. He stroked the top of my hand with his thumb as he hummed along with the radio.

"Downtown, your place, and I've been to Green Hills, where my dad lives, once."

"And you've been here since January?" I nodded. He glanced out the window and checked his mirrors as he merged onto the interstate. "Why haven't you gotten out to explore?"

"I haven't really been in an exploring mood." I tried to hide the nervousness in my voice as the Tuesday morning rush hour traffic deadlocked around us. Traffic jams weren't much of a thing in Wishing, unless there was a tractor or a runaway cow.

"You okay, Missouri?" he asked as if he were reading my mind.

"We don't have a lot of interstates in Wishing."

"Wishing?" He raised an eyebrow.

"Yeah, where I grew up. You knew that, right?" I asked. Judging by the look of amazement on his face, he didn't.

"You always just say Missouri when you talk about home. I pictured you growing up in a suburb outside of Kansas City. I'm a thousand percent sure I'd remember if you'd mentioned it was called 'Wishing,'" he said with a soft chuckle. "Is that really the name?"

"It is," I said, rolling my eyes. When you grow up in a town called Wishing, you get used to the questions people ask. "There's a wishing well at the center of town. Legend has it, it is magical. There's a festival every year, and you drop in a penny and make your wish for the next year."

"What did you wish for?"

"Depends which version of Abby you're asking."

"See those apartments up there?" Derrick asked and pointed out his window. I leaned forward and followed his finger. I nodded as I took in the faded, peeling paint of the nondescript building. "Noah and I lived there when we moved out."

"Looks a bit run down for the Bales."

He smirked. "Man, we had some good times there."

"Want to tell me about them?"

He shook his head. "Naw, I'd rather know what little Abby wished for."

"She wished for her dad to come home." Derrick gave my hand a soft squeeze. I conjured up an image of eleven-year-old me standing alone beside the well as my mom and sister roamed the different craft booths. Jacob was somewhere in the background; I was fairly certain he'd given me the penny I'd wished with that year. In fact, he'd given me most of the pennies I'd used to wish in the well. All but one. "I stopped there the night I left town."

"What did you wish for then?"

"Forgiveness. A fresh start. To meet a tattooed guitar player."

"How's that one working out for you."

"Two out of three ain't bad."

"You know, Meatloaf doesn't get the credit he deserves."

"My dad used to love that song. I hated it," I said, smiling. Derrick crossed to the far-right lane and pulled onto an exit. "Any clues yet?"

He glanced in his rearview mirror and shook his head. "It's a beautiful day."

The sky was a vibrant, cloudless blue. The sun, bright and high, shined down and warmed my face through the windows. I wasn't sure when we left the city or when the trees replaced the skyline and buildings, but the greenery welcomed me. I wasn't much of an outdoorsy girl. Camping was something I left for Jacob and his dad, same with the hunting and fishing they awoke at the crack of dawn for. I much preferred my new condo in the city to the house we'd shared, which was surrounded by cattle and pig farms. Despite this, trees and clear skies were a welcome sight. It felt like home but a bit less suffocating.

"What are you thinking about?" Derrick asked. He turned down a narrow road and smiled over at me. A small brown sign welcomed us to Four Corners Marina.

"How this reminds me a bit of Wishing."

"You know, if I'd known the name of your hometown, I might have called you Wishing instead of Missouri."

"No," I said, shaking my head, "I like the way Missouri sounds."

"Good," he said with a smirk, "I like the way it feels. But I like 'Abby' even better."

"Me too."

Derrick pulled the car into an empty parking lot. "Perk of working non-traditional hours? You get the lake to yourself." He got out of the car and walked around to my side to open the door for me.

I stepped out and the intense Southern summer heat hit me immediately. I gathered my hair into a ponytail and turned to look at the wide lake in front of us. There were a few rows of docks with every kind of boat imaginable—speed boats, pontoons, things that looked like mini yachts. "Do you come out here a lot?"

Derrick was at the back of the Jeep, unloading what appeared to be a picnic basket and a tackle box. "I try to, but I don't get out here as often as I'd like."

"Do you have a boat?" He led me towards the docks. We walked past row after row of boats. He took a left at the last row and nodded to a pontoon boat at the end.

"I got her the day Beau cut 'Her Eyes.'" He took my hand and helped me onto the boat. "Dad has a lake house up in Kentucky, but I've always preferred Percy Priest Lake. It's home. And I don't need three-story glass mansions destroying my view."

I knew better than to ask another question about his dad, so I let the comment roll. "So, you're taking me fishing?" I asked as he opened the tackle box.

"This is my sanctuary." He held his arms out wide like he was hugging the lake. "I come here to think or decompress. Before I moved into the house, I lived on my old houseboat out here. Right after—" he paused and shook his head as if he'd changed his mind.

"After what?"

"Nothing," he said, shaking his head, "I was in a dark spot for a few years, and I found peace out here."

"It's nice." I sat down on one of the light blue benches and was grateful for the shade the upper level provided. "You should know that I'm not touching any fish. Or gutting them." I gagged a little, and he laughed.

"I figured I'd fish, and you could sunbathe and sing to me."

It was my turn to laugh. "You want me to lay half naked on your boat and sing to you?"

"Maybe leave out the half part," he said. I swatted at him, but he dodged my hand. He handed me a life jacket and helped me slip it on. "No, I think we both could use some time outside and away from the bar and the city and all the drama."

I was about to argue that I no longer had any drama when he climbed behind the wheel and steered away from the dock. Neither of us spoke as he drove. I didn't bring a bathing suit since I didn't know we'd be out on the lake, but I was grateful to have chosen a tank top and shorts instead of the jeans I'd originally put on.

"Sunscreen?" I leaned over his shoulder and asked. He pointed to the basket he'd brought along. I held onto the railing as I walked back to it, careful to not let the motion of the boat knock me over. I opened the basket and pulled out the sunscreen. Derrick stopped the boat and appeared beside me. Without a word, he took the sunscreen from me and squirted a tiny amount into his hands.

"Close your eyes," he said, his voice thick. I did and shivered as his fingers massaged the lotion into my cheeks. He ran his fingers over my ears and down my neck, lingering for a moment on my shoulders before moving down my arms. He knelt down in front of me and hesitated. I opened my eyes and smiled down at him. He put more of the sunscreen in his hands and rubbed them together. He started at my ankle. His touch was light as a feather. He applied a bit of pressure as he worked his fingers and palms over my calves and up my knee and thigh.

The tip of his finger traced under the frayed edges of my shorts. I gasped when he didn't stop. "I don't think the sun is going there," I whispered.

"No, but I might." He brushed his lips over my knee and then kissed my thigh. He wrapped his hands behind me, cupping my butt, and pulled me to him.

Another boat whizzed by, creating a wake that nudged the boat. For a second, I'd forgotten we weren't on land. "Get a room," a voice shouted. Derrick pulled away and rose to his feet. He waved off the nosey passerby and shook his head.

"Damn, I was hoping we'd go straight to dessert." He cleared his throat and left me standing breathless in the middle of the boat. He returned to his seat and started driving again.

I pulled my hand over my mouth and stifled a giggle before joining him at the helm. "You, Derrick Robert Bale, are a tease."

He reached over and rested his hand on my thigh. "Oh, I have every intention of following through."

I didn't doubt him for a second, but I let his promise linger in the air. He pulled the boat into a shaded cove and dropped the anchor.

"Hungry?" he asked.

"Famished."

He'd packed sandwiches, fruit, vanilla cupcakes, wine, and plenty of water. My mouth watered as he laid out the spread. He poured us both a glass of wine, and I reached for a cupcake.

"How'd you know these were my favorite?" I held it up and ignored the fluttering of my heart when I realized they were from the same bakery as the ones on night we first kissed. He picked up the second cupcake and used his finger to remove the icing. He piled it on top of the one I was holding and held up his finger. Smiling, I leaned forward and took his finger into my mouth, licking it clean.

"That is something I will never forget." He took the cupcake from my hand and set it on a plate. Then, he took my head into his hands and kissed me. He pulled back and whispered, "I love the taste of icing on your tongue."

CHAPTER TWENTY-THREE

JESSIE FLOPPED ON THE COUCH AND THREW HER LEGS OVER THE ARMS, leaving nowhere for Claire or Leah to sit. Claire shoved her legs out of the way and made room for herself, while Leah went out to the balcony to drag in my lawn chair. I handed them each a glass of wine and took my usual spot on the floor. Niles, unsure of which female to claim for the evening, nestled himself between Claire and Jessie. It was amazing how different the energy in the condo was when it was filled with women.

I'm still not sure what came over me when I invited them all up to hang out after our shift this Wednesday night, but it was gross and raining outside, and I needed a little less testosterone in my life. They'd all eagerly accepted the invitation.

"This place is nice," Leah said and thanked me for the wine.

"Thank you," I replied. For once, I wasn't embarrassed by the place and didn't feel the need to explain that it was actually my step-mom's place.

Jessie lifted her glass and said, "Cheers to spending a night in with the girls."

"I'll drink to that," Leah replied. Claire and I each nodded in agreement, and we all drank.

"So," Jessie said as she continued sipping her wine, "spill it, Abby." She twirled a chunk of her platinum blonde between her fingers.

"Spill what?" I asked, knowing full well what she was asking.

"You and Derrick. You've sung together three weeks in a row now. New songs each week, I know you two are spending a lot of time together."

"And," Leah said jumping in, "I recognize that leather band on your bathroom counter."

My face flushed red. He'd forgotten it when he left earlier this morning. I'd been spending every waking and non-waking moment with him since he'd surprised me with the fishing trip. We were writing non-stop—ending your marriage and confessing your biggest regret has a way of unleashing the words. We didn't talk about Jacob or the past anymore. I was slowly working my way through everything with each lyric, melody, and chord we wrote. Despite this, I wasn't any closer to peeling back the layers of Derrick Bale.

"I know that face." Jessie giggled.

"What face?" I asked. As much as I hoped my face portrayed a hint of innocence, I knew my eyes were giving me away.

"The face that says, 'Derrick is a snake in the bed,'" Jessie said with a wink.

"What?" Claire asked. She glanced at me over her wine glass before turning back to Jessie.

"Derrick and I had a thing."

Leah choked on her wine and coughed. "When?"

"Last year sometime, just after I started." Jessie shrugged as if to say *"What?"*

"You and Derrick dated?" I asked her, unable to hide my shock.

"'Dated' is a bit formal for what we were. One of us would call for a hookup, and the other would answer. Only lasted for a month or two before I got bored."

"Geez, am I the only one who hasn't broken Noah's rule?" Leah asked. When neither Claire nor Jessie played along with her question, she shook her head. "I don't know whether to be offended or relieved."

I tried not to show the horror I was feeling, but I knew my face was as readable as a children's picture book. I caught Claire watching me and returned her stare with a raised eyebrow. I didn't suspect that she'd have had anything to do with Derrick given the way she looked at Noah, but it was hard to miss her silence on the topic.

"Wait, you didn't sleep with him back when you two were writing together?" Jessie asked.

Leah shook her head. "No. We wrote, and that was it. I was seeing Tony at the time, so I wasn't exactly giving off the 'easy' vibe. Not that he'd have cared that I wasn't single. He doesn't seem to have high standards."

"Ouch," Jessie and I said in unison.

"I didn't mean you two specifically, I just meant he's a man-whore."

"Still, ouch," I said, feeling an urge to stand up for him. "I get that he has a reputation, but I think there's more to him than that. He's a good guy."

As soon as I said it, I wanted to take it back. I meant it, but saying it out loud all but confirmed what they were assuming. While I knew Noah wasn't blind to anything, I worried Claire or one of them would blab to him and confirm that I had, in fact, broken his stupid rule.

"You say that now in the afterglow, but when he moves on to the next girl with shinier hair and a prettier voice, you might feel different," Leah said. She didn't even try to hide her contempt.

"Are you sure you didn't sleep with him?" Jessie asked Leah. "I'm getting a bit of a jilted-lover vibe off of you right now." Her tone implied she was teasing Leah, but Jessie's eyes bore holes into her as she said it.

"Absolutely positive I did no such thing, nor would I."

"Because you think you're better than the rest of us?" Jessie waved her hand around the room.

"I didn't say that," Leah snapped back. "Fuck who you want, just know when you're the one being fucked is all I'm saying."

Claire cleared her throat and said, "I'm with Abby, guys; Derrick is a good guy. I didn't come up here to razz on Abby or get the details on her private life."

"We're just having fun," Jessie said. "Right, Abby?"

I shrugged. I wasn't having any fun listening to this conversation while texts from Derrick lit up my phone beside me. I'd much rather be with him than to have to sit here and listen to all of his conquests that came before me.

"Alright, we'll move on. He's great in the sack, though."

To show I wasn't mortally wounded by the conversation, I raised my glass and nodded. That I could agree with.

"Just promise me you'll be careful with him," Claire said. Her nose wrinkled as if she were trying to hold something in. "He's more fragile than he looks."

"Oh, please, Derrick Bale can hold his own. I'm more worried about Abby. She is fresh out of a divorce and still has that wide-eyed country girl look to her." Jessie laughed.

"I can take care of myself," I argued, "and I have no intention of hurting anyone. Derrick is different around me."

"You two do write great songs," Leah said. "The one you sang tonight about the little girl and her dad, I thought I was going to cry."

"Okay," Jessie said, clearing her throat, "it was a great song, and I'm pretty sure your dad was crying into his beer."

I smiled. Dad had been showing up every week to watch Derrick and I sing. Last week, I even convinced Derrick to move our slot up so Dad could get home in time to tuck the boys in. I'd been surprised at how quickly he agreed. Derrick loved closing out the night, but he didn't hesitate.

"I couldn't look at him while I was singing." I'd slipped once and caught his eye when I got to the line *you may have missed the little moments, but you were there; you were always with me.* Derrick heard the quiver in my voice and took over the lead while I recovered.

"Are you two close?" Claire asked.

"We are getting there. It's a long story."

"We've got time," Leah said. She seemed grateful to have the focus shift away from her, almost as thankful as I was to have the topic move on to something other than Derrick. I still didn't know what we were to each other, but I knew what we had was more than what he'd had with Jessie. We spent a lot of nights just being together. It wasn't just about sex anymore.

"I'm not sure I want to get into it, but we reconnected when I moved here, and it's been a bit of a bumpy start. I think we're on our way now. Speaking of, Leah, I was wondering if you could swap shifts with me this week?"

Before Dad headed out tonight, he'd invited me over to dinner on Sunday night. "Bring your friend, if you want." He'd waved at Derrick and winked at me. When I'd tried to protest that we were just writing partners, he said, "No man looks at a co-worker the way he looks at you."

We fell into a comfortable rhythm of conversation after that. No one brought up Derrick again, but I couldn't shake the feeling that Claire was watching me closer than she had in the past. All night, I felt like she was on the verge of revealing something. She'd moved to the floor to sit beside me and would lean in as if she were going to whisper a secret into my ear, but she never did.

When they left around 3:00 a.m., I fell onto the couch and relished the silence. As much as I loved the quiet, I had to admit how nice it had been to have girl time. Back home, I spent a lot of Friday nights with my friend Melissa and my sister, Lindsey. Jacob had his boy time, and I got my girl time. With the two of them, I was able to be myself and confess all the things I never told Jacob. They knew all about my dreams of leaving Wishing. They'd heard most of my songs and supported me. Though they never came out and said it, I think they knew I was going to eventually leave. It was this unspoken agreement between us.

I imagine Melissa had been the first person Jacob called when he realized I was gone. In fact, I was more than certain it had been my leaving that brought them together. The image I conjured of the two of them together stung. She'd been the only person I ever really talked to about Jacob. She knew all about our arguments over starting a family. I'd shared my hurt with her when he told me my songs and dreams were childish. I'd also told her the intimate stories of our love and life together. Now, she was making her own story with him.

As long as they're happy. He deserved to be happy, even if I wasn't the one to give him that. She did too, probably more than he did. It still hurt to know they were moving on without me, and I'd never be the one she'd call to share her news with.

CHAPTER TWENTY-FOUR

"I made cookies!" I said as I walked into Derrick's house. I'd been there often enough that I no longer knocked. He met me at the door and kissed my cheek. I leaned into him and pulled the warmth of him into me.

"Chocolate chip?" He closed his eyes and inhaled deeply.

"Yup, my grandma's secret recipe," I said and handed him the plate. "There's rum in it."

He raised an eyebrow. "I like Grandma."

"I honestly think she just put it in there so she could drink while she baked."

"My kind of woman," he said and picked out the biggest cookie from the pile, "how was girls night?"

I hedged. When I crawled into bed and fell asleep, I'd been met with a torrid dream about Derrick and Jessie. I'd spent the morning baking and distracting myself while I tried to erase the images of their tattooed bodies dancing together.

"What?"

"You and Jessie, huh?" I asked. We'd grown close enough that I felt safe bringing this up with him. A few weeks ago, I'd have just left it to fester until I blew up on him.

He raked his hands through his hair and gave me a sheepish smile. "So, y'all talked about me?"

"Seems like you've slept with most of Noah's staff."

Derrick shoved the entire cookie into his mouth to keep from answering. The tiny upturn of his smirk told me all I needed to know. I waited as he took his time chewing. He reached for another, but I slapped his hand away.

"Your past doesn't bother me," I said.

"Then why bring it up?" he asked.

"Because I need to erase the mental picture I have of you in a threesome with Claire and Jessie."

"Claire?" He coughed and looked away from me. He took the cookies into the kitchen and set them on the counter. I followed behind him. When he turned back to me, his face was red and filled with guilt.

"So, you two did hook up!" I exclaimed. I'm not sure why I felt the need to sound so excited that I'd read her right the night before. She'd never come out and admitted it, but I gathered from the way she defended him and avoided the topic each time it came up. She also hadn't denied it.

"Don't say it like that, Abby."

"Well, that's what it was, right? Just like you and Jessie? And Shanna, or whatever her name was. You don't have to hide that from me, Derrick. I'm okay with you exactly who you are now and who you were then." To prove my point, I lifted onto my tiptoes and kissed him. Leftover cookie crumbs stuck to my lips when I pulled away. I cleaned them off with my tongue. "I like you a lot."

I'd hoped the callback to our first night together would pull him out of the mood my questions had sent him into, but it didn't. He brushed past me and marched into the living room. When he grabbed his guitar and motioned for me to grab mine, I didn't hesitate.

"Let's work on the one you started last week."

"I'm not ready." I'd written down a few lyrics to try and pull all of my thoughts and lingering issues with Jacob out of me, but it was still too raw to share.

"You are." He insisted. He grabbed my purse off the entryway table. He pulled out my notebook and flipped it to the page I'd earmarked yesterday. I tried to pull it from him, but he held it just out of reach. "'After Everything,'" he read before handing it to me. "Let's work on this."

"No, I told you, I'm not ready."

"You are." He looked at me with such intensity that a shiver ran down my back. I shook my head and dropped the notebook onto the ground, tears forming in my eyes. "Abby, you're ready."

Though his voice softened, I sensed his reaction had more to do with him than me. My questions about Claire had sparked something deeper than I'd initially realized.

I smoothed the piece of paper in my notebook and pulled my guitar onto my lap as I sat down. My heart pounded wildly in my chest. It didn't matter what he said, I knew I wasn't ready for this, but I wanted to be.

The way I'd heard the song in my head, it started with a cold intro. So, I held my trembling fingers over the strings and took a deep breath. *"Three hundred miles in, and I'm chasing a rising sun,"* I sang and then played the first chord. *"Your blue eyes in my rearview are darker than the fading moon, but they aren't calling me home because home isn't where you are. My heart isn't where you are."*

I barely made it through those few lines. I couldn't catch my breath. Derrick nodded for me to continue.

"I just have an idea for the chorus."

"I want to hear it." He must have picked up on my hesitation because he added, "Please?"

I sighed and focused my attention back on the guitar. *"After everything we've shared; after everything we've lost, we haven't been worth the cost. I gave you my heart. I gave you my soul. It used to be you, we used to be us. After everything is gone, I finally have it all."*

By the time I'd finished the first line of the chorus, he'd joined me in harmony. He sang the words as if he'd written them himself. When I stopped singing, he kept playing and humming. He pointed at the last few lines I'd scribbled and asked, "What is that?"

"An idea for the bridge." My voice was weak and timid. I was seeing a new side of him. Whatever wounds he had that he'd kept hidden from me were bubbling to the surface. I wanted to reach over and drape myself over him like a Band-Aid and seal him back up, to be the pain medication he so desperately needed.

"Will you sing it?"

I nodded. *"I wish I could take it all back. I wish I could do it all again. I wish I could tell you everything."*

"This is for Jacob?"

"No," I said, correcting him, "this is for me."

"How did writing this feel?"

"Cathartic, I guess?" The tear stains were still visible on the page. Tiny spots where the blue ink had dripped from one line to the next. Singing just now had felt a bit like that, bleeding.

He picked his guitar back up and started playing again. I recognized the song as the one he sang the first night I watched him play. "In her eyes, I can't do wrong. In her eyes, I'm her only one."

"I remember that one."

"The original line was *In her eyes there are lies of every shade of white.*"

"Whose eyes?" I whispered.

"Claire's."

I could've guessed that would be his answer. It was plain as day by his reaction to everything tonight. "Will you tell me?"

"We all grew up together: me, Claire, and Noah. You know we were in a band together?" I nodded, remembering his confession. "Well, Claire and I started it our freshman year of high school. She sang and I played. Noah joined us a year or so in. We played all over town and eventually caught the attention of the execs over at Big Cat Records, and they signed us. We were maybe twenty when it all started to get real."

I leaned back and looked up at him. He smiled down at me and said, "It was great at first. I mean, we were opening shows for Keith Urban. We were recording an album."

"You and Claire were together?" I guessed.

"Since seventh grade, as ironic as that sounds."

"I get that." I thought of Jacob and me and how there had been a sense of inevitability with us.

"She was my first everything. We were young and stupid and in love." He flinched and shook his head. "At first, I didn't notice all the time her and Noah spent together. I was busy writing songs and cutting demos. I could see our future plain as day. The Grammys and world tours, a big star-studded wedding, and then we'd be on stage together for the rest of our lives. I was so lost in the daydream of it all that I missed the train coming straight for us."

I stood up and moved to sit by him. He held his arms out, and I nestled into his lap, burying my head beneath his chin. With my ear pressed against his chest, his words thundered into me as he spoke.

"We'd just gotten back from a three-stop tour in the Carolinas. I headed straight for the studio to lay down one of the songs I'd written while we were on the road. I don't think either of them expected me home that night."

His heart thumped inside of his chest. I pressed my hand against him to see if I could feel it too. "You don't have to finish if you don't want to."

"You can guess what happened next. We lost our record deal because I refused to be in the same room as them, and I lost my mind. Things spiraled out of control for a few years as I watched my best friend and cousin get everything that was supposed to be mine. We didn't speak for years. It was Claire who brought us back together, but we still have our issues. He sees me as the screw-up who blew our shot, and I see him as the liar who stole my girlfriend. Neither of us is wrong."

"I don't think you're a screw-up. You were hurt," I said.

"That didn't give me the license to sabotage the band or myself. Abby, I was a different guy back then. It took me a decade to pull myself together. Some days, I wonder if I'm really any different."

He wrapped his arms around me, and I ran my fingers over his tattoos. I loved to follow the path of each one and trace them. Sometimes, he'd whisper their stories in my ear, other times he'd close his eyes and hum a song I didn't recognize.

"Do you still love her?" I asked, terrified to hear his answer.

"Not like I did, but I think there will always be a part of her with me."

"Yeah, I get that. There's something powerful about first loves."

"Even if the end is disaster and turns your life upside down."

I curled myself against him, fitting myself into every open spot. We were like a broken jigsaw puzzle. Some pieces were missing, some were broken, but the picture was still beautiful, flaws and all. Perhaps more so because of the imperfections. He took a deep breath in, and when he exhaled, I sank further into him.

"I didn't know you then, but I think I know you now, and you're more than anything I ever expected," I said. He rubbed his cheek against the top of my head. The tiny hairs of his beard tickled against my scalp.

"One-Night-Stand Derrick?" he asked. Though he sounded playful, there was a twinge of sadness in his voice.

"Not to me."

"Who am I to you?" he asked. My heart quickened, and I chewed my lip.

"You're the guy I want to invite to dinner at my dad's house on Sunday."

"You want me to meet your parents? I'm not sure I'm the kind of guy you bring home."

"You've already met my dad, and you are. You're exactly the guy I want to bring home." It wasn't a lie or a platitude. I wanted him there. I needed him with me.

"I'd love to," he said. He dragged his finger over my shoulder and down my arm. When he reached my wrist, he turned my hand over and ran the tip of his ring finger over my vein. "I'm glad you found your way into my life, Abby."

"Me too," I whispered. *I think I'm falling in love with you.* I didn't say the words out loud, but they lingered between us and sat on the tip of my tongue as I shifted to face him. I took his bearded face into my hands and kissed him. I ran my tongue over his lips, letting it transfer the words I wasn't ready to speak.

CHAPTER TWENTY-FIVE

Saturday night was always busy at the bar, but this Saturday night was pure insanity. By eight, the place was packed, and Noah had to call Derrick in to help back him up at the bar. It was my first experience working with him and made me wonder what he did when he wasn't writing songs or fighting with Noah over the bar's budget. He sure as hell didn't spend his time practicing bartending or memorizing drinks.

"Derrick," I shouted over the crowd and shoved the drink back at him, "the Gulch Shooter has pineapple juice, one shot of coconut rum, and two shots of spiced rum. This smells like it has vodka and orange juice in it."

"Whoops," he said with a sheepish grin. Noah groaned behind him.

"You came up with half the drinks, man. I don't understand what your problem is tonight." Noah pulled the bottle of Malibu from his hands and remade the drink for me.

"I know," Jessie said as she slid next to me. "He's been watching Abby run her ass off all night and wishing she were—"

I didn't let her finish. "Thanks, Noah." I took the drink and ran it out to the table. Derrick and I had stopped trying to pretend there was nothing happening between us, but I still didn't want to flaunt it in Noah's face. Or Claire's, for that matter.

"One Gulch Shooter," I said. I handed the shot over.

"Thanks," the customer replied. "I'm Randy."

I made a concerted effort to not roll my eyes. Randy, as he'd just introduced himself, had been camped out at my one and only four-top for three hours. He and his buddies showed up for happy hour and refused to leave even after my numerous attempts at closing them out.

"Enjoy your shooter, Randy." I threw him a wink for good measure. He may have annoyed the shit out of me, but I still needed a tip.

"Doing okay?" Leah asked when I retreated to the back for some quiet.

I nodded and asked, "Are you still good to swap shifts tomorrow?"

"Yeah, you're going to your dad's, right?"

"Yes, first time meeting his new family." I left out the part about bringing Derrick. I still couldn't believe he'd agreed. Things were going good between us, but this felt like an official step. Sure, he'd met my dad before, and they'd shared a beer at the bar, but this was different. Derrick would be there with me when I met my stepmom and half-brothers for the first time.

As hard as I tried, I couldn't stop myself from overthinking things. Derrick was the first real thing I'd felt in years. Maybe even more real than the first few years with Jacob. With Derrick, I could be myself. I didn't have to hide my insecurities or dreams. When we lay together at night with our hands intertwined and our bodies exhausted from worshipping each other, I could tell him everything. I could share how I imagined it would feel to hear my words being sung in an arena or over the radio waves and know that he wouldn't laugh.

He'd experienced both of those things and would encourage me to dream bigger. "Close your eyes and listen," he'd whispered into the darkness, "hear the crowd singing those words back to you."

Jacob would've just laughed and told me to grow up.

But Derrick wasn't Jacob. He was nothing like him and comparing the two wasn't how I wanted to spend my time. So, first thing Friday morning, I went down to the courthouse and filed a petition to get my name back. I changed my social media from Abby Rhodes to Abby Monroe and made my first post since moving to Nashville; a video of Derrick and me sitting on his couch singing a cover of a Little Big Town song. Everyone from back home either liked it or left a comment encouraging me. Everyone except Jacob and Melissa. This morning, I shared a selfie of me lying in Derrick's bed with a sleepy smile and messy hair. He wasn't in the frame, but he'd been sleeping next to me. I didn't add a caption. Words would never do justice to what I felt when I woke up beside him.

"Hey, you," he whispered into my ear as he came up behind me. He wrapped his arms around my waist, and I fell back into him. "You look lost in thought."

"I was thinking about this morning," I replied, giggling as his beard tickled the back of my neck.

He ran his hands over my stomach and pulled me closer. "What about it?" His voice grew thick with what I now recognized as desire.

"How much I love waking up beside you." I'd said those words to him many times before, but they always came as we were waking up. Now, miles away from his bed and in the stark neon lights, the admission felt like more than a flirtatious morning greeting. It felt like an admission of something neither of us had been ready to say aloud.

"I love falling asleep with you," he said. *I love.* We'd both just said those two words as if the third were implied. *You.*

I laid my hands over his and slipped my fingers between his. We stood there in the middle of the busy kitchen in view of anyone who walked in. The roar of a rowdy Saturday night crowd sang behind us as we swayed together. I closed my eyes and dropped my head against him. What I wouldn't give to be up in my condo or across town in his bed.

"You're a shitty bartender, though," I teased. A smile danced over my face when I felt his chest shake with laughter.

"I'm too distracted by you."

"Is it the smell of the grease from frying chips that you find so distracting or my—" I was interrupted by the sound of someone slamming into the kitchen.

"Abby!" Claire shouted. "The assholes at eleven are asking for you. I think they're ready to cash out."

"Sorry," I said and pried myself free from Derrick's arms. I offered an apologetic smile, but she brushed me off. I tried to ignore the pained expression on her face as she watched Derrick's hand linger in mine. He either didn't notice or didn't care because he squeezed my ass and pulled me back for a kiss before letting me go.

I stopped at the bar to collect myself before returning to Randy's table. Noah watched me closely as I printed out their check. Much like Claire, I wasn't able to read his expression. It was either annoyance or bewilderment.

"Hey guys, are we ready for our check or another round?" I asked, slipping their check into Randy's waiting hand.

Randy leaned toward me and grabbed my wrist. "What time is your shift over?"

I ignored his question and asked, "One check, right?"

The quieter of the men reached into his wallet and pulled out a credit card. "Yes, one check, please."

Randy didn't let go of my wrist, but I pulled it free. I took the credit card from the friend and thanked him. When I turned to head back to the bar to cash them out, I felt an unfamiliar, grabby hand on my ass. His chubby fingers gripped tightly and held on for a moment. His laughter exploded through the room and mingled with the shocked gasps of his friends. I was too stunned to move or react. In my two months working here, I'd never had a customer touch me. Four years at Lace & Grit had netted the same. I'd heard of it happening to my co-workers, but it had never happened to me. Bile rose into my throat, and my breath hitched. Every inch of me went on high alert. I jerked away, causing his hand to squeeze harder. I panicked and screamed. I don't know if actual words came out or just a desperate shriek.

I didn't see him coming but heard the aftermath. The crack of his fist against the soft skin of my customer's. The shouting and tumbling of their bodies colliding and crashing to the floor, followed by Randy's chair. The glasses from their last round of shooters shattered on the floor as the men scrambled back in shock. They stood and watched as Derrick—my Derrick with the soft, gentle touch—pummeled their buddy's face. It took a second for my mind to register what was happening.

"Derrick, stop!" Noah shouted and pushed past me. He grabbed Derrick by the waist and tried to pull him back, but Derrick shoved him off.

"Fucking prick," Derrick shouted. His face just inches from Randy's.

"Fuck you, man," Randy spat back. He managed to get a swing in but missed. Noah and one of the bar's regulars took hold of Derrick's arms and yanked him away from Randy, who crab crawled away from him. When he stood, Derrick lunged for him again but wasn't able to wriggle free.

It was Claire who pulled me out of the melee. She grabbed my arm and tugged me back just as another customer ran past us to help hold Derrick. My heart pounded hard and fast inside my chest, drowning out all other sounds. It was as if I'd been sucked into a vacuum. The world spinning into chaos around me.

"Breathe, Abby," she said as she held her face in front of mine. I studied her calm green eyes and followed her directions. "In…and… out." She took slow, measured breaths alongside me until I calmed.

"I'm sorry," I whispered. "Thank you."

"Don't apologize for that asshole." She nodded behind me. I turned just in time to see Noah and Derrick hauling Randy to the door. His buddies trailed behind him uttering their own apologies. "Let's go outside."

Though I wanted to stick around and wait for Derrick to come back, I followed her through the kitchen and past Jessie's and Leah's gazes. Claire held open the back door for me. The night air was thick with Southern humidity. The back alley behind the bar was still and quiet.

"Did Derrick punch him?" I asked after a minute or two of silence.

"Right in his face. Lots of blood. His nose might be broken."

"Shit."

"Yeah."

"Noah is going to fire me, isn't he?"

"Because that guy grabbed your ass?"

I shook my head. "I broke his rule."

"Abby, you've been breaking his rule for almost a month now. He's not going to fire you now. Besides, his rule exists to protect Derrick, and I'm not sure that's necessary with you."

"What? Why?"

"Oh, Abby," she said and put her arm around me. "We all see the way he looks at you. The way he is with you. I've never seen him like this before."

"Like what?"

"In love." My heart caught in my throat, and I blinked at her. "He's been wandering around lost for a while, but now he seems grounded. Steady."

"What about with you?" I asked, timid and unsure if it was the right thing to say.

"He told you, huh?" I nodded. "That was a long time ago, and I'm fairly certain he never looked at me like that. I mean, he caught me in bed with his cousin, and his response was, 'Oh, well, fuck.'"

I laughed and wiped my nose. I hadn't expected to pull my hand away tear soaked, but somewhere between Randy's nasty hands and this moment beside the dumpster with Claire, my eyes had started leaking. "Yeah, but after?"

"After was a mess, but even then, I don't think it was because of any lingering, deep love. He was pissed and betrayed."

"You and Noah seem happy."

"We are. I still feel awful about what happened with everything, but Derrick and I weren't meant to be. We're not right for each other."

Before I could respond, Derrick and Noah appeared in the doorway.

"You need to go home, Abby." Noah's voice was tainted with an anger I'd never heard before.

"Am I in trouble?"

"Just go home. You've done enough damage tonight."

"Dude, you're pissed at me, I get it," Derrick said, getting right in Noah's face. "Don't be a jerk to her."

"Both of you get the fuck out of my bar," Noah spat back.

"*Our* bar."

"Get out," he seethed. Claire place her hand on his forearm. He started and then calmed as he looked down at her. "Please."

Derrick took my hand and led me back inside. "Are you okay?"

"I don't know what happened," I replied honestly. "Why is he mad at me?"

"He's not mad at you; he's mad at himself. He'll get over it. Let's get you home."

CHAPTER TWENTY-SIX

"Do I have to go?" I asked as I traced my finger over Derrick's lips and down his face, smoothing his beard as I did. I never thought I'd be a beard woman, but there was something about his that I couldn't resist. Maybe it was the tiny, almost invisible, sprays of salt and pepper that I was certain only I could see.

"Not right now," he whispered.

"Noah is going to give me the biggest lecture. I just know he is. But we didn't do anything wrong. That guy was an asshole, but you were incredible. I've never had anyone jump to my defense like you did. It was hot."

"You mentioned that once or twice last night." He propped himself up on the pillow beside me and locked his gaze on mine. "Are you sure I didn't scare you?"

He'd asked me that no less than fifteen times since we got back to my condo last night. "I mean, you came out of nowhere, but I was more scared of what might have happened if you weren't there." I slid closer to him and brushed my nose over his. I closed my eyes and breathed him in. Heat radiated from my center, warming me from the inside out. I found his hand and placed mine inside it. "You could never scare me, you know that, right?"

"I just saw him grab you and then saw your face. I don't know what came over me. I could have strangled him." He exhaled, his breath hot as it blew through my hair. He slipped his hand from mine.

"You saved me," I whispered just as his lips found mine. I hoped he knew that the saving he'd done had been bigger than last night. He'd saved me over and over again before he broke Grabby Randy's nose. First when he put my guitar back in my hands. Then when he pushed me to find and use my voice again. And again, each time he gave himself to me. I no longer feared that I'd wake up to an empty bed. He wasn't going anywhere, and neither was I.

His lips released me, and I laid my head on his chest. With each breath in, my body rose with his. I sank deeper against him as he breathed out. His fingers teased at the waist of my panties. I shivered as he teased my skin. He'd dip lower, and just as I'd think he was coming close to the exact spot I wanted him, he shifted directions and trace circles around my belly button.

He explored every inch of my naked stomach. His touch was light but not tentative. He knew my body like a map he'd memorized. Each path he took was new and different, but they all led to the same place. I tried to relax and just enjoy his touch, but each time he neared the roundness of my belly, I flinched and tensed. He splayed his fingers over the small curve and asked, "Why do you keep doing that?"

My mind flashed images of the toned bodies of the women I knew he'd been with. Claire. Jessie. I hated that I did it, but I couldn't stop comparing their perfections to my imperfections. I'd never been completely comfortable in my skin or body. I think that's just how women are taught to see themselves. We start out being praised for our rolls and rolls of baby fat, then the praise turns into questions of whether or not we should be given the same portions as our skinnier siblings. From there, the suggestions that we tone and trim our waists, hips, and thighs begin. It's a downhill spiral meant to mold us into the shapes the world desires.

I shook my head. He didn't need to know what I was thinking. But, of course, he already did. He could read me better than anyone.

"You're beautiful, Abby," he whispered as he moved his mouth down my neck, laying kisses over each inch of skin he passed. He moved slowly and with an intent that sent my heart racing after him. When he reached my stomach, he braced his hands on either side of me and sat up. "I wish you could see what I see when I look at you."

"What's that?" My breath hitched when he resumed kissing his way south.

"A strong, independent, beautiful, talented woman who is finally freeing herself from the expectations of her past. A woman I—" He didn't finish the sentence. His mouth was otherwise occupied. As badly as I wanted to hear what else he had to say, I wanted his focus to remain exactly where it had shifted. Still on me, only using his tongue for something other than words.

I closed my eyes and let my mind wander back to the present. All thoughts of other women drifted away. Every nerve ending in my body was on high alert as I gave myself over to him completely. I ignored the rising sun and the ticking clock. Work could wait. The day could wait. I was his now, and that was more than enough.

"Derrick, I—" *I what*? I wondered. *I love you.* Those were the words that hung on my lips as the tidal wave rushed through me. The words as desperate as the rest of me. My mouth lost the ability to form a sentence, and I just whispered his name again, hoping the breathless syllables told him what I needed them to.

When his mouth found mine again, I no longer had the ability to form coherent thoughts or sentences. We didn't need words, my body and his had their own language that was meant for only us. I threaded my fingers through his shaggy black hair and pulled him closer, craving him. Sinking deeper and deeper into him until there was nothing but a thin layer between us. His lips left mine, and I sighed the kind of sigh that begs for mercy as he trailed his lips down my neck and over my breast. He flicked his tongue over my nipple and then pulled me into his mouth. His hands teased me as he slipped the condom on. I reached down and took him into my hands. I wasn't in the mood for slow. I needed him—all of him—and I needed him now. I guided him inside me and then wrapped my legs over his, pulling him closer. His breath tickled my ear as he exhaled a quiet *Abby*. I loved how my name felt as it blew past my ear.

His hands slipped below me, and he lifted my hips as he sank further into me. I dug my fingers into his back and raked them down towards his sides. I grabbed his hips and held on, guiding each slow, desperate, hungry movement.

I wanted to feel every inch, every second.

"Me, too," he whispered as he pulled away to stare down at me. I read his eyes and face, searching for the same words I'd been unable to say. I found them in the longing in his gray eyes.

Those two words pushed me over the edge. I tried to keep my eyes on him, but they blurred with unexpected tears. I clenched them closed and bit my lip as I came undone. I couldn't see him, but I could feel him losing control alongside me.

AN HOUR LATER, we stood outside the bar. I felt like a teenager walking in late for curfew smelling like beer and my boyfriend's cologne. Derrick leaned in and kissed my forehead. "Do you want me to come in with you?"

"No," I said and shook my head. "I have to do this. I mean, it's not like he doesn't know about us."

"If he's a dick to you, call me." Something flashed in his eyes that made me flinch. "Sorry."

"Don't apologize," I said.

"I won't hurt him. I'll just remind him that his beef is with me, not with his sexy, smart, talented waitress." I tickled his love handles, and he jerked away. He laughed and added, "I'll pick you up at three. Still up for guitar shopping?"

I nodded. I'd been putting it off for far too long, but I wanted to be able to bring my new guitar to dinner tonight. Every Monday morning and Wednesday night, my dad asked if I'd taken the rent money and gotten a new guitar yet. It was hard to miss the disappointment in his eyes each time I told him I hadn't. Tonight, I'd show off my shiny new toy and thank him.

"See you then." I gave him one last kiss and pushed open the door. I felt him lingering behind me, waiting to make sure Noah didn't attack me. I turned and waved him off. *I'm okay*, I mouthed. He hedged for a moment before nodding and heading out onto the street. I wanted him to stay but knew his presence would only agitate Noah.

The dining room was still dark, but I heard Noah's and Claire's voices in the back. I followed their low, hushed tones and found them huddled together in the kitchen. Claire stood behind him with her cheek pressed against his back. Her arms were wrapped around his waist. I stopped in the doorway and watched him for a moment, not wanting to intrude. But it felt weirder to watch the intimate moment than to interrupt.

I cleared my throat and said, "Good morning." Claire jumped and pulled away from Noah. She offered a shy smile that I returned.

"Abby," Noah said. He didn't bother to hide the annoyance in his voice. "What are you doing here?"

"I'm working the morning brunch shift."

"Oh, that's right. I forgot you'd swapped with Leah this morning." His face softened. "Let's go out front. I brewed some coffee."

"You two go, I'll bring the coffee," Claire said.

I didn't want to leave her. She always seemed to lessen the tension. When I first met Noah, we had an easy banter and a friendly rapport, but ever since Derrick and I got close, Noah's attitude toward me shifted. It didn't matter that I was good at my job or that, until last night, our relationship hadn't ever impacted the bar.

"How are you this morning?" he asked as he took the seat across from me.

I felt my face flush as my mind involuntarily drifted back to my bed and Derrick. "Good, I guess."

"You know I'm not mad about last night, right?" I shrugged. "We have a zero-tolerance policy when it comes to customers harassing or touching the staff. We also have a no-punching-the-customers policy."

"If it had been Claire, what would you have done?" It was his turn to not answer. I took his silence as an invitation to keep talking. "Look, I know you have your rule about not—" I couldn't say "fucking

Derrick" because that isn't what we were doing. We had something more than that.

"Abby," Noah said, shaking his head.

"No, let me finish," I said and thanked Claire for the coffee she'd placed in front of me. She sat down in the chair between Noah and me. "Your rule about Derrick is completely unfair to him. I know you think he's a womanizer or a player or whatever, and yes, you've known him longer than me, but you don't know him like I do."

"I think I know my cousin."

I glanced at Claire and hoped my eyes conveyed the apology I needed it to. "Well enough to sleep with his girlfriend? To blame him for his reaction to it? To treat him like a failure? To gossip about him and spread rumors about him?"

"That's not fair, Abby. You weren't there and don't know the full story."

"I know enough to know that he was left to hurt on his own. He'd lost his girlfriend, his cousin and best friend, and his career. And then he had to watch you two carry on as if he didn't exist. Maybe he could have handled it better, but I know better than anyone what it's like to feel alone and misunderstood."

"So, you sleep with him a few times and suddenly you're an expert on Derrick?"

I ignored his slight and said, "Yes. You know why? Because I listen to him. I listen to the words he says and the ones he doesn't."

"So, you know all about him breaking my nose? Or him getting so drunk he passed out on stage in the middle of a show? Or the time he drove his car into my parents' house because he was too wasted to realize he'd gunned the gas instead of the brakes?" The resentment in his voice darkened the air in the room. While we hadn't gone into the details of his post-breakup path of destruction, I knew the gist of it. The specifics didn't matter. That wasn't who he was now. It was clear Noah still held a grudge against Derrick for losing their record deal. He was all too eager to rehash every gory second, all while forgetting the role he and Claire had played.

"Noah," Claire warned, "just stop. Abby doesn't need to hear this."

He scoffed. "Abby, you think you know Derrick, but you only know a piece of him."

I didn't need to prove anything to Noah. I knew Derrick well enough to know what was inside of him.

"Abby can take care of herself, Noah, and so can Derrick." She put her hand over his and squeezed. "You need to put the past behind you."

He calmed under her touch. He glanced across the table at me and said, "Just keep it out of my bar. I won't have him trashing this place when he eventually pushes you away, too."

CHAPTER TWENTY-SEVEN

DERRICK TOOK MY HAND, INTERLACED HIS FINGERS BETWEEN MINE, and squeezed. I gripped tighter in the faint hope that I could somehow pull some of his strength into me. My nerves left my hands sweaty and my heart pounding. The brand new blue acoustic Epiphone guitar in the backseat suddenly felt like an added weight instead of the gift it was.

"Regretting not getting the pink one?" he teased.

"No, blue is more my speed." The pink one had conjured images of the towheaded blonde who had disappeared from my dreams the past few nights. She only seemed to appear when I wasn't curled up beside Derrick. Those nights, I tossed and turned and stared at the ceiling.

"You know we can't sit in the car forever, right?" he asked and nodded towards the front door where two boys stood watching us. *Adam and Eric.* I squinted and tried to study their faces. "They look a bit like you."

He wasn't wrong. We shared the same mousy blonde hair. From here, I couldn't see their eyes but somehow knew they were brown like mine and Dad's. They were both tall and lean.

"Let's go," I said and gave an extra nod to convince myself I was ready. I wasn't. I'd wanted this moment and had practically begged

Dad for it for months, but being here now felt like a heartbreak waiting to happen. Derrick climbed out of his Jeep and came around to my side. He opened the door and helped me out. "Should I bring the guitar?"

"I'm sure he'd like to see it." He was right, of course. He'd heard Dad ask about it every Wednesday night. "I'll carry it."

Derrick had this uncanny way of knowing exactly when my insecurities were swooping in to steal my confidence, and he always knew exactly what I needed from him. I bumped my hip against him as a silent thank you. He smiled down at me and for a split second, the fear melted away.

"She's here!" Two small voices shouted as we crossed the street. I let my gaze wander up the long stone walk. It was hard not to compare this manicured lawn with the dead grass and junk that filled the space outside of Mom's house. There were no plastic toys or broken Power Wheels littering this Monroe house. The pristine brick, two-story house felt like a castle compared to any place I'd ever lived in. Aside from my condo at RBX, which belonged to them as well.

"Abby," Dad's warm voice greeted me. He met Derrick and me at the door and held it open. He nodded down at the guitar case and asked, "Is that what I think it is?"

"I just picked it out today," I said with a nervous smile that shifted into a large, goofy grin as Dad started begging to see it. Derrick laid it on the ground and popped open the case. Dad admired it for a moment before asking me to play for them later. Derrick agreed before I could say no.

"Are these real tattoos?" the taller boy, whom I assumed to be Adam, asked. Both he and Eric were standing next to Derrick, gawking at him.

"Sure are." He held his arm out for the boys to get a better look, and I silently thanked younger Derrick for not getting curse words or naked ladies tattooed onto his skin. Tiny *ooh*s and *ahh*s echoed through the hallway as the boys touched and traced their fingers over his tattoos. They asked questions about each of them, and Derrick shared the story behind each piece of artwork. His voice shifted as he spoke, softening with each question. He was as patient and gentle with them as he was with me.

"How about a tour?" a voice I didn't yet recognize asked. I broke my gaze away from Derrick and the boys. Jenny had appeared beside Dad. He tucked his arm around her waist. I took in the sight of the two of them together. She stood tall and confident but barely reached his shoulders. Her long brown hair fell in loose, perfect curls around her face. If she was wearing makeup, she didn't need it. Her pale skin glowed even in the soft lighting of her perfect home.

I allowed myself to imagine Mom here instead. Her hard edges and bitterness wouldn't have meshed with the subtle pink-and-floral decor that adorned Dad's new home. Then again, her hardness had come from Dad's leaving, so perhaps there was a Laura Ashley–loving woman buried deep beneath the anger of being left to raise two girls on her own.

"I'd love a tour," I said with a forced smile. Derrick was lost in his own world, reliving his glory days as my half-brothers continued to obsess over his tattoos.

Dad walked beside me as Jenny led us through the four-bedroom house. She spoke with love and enthusiasm while she explained the details of each room, and I could tell she'd led more than a tour or two through their home. I could see her being the dinner-party-hosting type. Mom wasn't much of a cook, but based on the smells that had welcomed us when we walked in, Jenny knew her way around a kitchen.

After the tour, Jenny gathered Derrick and the boys to follow us into the dining room.

"I hope you brought your appetites," she said as she directed Derrick and me to the chairs across from Adam and Eric. The boys kept whispering to each other, lost in their own world. "Alan made quite the spread."

I took in the table and marveled at the lasagna with bubbling cheese and sauce. My mouth watered instantly. Garlic bread—with and without cheese—and asparagus flanked the main dish. A small bowl with salad sat by each plate and two expensive bottles of wine, a red and a white, stood proudly in the middle of the table. In my nearly thirty years on this planet, I'd never had such a fancy meal prepared for me. Restaurants excluded.

"Wow, you made this, D— Alan?" It felt odd to call him 'Dad' in front of the boys he was actually raising. Did they see me as their sibling? Would it be confusing for me to call my dad 'Dad?'

"He did," Jenny said. A wide, beaming smile spread across her face. "Spent half the afternoon in the kitchen."

"This looks amazing, Mr. Monroe," Derrick said. He rested his hand on my knee and gave it a gentle squeeze. I placed mine on top of his. "Thank you for doing all of this."

"Yeah, it looks great." Jenny took the bottle of red and poured herself and Dad a glass. She offered it to me. I nodded towards the white with an apologetic shrug and thanked her as she poured me a healthy glass. She must have sensed my need for it. When she returned to her seat, she raised her glass and said, "Cheers to finally meeting my stepdaughter."

I smiled and raised my glass. "As much as he talks about you, I feel like I already know you."

"Same. I hope we have many more dinners ahead of us," she said.

We spent the meal navigating our way through awkward pauses and stilted conversations. Jenny talked about her interior design business. Dad sprinkled in tales of the country singers whose homes she'd decorated in between mentions of his accounting firm. I talked about the bar and writing songs with Derrick while avoiding any mentions of Missouri or Dad's old family. Derrick filled in the gaps when I lost the ability to behave like a normal human being. My half-brothers knew their way around a dinner table and didn't hesitate over which fork to grab and when. They said please and thank you and grilled Derrick about music. Occasionally, they shot a question in my direction, but it was clear they, like me, were quite infatuated by my tattooed and bearded boyfriend.

Boyfriend.

I wasn't sure if we'd reached the label stage of whatever we were, but the thought comforted me. We were more than writing partners. We spent more time out of bed than in it. We talked and shared our lives, past and present.

If I'd been feeling something akin to *love* toward Derrick, watching him interact with my family sealed the deal for me. I was in love with him. There was absolutely no denying it. I couldn't know for sure if he was having the same thoughts or feelings, but I kept catching glimpses of the answer to the question I hadn't asked in his eyes.

After dinner, the boys insisted Derrick join them for a game of *Animal Crossing*, which was their latest obsession. He joined without hesitation.

"I'd love to hear you play something on the new guitar," Dad said when Jenny left us to clean up.

"Oh, I don't know," I hedged. I glanced around the dining room, suddenly unsure of myself.

"We can go up to my office. We won't disturb anyone there." His suggestion did little to calm my nerves. It was one thing to have him watch me perform at the bar—my territory. To sing in the home he'd built without us shook something inside of me and rattled every nook and cranny where I'd shoved my insecurities.

Still, I nodded and said, "Okay."

I retrieved my guitar from the front hallway and followed him up to his office. The room, lined with dark wood bookshelves and hundreds of books, was inviting. A large ornate desk stood at the center with two leather armchairs placed in front of it. The space was an exact reflection of my dad. It exuded his warmth and sophistication. I lay the guitar on the floor in front of his desk and walked around the room, running my hands over the books.

"Your house is gorgeous. Nothing like the trailers and apartments we lived in growing up." Alone with him, I felt free to mention the past. It was difficult to stand in the middle of so much excess and not be reminded of all that we'd done without. I didn't need to rehash any of it with him, I'd said my piece months ago. But it still stung.

Dad didn't say anything, but his gaze dropped to the floor. He leaned back against his desk and crossed his arms over his chest.

"I'm sorry, it's just kinda hard to see all of these things we never had and not be a little jealous. I'm not mad at you anymore. I guess I don't understand." I sank into the plush leather armchair and sighed. It was as smooth as butter but felt like a warm hug. I decided I could live in this chair.

"Understand what?" he asked.

"This," I said and waved my hands in front of me, "I can't reconcile that the man standing in front of me with the man who walked out on his family without so much as a goodbye. Or how the dad who abandoned his daughters can be the same dad who has given his new sons everything. I mean, I bet they never spent a birthday wondering how their dad could've forgotten about them." Tears sprung to my eyes. I didn't bother fighting them. I wasn't mad. I was hurt. It was like we were his disposable family and this new one was his upgraded, permanent family.

"I never forgot about you, Abby, or your sister." He knelt in front of me and pulled my hands into his.

"Then why didn't you at least write to us or send a birthday card?" I shook my head at him. "I mean, maybe you didn't trust Mom with child support, or you didn't have the money back then. All of that I can forgive; we made it work. But spending birthdays and Christmases without you sucked." A tear rolled down my cheek and dropped onto his hand. He reached up and ran his thumb under my eye to swipe away the rest.

"Oh, Abby," he whispered. "I sent cards and presents. Every October tenth for you and every March fifth for Lindsey. I sent Christmas presents, too."

"What?" *No*, I shook my head and thought, *he didn't. I'd remember that.*

"Every year until your eighteenth birthday. Any time you moved, my mom and dad would send me your new address."

"I didn't know that. How could she keep that from us?" Anger bubbled inside of me, burning from my heart down through my legs and up to my ears.

"I sent money, too. A thousand dollars every month until you and Lindsey graduated."

I jumped out of the chair and stepped back. "This doesn't make sense." None of it did. Every month when rent was due, Mom would lose her shit and complain about how she was on her own and had no one. She worked two jobs, sometimes three. Lindsey and I worked to help pay the bills when we were old enough. Mom always blamed Dad when we got evicted and had to move. I shook my head back and forth. My hair stinging my brown eyes with each movement. "No, she wouldn't lie to us. She wouldn't."

She'd spend two decades making my dad a villain. She told us lie after lie with a straight face and a seemingly guilt-free conscience. She hid the presents and evidence that he'd not forgotten us. Did Lindsey know?

"Why didn't you tell me this when I yelled at you that day?"

"You were already hurt; I didn't want to hurt you more. Your mother is a good woman, Abby, but I can't for the life of me figure out why she'd have kept this from you."

I considered this for a moment, but the truth was obvious. My mother never wanted to be the bad guy. She was the victim. The one who'd been jilted and left behind. It was why she never understood why I left Jacob and why she took his side when I told her about the pregnancy.

"She never forgave you for leaving and wanted to make you pay. When she found out I'd come here and found you, she told me you'd lie and fill my head with nonsense that made her seem like the bad person. But you didn't. You never spoke a bad word about her."

"I don't want you to be angry with her, Abby," Dad said. "I'm sure she had her reasons."

"She kept us from you!" I seethed. My body flushed with heat as I tried to hold in my anger. "I could have known you and been a part of your new life, Dad. She robbed me—and you—of that chance. I spent years hating you, but it was her I should have hated."

"I can't tell you how to feel, but you need to talk to her. I didn't tell you this so you could take it out on her. I wanted you to understand that you were always loved and wanted and never forgotten."

"No, but I thought I was. And so did you." The realization of this caused the words to catch in my throat. He'd spent most of my life thinking we'd rejected him. "If I'd have known you were out there waiting for me, I'd have come sooner. I never would have stayed with her."

"I'm so sorry," he said and pulled me into a hug. I fell into his embrace and let him hold me, but the longer I stood there with this new knowledge, the angrier and angrier I grew.

"I have to go," I said and wriggled myself free, "I'm sorry, Dad, I need…I don't know what I need but I have to go."

"Okay," he said. His voice trembled enough to let me know that it wasn't okay, but he let me go, nonetheless.

CHAPTER TWENTY-EIGHT

I DROPPED MY PURSE ON THE KITCHEN COUNTER, SULKED INTO THE bedroom, and face-planted onto my unmade bed. I took a deep inhale and breathed in the lingering scent of Derrick's cologne. He'd spent so much time in my bed, it smelled more like him than it did me. The mattress shifted as Derrick sat next to me. He rubbed my back and sat silently while I tried to wrap my head around everything. On the car ride home, he sensed something was wrong but knew better than to ask. He didn't question me when I turned the music all the way up and didn't bother singing along. When I started biting my fingernails, he reached over and held my hand until I stopped shaking. I wasn't sure how he knew exactly what I needed, but he did, and I was grateful.

"Do you want to talk about it?" he asked in a soft whisper.

"No," I said and sat up. I tucked my legs into crisscross applesauce and folded my arms over my chest. "Do you know what he told me?"

Derrick shook his head. He reached over and brushed my hair out of my face and tucked it behind my ear. His touch was light as he dragged his hand over my cheek, wiping away the tears as he did.

"She lied to me! For twenty years, she fucking lied! She told us he left and never called. She said he didn't help. She said she worked her ass off for us because *he* didn't do a damn thing for us. She said he forgot about us and moved on. She fucking threw him under the bus and bragged about how she'd stuck around while he wiped the slate clean," I said and took a deep breath. "He didn't deserve that! *I* didn't deserve it, either!"

"So, you do want to talk?" Derrick teased. He caressed my arm; dragging his fingers over my skin in slow, deliberate movements.

"I hated him for so long. I came here with a giant chip on my shoulder like he owed me something, and he didn't. He tried! He sent presents every year, Derrick. Every year!"

"Maybe she thought she was protecting you." The suggestion was a legitimate one, but I wasn't having it. I knew my mother and nothing she ever did was for anyone but herself.

"Nope," I snapped, "that's not her style. She's selfish, and she wanted to be the fucking hero."

"I'm sorry, babe," he whispered into my ear and then kissed my shoulder, "I know now isn't the right time, but I think you should talk to her. Let her explain."

"Explain what? How she stole the good from my life? How she's an ungrateful bitch? A thousand bucks a month for nine years. That's like a hundred grand!"

The math was overwhelming. Sure, she spent more than that on food, rent, clothing, and whatever for nine years but it wasn't the "nothing" she claimed. If he'd sent money, she didn't need to work two jobs or overtime. Lindsey and I weren't high-maintenance kids. We didn't do sports or go out. We had jobs to pay for our date nights. I paid for all of my music lessons and instruments. Lindsey footed the bill for her cosmetology classes, and I'd won scholarships and worked to pay for college. I tried to drag up any memories of Mom writing a check for a single thing for us and came up blank.

Not even my wedding. Jacob's family had paid for that.

"She kept him from me," I said in defeat. "Her lies kept me from him."

It wasn't just the money. The money hurt, but knowing she'd hid the things he'd sent to us gutted me. She'd sat and watched me cry myself to sleep on my birthday. She played with my hair and reassured me that she loved me enough to cover the loss. According to her, we didn't need Dad any more than he'd wanted us.

"We're just fine without him. Better even," she'd said to me on my sixteenth birthday. I'd had to watch as all my friends got fancy new cars; I hadn't even gotten the keys to an old clunker. That was the year I learned from Grandma Grace, Dad's mom, that I had a new stepmom. We didn't see the Monroe family often; Mom always made sure of that. Back then, I thought it hurt her too much to be near them. Now, I knew it was because she was afraid they'd expose her lie. But Grandma Grace found ways to update us. I learned I had a baby brother from her when Adam was born, and then again, a few years later when Eric came along.

"It's not fair!" I'd cried into my pillow, curling my body away from her. She tried to lay beside me, but I begged her to leave.

"No, your daddy leaving and starting over while we're barely scraping by isn't fair. He made his choice, Abby, and he didn't choose us."

He didn't choose you. She may have said the word "us" but all I heard was "you." He didn't choose me. He'd left Mom and Lindsey too, but neither of them seemed to miss him like I did. We'd been closer, I used to reason. Lindsey was Mom's daughter through and through, and I'd been Daddy's girl. He was the one I went to for skinned knees or math that didn't make sense. So when he left, it felt more personal. It felt like he'd left me and only me. Maybe Mom knew that and saw her opportunity to swoop in and fill the role.

"Stop watching the mailbox," she'd say to me on Christmas Eve. "I can't believe you're still waiting for him after all this time."

On the eve of important days like homecoming, prom, graduation, and my wedding, she'd lose her patience. "I'll never understand you, Abby. He gave up on us. I'm the one here, and I'll never be enough for you, will I?"

I'd always lied and told her it wasn't him I was looking for in the crowd. I'd take her hand into mine and reassure her that she was more than enough, knowing all the while that I wanted more. I'd wanted him. I'd needed him. He'd have seen through Jacob's compliments and facade. He'd have been my soft place to land, just as he'd done when I showed up at his place on Christmas morning. I should've seen it all then. Maybe I'd known all along that he hadn't abandoned me. I drove five hundred miles to find him without a plan. I flew into his life expecting him to be there for me; no, knowing he'd be there for me, because I knew my dad. I knew the man he'd been when I was growing up. I never forgot the feeling of his arms around me. He was always with me.

I opened my eyes as yet another round of tears broke free. Relief washed through me when I saw Derrick sitting silently beside me.

"My dad loved these buildings more than he loved us," Derrick said, clearing his throat. "He wasn't home much, but when he was, he and Mom fought all the time. Not just screaming and yelling but dishes flying and doors slamming. It was like World War Three in our house. Thankfully, we had a big house, and I was an only child. Most nights, I'd hide in my room under my pillow and wait to hear his truck peel out of the driveway. He'd come home the next morning smelling like Bud Light and cheap perfume. Mom would slap foundation and concealer over the dark circles and bruises and welcome him home as if nothing had ever happened. He and Mom would disappear upstairs, and then he'd head off to work for it to start all over again."

As he spoke, I could see a clear picture of my life with Jacob had I stayed. Bitterness, anger, resentment. While Jacob never laid his hands on me, he wasn't timid about using his words as weapons. He could cut me down to size with a look or carefully crafted sentence. He knew how to hurt me, and he never shied away from an opportunity to remind me of my place.

"He always had a dozen red roses for Mom. She'd usually throw the roses away as soon as he left for work," Derrick said.

"Is that why you never bring me roses?" I asked. I sniffled and wiped my nose.

He nodded, and he smiled as if he'd been caught. "I spent a lot of years wishing I could grow up to be like my dad. For a while, I followed in his footsteps. Too much beer, too many women chasing after the Bale name, and a lot of anger I couldn't control. For a while, I fooled myself into thinking I was having fun. I'd put Claire and Noah behind me and was enjoying the single life. Then, one day I realized I wasn't having fun, and I didn't want to be like my dad."

"What changed?"

"I met a girl from Missouri who made me want to be the kind of man she writes songs about."

My face flushed, and I pointed at myself and asked, "Me?"

"Yes, you. You with your deep brown eyes that make me wish I had all the answers."

"But," I said to Derrick, "I'm a mess."

"I love you and all of your messes," he said. My heart jumped into my throat, and I turned to face him. I couldn't have heard him right. As I studied his face, a slow smiled spread across his lips. It stretched up and reached his gray eyes. The warmth I found in them soothed me momentarily.

I opened my mouth to say the words back to him, but nothing came out. I felt every single letter of those three words. They burned as I held them on my tongue. "I—"

"I know," he said as he wrapped his arms around me. "I know."

I leaned into him and buried my face against him. "I love you," I whispered into his chest. I wasn't sure if he heard me, but I felt his chest expand as he sucked in a deep breath and then released it slowly. I wasn't anywhere near okay with what I'd just learned, but with Derrick, I was content with it. I'd deal with my mom tomorrow. Tonight, I needed to listen to his heart beating and take in the song that was us.

CHAPTER TWENTY-NINE

SUNDAY NIGHT FADED INTO MONDAY MORNING. DERRICK STAYED WITH me as I moped around the house and went through the motions of pretending to be a normal, well-adjusted human. He made us coffee and brought me snacks. When I flopped onto the couch to watch hours of shitty reality TV, he planted himself right next to me and held me. He didn't complain when I whined about not knowing what to do, but he gently nudged me to call my mom. He was right. I needed to call her, but I wasn't ready.

When I pulled out my guitar Monday night and carried it into my room, I shut the door behind me. Derrick didn't follow me. He sensed I needed time to write and be by myself. I could still sense him sitting on the other side of the door and let his presence be enough to remind me that even though everything I knew about my life had been upended, I hadn't changed. I was still me. I was still Abby.

I emerged two hours later and asked him to come listen. "It's rough, but I think it's going somewhere."

He smiled and sat on the floor in front of the bed. I shifted my guitar into place and started to sing while I played. "*Mama said to guard my heart. Never let a boy take it and tear it apart. Mama said to be careful. Don't let my dreams be too small. Mama said don't give into day drinking or wishful thinking. Mama said to give it my all."*

I didn't have much more than that. There was a rough sketch of a chorus in my mind, but I wasn't ready to finish it, yet. Derrick took my guitar and played back what I'd just shared with him.

"Can I?" he asked. I nodded in response and fell back onto the bed and stared at the ceiling as he tinkered on my guitar and worked on a complicated melody for the words I'd written.

While he played, I thought about Mom and all the lessons she'd tried to teach me over the years. None of which matched up with the Mama I'd just written about. No, my mom practically pushed me into Jacob's cold embrace. She insisted my dreams were too big. She was a proponent of day drinking and, apparently, telling big white lies. All writing had managed to do was expose more of her lies.

Derrick sensed my lack of commitment to the song. He set my guitar aside and climbed up onto the bed beside me. I lay my head on his lap and closed my eyes while he stroked my hair. *"Missouri has my heart,"* he sang softly, *"and she's calling me, calling me, calling me home."*

I'd never heard him sing that song before. He didn't have the rest of the words, so he hummed the melody where the words would eventually live. I didn't fall asleep, but I fell into contentment. The rest of my world may have been unraveling around me but at least I had Derrick to help me hold the threads together.

Tuesday morning, I woke up feeling hungover and dead to the world. I shouldn't have agreed to take Leah's Tuesday night shift, but Derrick was helping his mom with something, and I couldn't spend another minute staring at my phone, waiting to find the courage to call my mom. So, I opted to distract myself by working on the slowest night of the week. Surprisingly, it didn't work.

Each customer who came in somehow reminded me of my mom or dad. I grew short and impatient, snapping at Noah, Claire, and the customers, which meant my tips were shit. I made mistake after mistake and input every wrong order imaginable. By eight, I was over it and ready to shrink back up to my condo.

"Noah!" I yelled back into the kitchen. "Can you remake table 7's Nashville Mule?"

"Again?" he asked, exasperated.

"Yes," I said with a sigh.

"What did you fuck up this time?"

"I forgot to ring it in as top-shelf, and they can *taste the difference.*"

"What is with you tonight?" he asked as he met me at the bar. "This is the fifth drink I've remade for you, and you've only had five tables."

I shrugged. I wasn't about to get into my personal family drama with Noah.

"You and Derrick have a fight?"

"I love how you instantly assume this has anything to do with him."

"Well, I know my cousin, and you aren't the first waitress to bring his drama into my bar."

"It's his bar, too," I said, choosing to ignore his other comment.

"Do you see him here working?"

"Not tonight, but I see him out promoting the bar and driving business every week."

"I see he's completed his brainwashing. I thought you were different, Abby; I really did. Turns out, you're just like the rest of them."

"Shut up," I spat back. "Just make the drink and don't be an asshole."

"You do realize screwing the co-owner won't prevent me from firing you, right?"

While I didn't think he'd actually fire me, his words and harsh tone took me by surprise. We hadn't been on great terms for a while, and I was starting to miss the fun banter we'd had when we first met. I huffed and grabbed the drink from him, bumping into Claire as I did. "Sorry." My mumbled apology wasn't even half-hearted. I needed to get out of there.

I needed to call my mom. I couldn't let my new knowledge fester inside of me. I'd learned my lesson with Jacob. The longer I let things rest, the less rational my decision-making became. I'd spent much of last night tossing and turning and imagining what I'd say to her. It wasn't easy to find the words to ask your mother why she'd lied to you for two decades. Each rehearsal grew angrier and angrier. By the time I fell asleep as the sun was coming up and Derrick was getting out of bed, all I'd come up with was, *Mom, why are you such a bitch?*

That opening would get me nowhere with Susan Monroe. I'd hoped distracting myself with work would give me the time I needed to work on a better icebreaker. So far, I'd managed to add only one word. *Mom, why are you such a fucking bitch*? Definitely worse.

Claire came up to me as I was cleaning my last table. She plopped down into the chair and asked, "Do you want to head out?"

"No, I agreed to cover Leah's shift, and she was supposed to close."

"I hope I'm not stepping too far out-of-bounds, but there is clearly something going on that is distracting you. Go, take care of it. I can close."

"It's fine." I didn't want to be here alone with Noah, but his wrath was far easier to manage than my mother's.

"Look, Noah asked me to stay and close. Go home."

I sighed. "He's going to fire me, isn't he?"

"Probably not," she said and tried to smile, but it fell flat. "Look, things are complicated between him and Derrick. Their history goes back years beyond me. Neither of them talks about it but Derrick didn't have the best childhood. His dad and Noah's are brothers, but they're nothing alike. I've met both men, and if I had to choose who I'd be stuck within an elevator, it wouldn't be Rob. Noah's dad was always stepping in to help Derrick and his mom, which meant he sometimes wasn't there for Noah. He resents that and often blames Derrick for his father's actions. Especially when it looked like Derrick was about to follow in his dad's footsteps. The Bale family isn't all they're cracked up to be."

I knew from Derrick's story last night that his life hadn't been perfect. He'd left out any mention of Noah or his uncle. I could see why Noah might have underlying resentment towards Derrick, but it was unfounded. Derrick wasn't his father. At least, not the Derrick I knew.

"You know I didn't mean for this to happen." By "this" I meant falling completely head-over-heels in love with Derrick. Claire, of course, knew this.

"Neither did I," she said. "I never meant to hurt Derrick or become the wedge that lived between him and Noah, but I did. We can't always control who we fall in love with or when, even if we end up hurting those we love the most. Sometimes you just have to take a leap and hope you don't splat onto the concrete."

Her words sparked something in me. I'd taken that leap when I came to Nashville to find Dad and to try and find my voice. Dad had done it when he met Jenny. "Are you sure you don't mind closing?"

"No, go," she said. I watched her for a moment to make sure her words matched how she felt. She answered with a wide smile. I thanked her and cashed out as quickly as possible.

"Noah, I don't want my relationship with Derrick to change everything between us," I said as I left. "He's a good man and nothing like his father."

Noah offered a slight shrug and dismissed me.

CHAPTER THIRTY

A͏FTER C͏LAIRE AND N͏OAH SENT ME HOME, I͏ SPENT FAR TOO LONG sipping a glass of wine and sulking on my balcony. I paced back and forth between my couch and the railing. The city moved at its usual pace on the street below, but the familiar sounds didn't comfort me like they usually did. The longer I paced, the less certain I was.

Call her. Derrick texted when I told him I was home from work early.

Come over?

Call her, he insisted.

Please, I'll make it worth your time.

I tried in vain to tease him over with a string of explicit emojis and GIFs, but he wasn't having it.

I'll come over to sit with you while you call your mom, but that's it.

Fine. I'm calling. See you tomorrow night?

Which song are we singing?

I thought for a moment and considered the options. I wasn't sure I was ready for it, but I suggested "After Everything." We'd only played it together a handful of times. Our voices played well together as we traded off, turning my breakup song into a duet.

You sure?

Yes. It's time.

You know what else it's time for?

Calling her now.

Mom didn't answer the first time I called. She didn't pick up until the fifth time I dialed her number. I could tell by the deep sigh she answered with, she was neither asleep nor in the mood to talk to me. She was still angry over my own lie.

"What do you want, Abby? It's nearly ten."

"Hello to you, too, Mom."

"Are you calling to apologize for lying to me and your husband about your pregnancy?"

I flinched and shook my head. "No, Mom, I didn't lie about that. I didn't lie to you about the pregnancy, I just didn't tell you about it."

"A lie of omission is still a lie." Listening to her lecture me about lies of omission was a lot more to stomach than I could handle.

"What do you call a lie that is both an omission and a blatant misrepresentation of the truth?" I asked. I rubbed my palms into my eyes and pressed them down until tiny sparkles appeared in the darkness behind my eyelids.

"A lie is a lie, Abby, regardless of how it is delivered."

"How about a lie that's been told for twenty years? Does that change the severity of the lie? Does it make it better or more palatable?"

"If you're trying to get at something, just say it."

"I had dinner with Dad on Sunday." I didn't want to just come out and reveal what I'd learned. I wanted her to admit it, to somehow be forced into facing her own lies.

"You meet Pilates Polly?" she asked with a yawn.

"I met Jenny, yes."

"Was she all prim, proper, and perfect? Better than me?"

"She was nice," I said and could practically hear Mom rolling her eyes over the phone.

"I'm sure."

"Why didn't you tell me Dad and Adam were close enough for him to name his son after him?"

"Did he tell you that he was driving the car that night? Or did he just tell you the feel-good parts?"

He hadn't included that part of the story, no, but I wasn't going to give her the satisfaction of knowing he'd left out that detail.

"No, I guess he wouldn't tell you that. I never should have forgiven him."

"You did, though, enough to fall in love with him and marry him. He gave you us, remember?" She used to say that the only gifts Dad ever gave her were Lindsey and me. Unless, of course, we were being demanding or misbehaving, then she'd say we were just another curse he'd left on her.

"I suppose he did." I listened to her slow, rattled breathing and ignored the nagging urge to fill the silence with angry accusations of my own. This was her admission to give, not mine. "What's his house like?"

"It's pretty."

"Nicer than ours?"

"Sure, a little." I gave intentionally vague answers. The fewer details I gave, the more curious she would be.

"Is he filling your head with nonsense?" she asked, picking up on what I wasn't saying. "You didn't fall for Alan's charms, did you?"

"Dad has been great," I said. "He's been showing up for all of my open mic nights."

"Wow, Dad of the Year." She snorted and laughed.

"You should see him with Adam and Eric, Mom. He's a great dad."

"Cut the shit, Abigail. You know the kind of father that man wasn't. He wasn't there for you or Lindsey. Being a decent dad to his whore's children doesn't change anything."

I shook my head. "What if he'd sent Lindsey and me birthday and Christmas presents? Or sent a grand in child support each month? Would that have changed anything?"

I held my breath as I waited for her response. My stomach twisted into knots as a wave of heat and nausea passed through me.

"What did you say?" Mom coughed into the phone, and I pulled it away from my ear. The hollow, tin sound echoed through the line and pulled at my ears.

When she finished coughing and regained control of her breathing, I said, "Answer the question."

"I don't like these little word games. Just spit it out, child."

"You lied to us, Mom. You told us he didn't want us and that he'd never sent a dime, but he did. Didn't he?"

"I don't know what you're talking about."

"You know, I've really gotten to see a side of Dad I never could have imagined. He was there for me when I needed him, when I didn't even realize I needed him. He showed up for me and supported me. The whole time, I struggled with reconciling the man I knew him to be and the man I saw him actually being. When I was little, he was always the one who took care of me. He held me when I cried and sat in the front row of every play I was in while you grumbled and whined about missing a show or Bridge night with your friends."

"It doesn't take a whole lot of work to father a grown woman. Of course, it's easy for him to be a good dad now."

"But that's the thing, Mom. He was always a good dad."

"Good dads don't leave their wives and daughters to start over with Pilates Polly."

"Her name is Jenny," I said again, "and she's not the bad guy here. Neither is Dad."

"You're just like him. A spineless coward. You both took the easy way out and ran in the middle of the night when things got hard."

"Maybe I am just like him, but he's better than me because he still tried. He didn't just disappear. See, I thought I was doing what he'd done because you spent my entire life telling me all the things he didn't do. But none of that was true, was it?" My voice was far calmer than I'd anticipated. The anger had melted away somewhere between her grunted greeting and my defense of Dad. I was still upset with her but was no longer feeling the blind rage.

Mom didn't answer immediately. I wished I was there with her to watch her face transform as she realized there was no other way out of this lie. The truth was her only option. I closed my eyes and pictured her sitting at the kitchen table. A glass of bourbon in one hand and a half-smoked cigarette in the other.

"What do you want from me?" she finally asked.

"I want you to tell me why you lied."

"He left. Don't forget that detail. *He* walked away from us and started over."

"No, Mom, he left *you*. He tried to be there for us, and *you* took that from him. You let me believe he didn't want me."

"He left," she said again. "I was the one who had to pick up the pieces and keep you girls fed and happy. *Me,* not him. He didn't get to be the birthday hero. He didn't get credit for the work I did."

"So, what? You threw away all those gifts?"

"No. I gave them to you."

"What?"

"I unwrapped them all and then rewrapped them to give them to you."

I blinked and chewed my tongue. "So, all those times you bitched about working overtime to afford Christmas, you were just regifting the things he'd bought while making yourself a martyr?"

She gasped as if she'd been caught again. "You have every right to be upset right now but—"

"No, you don't get to make me feel bad about this, Mom. You don't get to justify your lies by blaming him or me for something."

"What do you want from me, Abby?" She sounded tired. More tired than usual.

"I want you to tell me why you lied. I want to know what you did with the money."

"I spent it, okay?"

"On what? Cigarettes? Jim Beam? Trips to the nail salon?" The anger in me that had subsided roared back to life. "Did you actually work two jobs? Or, was that another lie designed to make us see all the 'sacrifices' you made for us?"

"I worked!" she shouted, "I busted my ass for you, and you never appreciated me."

"He sent $1,000 a month! That wasn't nothing! Yet, you acted like it was all you. What did you do with it, Mom?"

"Does it matter?" she asked after a long pause. "The money he sent wasn't enough to make up for him leaving. You get that right? He left. I raised you two on my own. Yes, I worked two jobs. Maybe I didn't work all the overtime or weekends that I claimed to, but I did work. Then I came home to *his* daughters and was completely on my own."

The pain in her voice reached through the phone and wrapped itself around my neck. I closed my eyes and tried to ignore the guilt that was building inside me. Mom always had a way of making her wrongs become someone else's.

"No, I guess it doesn't."

"If you want an apology, don't hold your breath. I refuse to feel bad about doing what I thought was best to protect your girls."

I clenched my teeth to keep from spitting out the nasty words and thoughts that exploded into my head. "No, what you did was meant to hurt Dad and to pay him back for leaving you. You were protecting yourself."

"No," she yelled into the phone, "you don't get to make me the bad guy here. I won't tolerate that from you. Not after what you did to Jacob."

I could feel her contempt radiating through the phone. I sucked in a deep breath and closed my eyes. "You need to talk to Lindsey, Mom. I won't tell her yet, but she needs to know."

Instead of responding, Mom hung up. I pulled the phone away from my ear and glanced down at the screen. For a split second, I debated calling her back. It wouldn't do any good. She wouldn't answer, and I didn't have anything to add. I unlocked the phone and clicked on Derrick's name, then turned off the phone.

I needed more than his voice. I slipped on a pair of shoes and grabbed my keys. I didn't bother texting him to tell him I was on my way. Tears blurred my eyes as I drove across the river to his house in East Nashville. I didn't bother wiping them away. If I had, I'd have noticed the red Kia parked on the curb outside his house.

CHAPTER THIRTY-ONE

Derrick's bedroom light was on, so I knew he was still awake. I didn't bother knocking. I never did. I let myself in and was greeted by an unusual silence. His house was never quiet. There was always music or the TV playing in the background. I made my way through the dark living room and down the hall. His bedroom door was closed. Before I pushed it open, I stopped to wipe my eyes and nose and smooth my hair down. I took a deep breath to cleanse away the anger from my conversation with Mom.

The call had gone exactly how I'd expected it to. Badly.

On the other side of the door, Derrick's low voice spoke in a rushed tone. I assumed he was on the phone, so I made sure to be extra quiet when I turned the knob and pushed the door open. I didn't say anything when I walked into the room. As my eyes adjusted to the light, I scanned the room to see where he was. I found him with his back to me. He stood beside the bed with his head bent down. He was wearing his usual bedtime attire. Boxers. No shirt. Except instead of bare skin, there was a pair of tanned, thin arms around him. Her arms crossed behind his back while her fingers caressed his shoulder blades. His own arms were around her as they swayed in a slow, seductive rhythm.

I found myself mesmerized by the sight. I couldn't look away. Without music or sound, they seemed to be making their own beat.

If they heard me, neither reacted. With each sway, I got a tiny glimpse of the woman he was holding.

My heart stopped.

I shook my head and stepped back.

Her small head was pressed against his shoulder. I could only see her hair, but I'd recognize that pixie cut anywhere. The undeniable truth slapped me in the face.

Tears pricked my eyes just as I wondered if I had any left to cry. Turns out, I did. It was like this single sight opened the dam and released a fresh surge of saltwater. Watching him hold her in a way he'd never before held me dug into every doubt I'd ever had about him or us.

Anyone but her. I'd have preferred to have found him completely alone, but if he were to be with someone else, it might have hurt less if she were a stranger. I closed my eyes and then opened them again. I couldn't blink away the truth. I'd have given anything to walk back out of this house and go back home and pretend I'd never driven here, and that I'd never caught them in such an intimate moment.

"No," I whispered. I stepped back again, shaking my head. I bumped into the corner of his dresser and knocked something to the floor. I knew from the countless times I'd stared at this dresser while lying beside him in his bed that it was the framed photo of him, Noah, and Claire on stage at the Ryman. The irony was not lost on me.

"Abby?" Derrick questioned as he turned around. His eyes grew wide with shock. They were puffy and his left eye had a dark circle around it as if he'd been punched. "What are you doing here?"

"No," was all I could say. The one word over and over. "No. No. No. Not her. Not you. No."

Tears streamed from my eyes as I looked from him to her and then back to him. I couldn't focus on either one of them without feeling the knife plunge deeper into my back.

"Abby," Claire said and took a step forward. I backed into the doorway. "This isn't what it looks like."

I locked my eyes on Derrick's and read the guilt in them. *This* was exactly what it looked like. Derrick half dressed, standing beside his unmade bed at midnight and embracing the woman who'd broken his heart could only be one thing.

My heart felt as though it had left my body and fell to the floor. It shattered into a million irreparable pieces that landed at his feet. I fought the urge to fall to my knees and beg it to come back to me, for him to gather the fragments and stitch them back together, just as he'd done before. But now some of the pieces were too small to see. Too small to repair.

"How could you?" I shouted at him. Snot and tears ran down my face. I didn't bother to stop any of them.

"Please, Abby just listen to me," he begged. Claire stood beside him, her body looking limp and used.

"And you," I said and pointed at her, "you of all people! How could you do this to me? After everything we talked about today?"

"Abby," she whispered. Her lips parted as she started to speak again. I held up my hand to silence her. I didn't want her excuses any more than I wanted his.

"Stop saying my name!" My body shivered as I tried to find my bearing. I had to get out of here, but I couldn't stop staring at the evidence in front of me. Derrick took two large steps towards me and pulled me into his arms. I broke free and shoved him away from me. "You're just like him, aren't you? You're just like everyone said. God, I'm an idiot! How could I have possibly fallen for your lines? Someone like you—someone like your dad—doesn't change for a girl like me."

"Please don't do this." He reached for me again. I felt the desperation ooze off of him. The longing in his voice almost broke me. *Almost.*

"You used me! You made me believe we were special, that I was more to you than the others. Deep down I knew better, I did. I knew it, damnit, and I still fell for you. I gave myself to you, completely," I cried and gasped to catch my breath, "while you two laughed at me."

"You have it all wrong," Claire said again. "I came here to—"

"No." I shook my head. I had eyes; I could see the truth standing in front of me. "I was wrong about you, Derrick. You were right. You're no good for me."

I turned to go. I made it halfway down the hall before he reached me. "Wait, Abby, don't leave. Please, talk to me."

I turned to face him and flinched. His eyes were red and brimming with tears. They pleaded with me to stay, and I almost gave in. Claire appeared behind him and pushed past us. His gaze followed her as she left. He chose to look at her rather than face me.

"Fuck you, Derrick. You fucked me, and I'm a fucking fool."

"You're not a fool, and it wasn't like that. I love you, Abby." Any other time, those three words strung together in that exact structure would have stopped me. Not now. Not after I'd just caught him with the one woman he used to love. The one he'd once confessed he would always love.

"Save your lines for the next gullible girl." His fingers brushed over my arm. His touch was soft and desperate. My stomach knotted. I yanked my arm back and held it against my stomach. "Don't touch me."

He shrank back, wounded. "I'm not going to hurt you."

"You already did. Why her?" I asked through my tears. "You could have any random girl and you picked her—the love of your life. The one I'll never measure up to. Were you trying to completely destroy me?"

"I'm sorry, Abby, what can I do? How can I get you to listen? Let me explain."

"You can't! I saw you with her. I saw you together and the way you looked at her," I said and reared back to deliver my final words to him. "Don't bother showing up with a dozen roses, Mr. Bale. I'm not your mother. I won't lay in your bed and let you have me while you have every other woman."

Wounded, he stepped back. I ignored the pang of longing in my chest as the tears broke free from his eyes and rolled down his cheek. My hand itched to wipe them away just as he'd wiped so many of my tears. I'd intended for my words to hurt, but now that they were out in the open, they hurt me too.

No. I was done feeling guilty for everyone else's mistakes.

I gave him one last look and then left him standing alone in his house without saying goodbye. I walked through the dark night, the air thick with humidity. Claire was long gone by the time I reached my car. I stopped to glance back at his house and flinched when I caught Derrick's gaze. I read his face and could sense that he wanted to follow me. I folded myself into my car and drove away.

"Damnit!" I screamed as I slammed my palm against the steering wheel. As much as I hated him, I hated myself more. I knew better than to trust him. Everyone had warned me that he'd do something just like this. It had been Claire who'd insisted he was different. She'd been the one person who'd been on his side. Now, I knew why. She never stopped loving him either.

No wonder Noah carried such a chip on his shoulder for Derrick. His fiancée was still in love with him. I don't know how I missed the signs. They were there all along buried in her actions. She was always the first to defend him from Noah and the girls.

I pulled into the parking garage and parked in my assigned spot. Everything in this building reminded me of Derrick. As I walked into the lobby and then the elevator, I recalled every kiss we'd shared all those times we'd been too impatient to wait until we were upstairs. I swiped at my eyes and brushed away my tears. He didn't deserve them.

I was done crying over the lies. I was done with lies in general. But most of all, I was done hurting.

CHAPTER THIRTY-TWO

IT WAS NEARLY ONE IN THE MORNING BY THE TIME I MADE IT BACK into my condo. Niles greeted me at the door and meowed to remind me I hadn't yet fed him.

"Sorry, buddy, it's been a shit day." He nudged into my leg as if to tell me everything was fine. He could see the streaks left by my tears, which adorned my face. I scooped him into my arms and nuzzled my cheek against his soft fur. "You're the only man I can trust."

"Meow," he replied, and I resigned myself to swearing off men and adopting more cats. Cats don't try to force you into pregnancy or screw their exes behind your backs. Sure, litter boxes are nasty, and they like to shove their buttholes into your face, but they'd never break your heart. Niles purred in approval as if he understood this revelation I'd just had. I filled his food dish and then pulled a pint of ice cream from the freezer.

Vanilla Cupcake. I'd bought it because it reminded me of my first night with Derrick. I ran my tongue over my lips as if I could still taste that first vanilla-frosting kiss. If I closed my eyes, I could almost feel it. Part of me wanted to feel it so I could go back in time and retrace the steps that had led me to this point. Every kiss, every midnight whisper, every song we wrote together. I'd take it all back and undo it. I wouldn't get tangled up in his gray eyes or stupid tattoos. His beard would never have tickled my skin. I didn't want to know how captivating it was to be caught under his spell.

I grabbed a spoon and wrapped a paper towel around the carton. There would be no need for bowls tonight. Tonight, I'd freely dip my spoon into my pity party and eat every last drop of ice cream. Guilt free. Just like the way I was vowing to move forward.

I took the carton out to the balcony and soaked in rare silence. It was now Wednesday morning, and the city had gone to sleep. Lovers had taken to their beds. Mothers and fathers had long ago tucked in their littles ones. I imagined even those with broken hearts like mine had crawled beneath their covers and curled their bodies around pillows wishing the fluff were something sturdier.

With each bite of ice cream, I sank deeper into contentment. Unlike Jacob, I'd only given Derrick a few months, but in that time, I'd given him far more of myself. I didn't paint over my flaws. I left each tear in the canvas wide open and invited him in. I'd believed we shared those moments. He'd opened up to me, too. It felt like we'd found kindred spirits in each other. He listened to me and shared in my grief. I offered him a shoulder to lean on when his own weight became too much to carry.

I'd miss our early morning chats and cuddles. I'd miss waking up to his beard tickling my bare shoulder. I'd miss his lips and his hands. But most of all, I'd miss who I was with him in those moments when it was just us. I wondered if I'd be able to pick up a guitar and just play it again. Or if I'd find someone whose melodies flowed naturally with my words. With Derrick, I could start a line, and as soon as I lost direction, he would jump in and finish it perfectly. He always knew what I wanted to say and could sometimes say it better.

I scraped the spoon over the sides of the carton and took the last bite. Taking one last breath of the night air, I stood and returned to the empty condo. I didn't bother cleaning up or throwing the empty carton away. I left them all to deal with tomorrow.

My phone buzzed on the counter. I picked it up, expecting to see Derrick's name.

Mom.

I shook my head and declined the call. Not today, Satan. I was done dealing with drama. Before I turned off the phone, my curiosity got the best of me. I checked the missed call and text notifications. Mom and Lindsey had both called a handful of times, which I assumed meant she'd taken my advice and had told her the truth. *Good.* Between those calls, there were a handful from Claire and Derrick. Next, I scanned the texts.

Mom and Lindsey had both sent *Call me* messages.

Derrick sent just one text. I read the preview and decided to put off reading the rest of it until the next day.

Abby, I know you won't read this yet, but I

It took every ounce of strength I had to not read it. I turned my phone to silent and plugged it into the charger. I could deal with everything after work tomorrow. I just needed time and space to think and wallow. Besides, Wednesday was one of the better days at the bar. Wednesday was … my heart sank as I remembered why Wednesdays were my favorite.

Open mic.

It hit me like a cannonball right in my gut. Derrick and I were supposed to sing together tomorrow. I was working a shift with Claire and Noah. Dread filled me. I couldn't face the thought of spending eight hours next to them. Or watching Derrick play and sing as if nothing had happened. I couldn't do it, I decided. There was no way I could keep my job at the bar. I had to quit and walk away from all of it. The steady income. The songwriting. Derrick. I didn't need any of it. I knew how to start over. I could go crawling to dad and beg to live in his basement. Now that I'd met his new family, I was sure he'd welcome me.

The idea of going to live with Dad and Jenny was not at all appealing, but it was far better than being in a tiny bar with Claire and her Bale brothers.

I couldn't solve this problem now. I didn't have the energy. I didn't care. I was spent. I turned off the light and fell into bed without changing my clothes. I didn't bother pulling the covers back because his intoxicating scent would greet me. Not trusting myself not to crave more of him, I opted to lay exposed on top of the blankets. Niles curled up beside me and nestled himself into my stomach. I was willing to bet he missed Derrick too. Lately, he'd gotten more attention from Derrick than from me.

"Sorry I haven't been here for you, Niles," I whispered through gritted teeth as I felt a fresh round of tears starting. I closed my eyes and ran my fingers through Niles's thick fur. "I promise that changes tonight."

That night, the little girl returned to my dreams. She'd grown from the infant who I'd lost to the black hole crib into a toddler. Her hair, still a familiar shade of blonde, fell in curls around her round cheeks. Her eyes had changed from blue to gray, and she toddled around my condo chasing Niles and me. This dream was filled with giggles and very few tears. Gibberish poured from her tiny mouth a mile a minute, but I couldn't understand a single word. We played together for hours and ignored the world outside. As night fell in my dream world, she tuckered out and climbed onto the couch. She laid her head on my lap, and I stroked her hair and sang to her as she drifted off to sleep.

There was someone else there on the couch with us. He didn't have distinct features, just the outline and shape of a man I knew far too well. Her little legs were tucked against him. As I began to sing her to sleep, the shadow man joined me. As his voice blended with mine, my dream daughter sighed, and her eyes fluttered closed. Dream me smiled at the man.

I watched in horror as each of my teeth fell from my mouth. One by one the tiny white chunks fell from my mouth and into the little girl's hair. She cried then. Her wails broke through the silence. She jumped from my lap and ran for the balcony. I tried to stop her and pull her back. But I couldn't reach her. She stopped for a second and turned back to me. Her eyes softened as she watched me calling her. Her tiny hand wrapped around the railing. She floated up and hovered above the emptiness. The world outside had evaporated. It was just blank and empty. From prior dreams, I knew how this ended and was desperate to stop it, even if I knew I couldn't. It was inevitable. I'd already chosen our fate. I held my eyes on her and watched her fade away. She didn't fall or cry as she left me. Her fingers curled into a tiny wave, and then she was gone.

CHAPTER THIRTY-THREE

NILES STARED ME DOWN WHILE I DRESSED JUST AFTER DAWN. I WAS never up this early and he was clearly suspicious. I slipped on a pair of ballet flats and sucked in my stomach while I tried to fasten my pants. I'd gotten far too comfortable with Derrick. My jeans were snug, and the button dug into my stomach. I kicked off my shoes and tugged the jeans free. I threw them into the back of the closet and yanked a loose dress off the hanger.

"It might be time to buy some new jeans and cut back on the ice cream or cupcakes," I mumbled to Niles. I gave him one last scratch and grabbed my purse and keys. While the walk to Dad's office was much needed, I'd learned my lesson last time. I'd save those walks for autumn.

Niles flopped himself in front of the door to try and block me from leaving. "Look, I know we had a moment or two last night that might have made you think I was never leaving the condo again, but I have to do this," I said but he didn't budge. "I'll be back before work. I promise."

I stepped around him and unlocked the door. He pushed against my leg, and I gently nudged him to the side. He meowed but retreated.

When I opened the door, a familiar scent tickled my nose and pulled at the emptiness that had begun to consume my insides. *Derrick.* I glanced down the hall. His body was slumped against the wall beside my door. A small part of me was relieved to see him. He didn't have a dozen roses in his hand. It was just him. I hated to admit it, but seeing him there outside my door and knowing he'd slept on the concrete floor all night comforted me. I shook off the warm, fuzzy feeling and stared down at him. His being here didn't change what he'd done. The bruise around his eye had darkened overnight; it was swollen and looked tender. I flinched. Whether it was from knowing he was hurt or from the lingering splinter he'd left in my heart, I didn't know. I watched him breathe for a second or two and debated kicking him to wake him up. Instead, I left him there and pulled the door shut behind me, careful not to slam it. The soft click was enough to wake him.

"Abby," he said, his voice thick with sleep. "You're up."

"What are you doing here?" I asked. I didn't bother to hide my anger. "You look like shit."

"I feel like shit," he said. He stood slowly, wincing as he lifted himself off the floor. I clamped my arms at my side to keep from reaching for him.

"What happened to your eye?" I hated that I was worried about him. He didn't deserve it.

"I got into a fight with my dad last night."

"Your dad did that?" A lump rose in my throat.

"Yeah," he said and took a step towards me. "That's not important. Abby, you have to know nothing happened last night."

As soon as I started walking, he fell into step behind me and kept talking. "After Dad and I got into it, I called the bar to talk to you because I knew you wouldn't have your phone on. Claire answered and said you'd gone home. She heard my rage and talked me down. When I told her what happened, she came over. I didn't ask her to, she just showed up."

"And what, your clothes just magically melted off of you? You two just happened to fall into an intimate embrace?"

"No, I was asleep when she got there. I thought it was you at the door. When I opened the door and she saw my face, she insisted on coming in."

"In your bed?"

"We weren't in my bed."

"Fair," I said and pushed the down button on the elevator. "Beside your bed. Half naked."

"Look, Claire knows my dad. She knows how he is. She saw I was upset and tried to comfort me."

"With her boobs?"

He touched my arm. I whipped around to face him. "No, it was a hug, Abby. That's all."

"But it wasn't just a hug, Derrick! I saw you two swaying together to a song I couldn't hear. You two have a deep history. That was more than just an innocent hug."

"You're right," he whispered in defeat. "I'd just told her that I loved you."

"Stop saying that!" I shouted at him. The elevator doors opened, and I stepped inside. "You do see the problem here, right? What if it had been me and Jacob you walked in on like that? What would you have thought? What would that have looked like to you? You don't get to throw out 'I love you' and think that somehow magically changes what I saw."

The doors closed before he could respond. I sank back into the corner and clenched my eyes closed. My shoulders shook as I folded forward, clutching my stomach. A sob tore through me and exploded into the empty elevator. When the doors opened on the tenth floor and a man I didn't know walked in, I righted myself and wiped my eyes. He furrowed his eyebrows and then turned his back to me.

Derrick's words played on repeat in my mind. *I love you. It was just a hug. Claire knows how my dad is.* Claire knew parts of Derrick that I never would. She was ingrained in his family and history. I couldn't change that. She would always be a part of him. But I'd seen the truth in his eyes as they pleaded with me to listen to him. He wasn't lying. I felt that in my core. I may not have known him like she did, but I still knew him. He didn't say the L-word lightly.

Did it change anything? That was the question I wasn't sure I could answer. Claire would always be a source of insecurity for me.

It didn't matter now. I'd walked away and left him standing on the other side of the elevator.

After navigating my way through the morning traffic, I paid $10 to park in the garage beneath Dad's building. It was just after nine when I walked into the lobby. The accounting firm's name was etched into the glass. Davidson, Monroe, & Burk. I'd known Dad was a partner at the accounting firm, but it was different seeing the evidence plastered in front of me. Back in Wishing, Dad had worked at a national tax accountant chain. He sat at a desk inside Walmart and did taxes for all my friends' parents every tax season. The difference between the past and the present was jarring.

"I'm here to see Alan Monroe," I said to the bubbly blonde receptionist. I took in her perfectly painted, youthful face and wondered if Jenny was ever jealous.

"Do you have an appointment?" she asked without looking away from her computer.

"No, I'm his daughter." This got her attention. Her mouth fell open as she took me in. The features I shared with my father sparked a look of curiosity in her eyes. "My name is Abby."

"Um," she said, stuttering, "one moment." She pushed her chair back and left me standing alone in the lobby. She reappeared a minute later with Dad in tow.

"Abby, what a pleasant surprise."

"I'm sorry for just showing up," I said. On the drive over, I'd resolved not to cry. Now, standing in front of him, I broke. He pulled me into his arms and guided me back to his office.

"What happened?"

I wasn't sure where to even start. "I talked to Mom," I said after I caught my breath. "She didn't deny it. She blamed you, and I'm pretty sure she hates me."

I reached into my pocket to pull out my phone to show him the texts from Mom and Lindsey, but it wasn't there. I must have left it at home.

"I think she told Lindsey the truth. I threatened her that I would if she didn't. They both keep calling. And then I walked in on Claire and Derrick," I said and swallowed back a fresh burst of tears, "and we broke up, I think. I mean, I don't know if we were even together officially. I can't go back to work. I can't face them again. Not after what happened."

"Slow down," Dad said and handed me a cup of coffee. I looked down and smiled. It was the perfect shade of milk chocolate. I took a sip. He'd somehow managed to make it just how I liked it. "You talked to your mom?"

I nodded. "I asked her about the presents and money. She admitted to it all. She would take your presents and rewrap them and pretend they were from her."

He laughed and said, "I wish I could say I'm surprised. I'm just glad you girls got the gifts."

"It doesn't make you mad that she made you the villain?"

"No, Abby, I made myself the villain when I left. I accepted that a long time ago."

"It's not fair, though."

"Maybe not. That's just how it is. When I left, your mother made it clear to me that I was to have no part in your life. She took the child support and reminded me that I wasn't good for you girls."

"She was wrong," I said. I pulled a tissue from the box on his desk and blew my nose.

He shrugged. "Now, tell me what happened with Derrick?"

"Ugh," I groaned. "I don't know. I was upset after talking to Mom and drove to his house. I found him and his ex together."

Dad cringed. "I don't know if I need to hear this."

"Not like that. I mean, I thought they were or had been, you know, but he insists they weren't. He'd had a fight with his dad, and she consoled him. He should have come to me, though, right? I mean I know they were close, and she knows his family, but I'm his ... whatever I am."

"Is this the long-term girlfriend?" Dad asked. I'd told him about Derrick and Claire when we'd last had coffee. I nodded. "I know it's not the same, but if I'd have ever needed to talk to someone about you or Lindsey being hurt or hurting me, I'd still think of your mother first because she and I still share that history. It doesn't change how I feel about Jenny or our relationship."

"You'd really call Mom?"

"I would and I did."

"What?"

"Christmas morning, I called your mom when I saw you out front. I talked to her before I told Jenny you were here."

"Oh," I whispered.

"We all have a history, Abby. You and Jacob. Me and Susan. Derrick and Claire. Sometimes we have to tap into that to find answers or comfort. It may not be the right answer, but it can help lead us where we need to be."

"You have a point, I guess. I'm still mad and hurt."

"I expect so. You're clearly in love with him," he said, "and he's head-over-heels for you."

I glanced up at Dad and tried to read into his smile. "How do you know?"

"He showed up for you. I see the way you two are together. I've told you that before. But I didn't really see it until he came to the house with you. No man would put himself in that situation for a girl he just casually liked."

Derrick hadn't even hesitated when I invited him to dinner with Dad and his family. He didn't flinch when I dumped my family drama on him. He didn't run when I'd said those horrible things to him last night.

"I said something horrible to him last night," I admitted. "I didn't even try to hear what he had to say. I assumed the worst."

"He'll forgive you if he hasn't already."

An image of Derrick sleeping against the wall outside my condo flashed in front of me. "I have to go," I said and kissed Dad on the cheek. "Thank you."

CHAPTER THIRTY-FOUR

I was in love with Derrick. As in completely, hopelessly gone. This was the truth I'd realized as I sat crying in my dad's office. It was the truth that drove me back across town and up the elevator to my condo. But, like me, Derrick was gone. I'd been naive to think he'd still be waiting for me. I'd shut him out twice in the past twenty-four hours. He didn't want anything to do with me.

Though he was no longer on the floor beside my door, he'd left a small brown bag. I opened and pulled out the note.

Abby - I'm sorry.

That was all he'd written. I stuck my hand into the bag and pulled out a box. When I opened it, I found a single vanilla cupcake. One cupcake. Not two. One. The significance of one lonely cupcake left along with the *wrong* three words wasn't lost on me. I'd hurt him. My words had done the trick. He wasn't waiting for me. He might as well have written, "Enjoy your life without me."

I pushed open the door and threw the cupcake into the trash. I didn't want it. I never wanted to see, taste, or smell another vanilla cupcake. I was done with cupcakes and frosting and Derrick. I retreated into my bedroom and curled up with Niles. I closed my eyes and tried to ignore the stinging of the tears I refused to dignify. I was done crying. And this time I meant it.

I hadn't meant to fall asleep, so when I awoke five hours later, I had just under half an hour to get ready for work. Niles whined when I shoved him off of me. "Sorry," I mumbled. I raced into the bathroom and took a quick shower. I didn't bother drying my hair, opting to twist it into a wet, messy bun. I fished out a clean(ish) black tank top from the hamper and threw on the jeans I'd worn the day before. The button was a little less offensive than it had been this morning.

By the time I walked into the bar, I was fifteen minutes late. Claire and Noah were standing by the front door reviewing the open mic list. I didn't bother saying hi or acknowledging them.

"Hey, Abby, wait," Claire called after me. I ignored her and went to the back to put my phone and keys into my cubby. I glanced at the screen and noticed I'd missed more calls and texts from Mom and Lindsey. None from Derrick.

"Can we talk?" Claire stood behind me, waiting for me to turn around.

"Look, I know you and Derrick didn't do anything last night. I fucked up; I'm sorry."

"Okay, then why are you pissed?"

"I said some pretty horrible things to him and now he wants nothing to do with me. And I love him, okay? I love him, and he trusted me with his secrets, and I threw them in his face at the first opportunity I had. Now, he hates me."

"He doesn't hate you."

"He does," I said. I shoved my phone into the cubby just as another call lit up. This time a name I hadn't seen in while popped up. *Melissa Raven.* I hesitated for a second and considered answering. *No.* Mom had probably gone to her when she couldn't reach me. I had enough going on without adding Jacob's new girlfriend to the mix.

"Are you sure you want to be here?" she asked, putting her hand on my shoulder. I nudged her off and nodded.

"Yes." After everything that had happened, I didn't expect to see Derrick tonight. He knew I'd be working. "What section am I in?"

"Two," she said, "it's just you and me tonight. Leah has a gig across town, and it's Jessie's mom's birthday or something."

"Great, I'm going to go get ready for the rush." I breezed by her and grabbed the bucket of silverware. At first, I didn't notice him sitting at the bar. I had my eyes down and my mind focused on the task at hand. My mind could only handle one small task at a time.

I set up the silverware and laid drink menus on each table. When I reached the last table, I realized I was out of menus. There were more at the host stand, and when I grabbed one from the pile, I caught a glimpse of the night's set list. My eyes moved down the page as if they had a mind of their own.

Derrick Bale ~~& Abby Monroe~~

There it was, plain as day. The end. My name beside his. My name scratched out. He couldn't erase me, but he could remove me.

"Fucking perfect," I said. I turned around and dropped the menu on the table. If Jessie or Leah had been on with us tonight, I'd have left right then and there. But I couldn't leave Claire and Noah alone.

The happy hour crowd was starting to slowly trickle in. I greeted two men in business suits.

"What can I get y'all?" I asked, forcing a smile, "Drafts are two for one tonight."

"I'll take a Blue Moon draft," the one with blue eyes said.

"Bud Light," his friend replied.

"I'll be right back with those." I headed for the bar and stopped when my gaze lifted from the floor. His dark, shaggy hair and broad shoulders were unmistakable. My heart stopped. I couldn't move or breathe. I stared at the back of his head and tried to shove myself forward. It was as if I were frozen. I'd just seen him a few hours ago, but it felt like a lifetime had passed. It had. I'd lost him in those few hours, and now here he was again.

Of course, he was here at the bar he owned on the night he always performed. He'd scratched my name out, but his name was still on the list. He intended to carry on without me. I sucked in a deep breath and wished I'd followed through on my plan to ask Dad if I could quit my job and move in with him. Instead, I'd let him remind me that I loved Derrick and believed that he loved me.

Look where that left me.

Speechless and frozen two feet behind him.

"Need something, Abby?" Noah asked from the bar. Derrick turned around at the mention of me. His cheeks and eyes were puffy as if he'd been crying. He frowned at me and dropped his gaze.

I shook my head at Noah, and then nodded. "Blue Moon and a Bud Light for table 10." Still, I didn't move any closer to the bar or Derrick. I watched from afar as Noah poured my drinks. He held placed both on the bar and looked at me, then at Derrick. When he realized I wasn't moving, he sighed and rolled his eyes.

"This is why my rule exists," he said.

"Shut the fuck up, man," Derrick growled. He slammed his hand down on the bar and shoved his stool back. He didn't look at me as he brushed past. I watched him walk out the door as tears sprang to my eyes.

I took the beers from Noah and delivered them to the table. Noah called me back to the bar.

"I don't want to talk about it," I said and slid onto the barstool. "You were right. I get it. I should have listened to you."

"That's not what I want to talk about."

"Okay. Can I have some water?" My throat ached from crying and talking so much. Noah handed me a glass. I took a big gulp and cringed as the icy water slid through my mouth. "What do you want to talk about?"

"Claire told me what happened last night."

"So, that is what you want to talk about."

"Yes and no. He's told you about his dad, right?"

"How he's an ass and gave him that black eye?"

Noah nodded. "Their fight last night was about you."

"Me?" That didn't make sense. I'd never met the man. How could he have an opinion about me? Much less one that resulted in giving his son a black eye. "I don't understand. Why would they fight about me?"

Noah sighed and leaned forward. "I know better than to insert myself into Derrick's business, but he's hurting, and I don't know how else to help him."

"What do you mean?"

"Last night, Derrick went to Uncle Rob to ask him about our grandmother's ring."

Ring? Did he just say ring? I gasped and met Noah's gaze. My eyes widened as he nodded. "Like, a *ring* ring?"

"Yes. Grandma had two rings from Grandpa; their engagement ring and then the ring from when they renewed their vows. She left one to each of us. Claire has the vow-renewal ring, and the engagement ring was left for Derrick. He wasn't asking him for it yet, just wanted to make sure the ring was still in the family safe and waiting for him. Just in case."

"Just in case." *He was asking about a ring.* If I'd felt guilty earlier, this was a whole other level of remorse. *I am an actual asshole.*

"Uncle Rob apparently lost his shit when Derrick asked. Told Derrick he had no business claiming family heirlooms when he'd walked away from the family business. He told him the ring wasn't his anymore. Derrick asked again, and then accused him of selling it or giving it to someone he shouldn't have. Things went sideways from there."

I shook my head. I didn't know how to process this. He'd gotten into a fight with his dad because he'd asked about a ring I assumed he intended to give to me eventually. Then I accused him of cheating on me and being exactly like his dad. I'd been wrong, so, so wrong. He was nothing like his father. He was his own man, and I knew that. I always had.

"Noah, I messed up, didn't I? I ruined all of this." I dropped my head into my hands and rubbed my eyes. "Shit."

"I can't answer that. He's hurting, Abby, and when Derrick is hurt, he shuts down."

I started to ask him if I could go after him, but the door chimed as more customers came in. Claire greeted them and sat the first in her section. Another couple came in, followed by more. The open mic regulars started to slowly make their way in. I couldn't leave now. I scanned the door to see if Derrick had made his way back, but he hadn't. He probably wouldn't.

"He'll come around," Noah said to me before I slipped away.

I wasn't so sure I believed him.

CHAPTER THIRTY-FIVE

The bar filled up quickly and stayed busy. Claire and I ran back and forth between the bar and kitchen fetching drinks and chips. We could barely keep up. I'd tried my best to pretend it was any other night and not open mic night, but the regulars kept asking what song Derrick and I were playing tonight. I didn't have the heart to tell the truth, so I lied and said I didn't know.

It was harder to lie to Dad. He knew what had happened last night, so he didn't ask. He took his usual seat and squeezed my hand every time I stopped by to check on him. He had to know something was up when Derrick didn't appear for the start of open mic. We'd been taking the earlier slots lately, but not tonight. Tonight, we wouldn't be taking any slots. At least not together.

Just before nine, all of my tables had settled into a comfortable groove, and I was finally getting my footing. I couldn't erase the image of my name beside Derrick's with a giant, angry slash through it. I smiled at Dad, hoping it reached my eyes and would convince him that I was fine, even if I wasn't anywhere near fine. His concern was sweet, but it also made everything else hurt just a little bit more.

"Abby," Claire said and grabbed my arm, "your fucking phone is blowing up."

"I put it on silent."

"I can hear it vibrating every time I'm in the kitchen, and it's making me insane."

"Sorry, I'll go turn it off." The front door opened again, and I mumbled a curse word under my breath.

"He's here," she whispered. I barely heard her over the guy screaming into the microphone. He was one of a handful of new artists this week, and I sincerely hoped he didn't become a regular. Claire bumped my shoulder and pointed at the door.

Derrick stood in the doorway. He had his guitar in one hand and was running his other hand through his hair. Our eyes met for a second before he looked right past me. I tried to silently convey my apology, but his attention was already pulled elsewhere. A few girls from a nearby table jumped up and ran to him, pulling him away. He'd barely even acknowledged me.

"I'll go get my phone." I tucked my wounded pride aside and tried to ignore the sting. He'd looked right through me as if I didn't even exist. I tried to pull in a deep breath, but my lungs refused to cooperate or expand. A tight iron cage clasped around my chest and squeezed.

Once in the safety of the kitchen, I bent over and braced myself on my knees while I tried to find my breath. My phone buzzed in the cubby. The insistent sounds pulled me back to reality. When I retrieved it, my mouth fell open. My screen filled with missed calls from my mom, Lindsey, Melissa, and Jacob's parents. Something was wrong.

"Hey," Derrick's voice boomed through the microphone. Any and all chatter that had filled the dining area ceased. "How are we doing tonight?"

I dropped my phone into my apron and stood in the doorway. My heart raced at the sight of him standing on stage. He looked almost exactly like he did the first time I bumped into him outside of the bar. Only now, his steel-gray eyes wore a deeper sadness, and I'd been the one to put it there.

My phone buzzed again, but I ignored it as he started to speak again.

"Most of you know I normally have someone up here with me but tonight, I'm flying solo." I flinched. "Abby, this one's for you."

He lifted his guitar into position and closed his eyes as his fingers hovered over the strings. As soon as he played the first chord, I recognized it. It was the melody he'd been humming and mumbling for weeks. It vibrated through me, rattling loose the tears I'd been fighting.

"*Missouri has my heart and she's calling me, calling me,*" he sang, "*calling me home.*"

I leaned into the door frame and continued to ignore my phone as it buzzed frantically in my apron. I focused on Derrick and the way he seemed completely lost in the song.

"*She pulled me in with those deep brown eyes. Held me in her loving arms. She set me free and captivated me with just one kiss.*" The more he sang, the more devastated I became. That melody and those lyrics belonged to me. He'd written them for me; I'd been in his arms as he worked through them. I didn't know it at the time, but hearing his guitar, I knew it now. I'd pressed my ear against his chest and felt the vibrations just like I was feeling them now. Under different circumstances, those words might have given me hope, but I knew him singing them tonight was his way of letting go. He was saying goodbye.

He finished the song and the room exploded into cheers. He didn't stand around and wait for them to finish. He pushed past them all and made a beeline for me.

My phone wouldn't stop ringing. I glanced up and saw Derrick coming closer. Dread filled me as I imagined the words he was coming to say. I'd heard his goodbye song; I didn't need to hear the words *it's over* from him. I couldn't handle it. Not now. I drew in a deep breath and reached into my apron to pull my phone out. This time, it was Melissa. I don't know what possessed me to do it, but I clicked the green answer button and lifted it to my ear.

"Abby?" Melissa's voice shook as she whispered my name.

"Tell my mom I'll call her when I'm ready."

"What? No, I'm not calling for your mom. It's Jacob, Abby." I could barely hear her over the crowd.

"Jacob?"

"There's been an accident."

"Is he okay?" Panic seized control. I gripped the phone tighter to my ear and pushed through the back door to find a quieter spot.

Melissa sobbed into the phone, and my stomach dropped. "No." That one word undid me completely.

"What do you mean no? What happened?" Now that I was outside, I could hear the familiar sounds of a hospital in the background. If she was in the hospital, that meant he was still alive. I let the single thought be the one I focused on.

"He was driving home after work yesterday and—" she said, unable to get the words out without more tears. I knew then that she was in love with him. I heard it in her voice as her love mingled with fear. She took in a long, slow, ragged breath. "It's not good, Abby."

"I'm so sorry, Mel," I said and sighed, "but I don't know what I can do."

"You're still listed as his next of kin and power of attorney." When we'd gotten married, Jacob had insisted on making sure both he and I were in control if anything ever happened to the other person. I'd thought it was ridiculous at the time, but Jacob was always a planner, and I'd been a pleaser.

"We're divorced."

"It's not final for another week."

"What do you need?" I already knew what she was asking before she said the words.

"You need to come home. You have to sign control over to his parents. They did emergency surgery, but they can't do much else without your signature."

"Can I just talk to someone?" I asked. It sounded callous, but I didn't want to go home. I didn't want to see him or my family.

"Abby," she said with a deep exhale, "you need to get here. He needs you. For once in your life, stop being selfish." She hung up before I could argue. I stared at my phone and willed it to ring again. It didn't.

"Is everything okay?" I looked up and found Derrick standing in front of me. His wide smile was a jarring sight. How could he possibly be happy right now? Did the idea of dumping me so publicly make him giddy?

I couldn't breathe or find the words to answer his question. I reached up and touched his face. He closed his eye and leaned into my hand. "I'm sorry," I whispered, "I have to go."

"Wait, Abby!" he called after me.

"I know I messed up, and I know I was wrong. I can't take back what I said, I get that and understand why you hate me." I pulled the door open and rushed into the kitchen. Claire was standing at the fryer. I grabbed her arm and pulled her aside, ignoring Derrick as he shouted my name. "I hate to do this, but there's an emergency back home, and I have to go."

"Now?" she asked. Her eyes grew wide as she took me in. Tears streamed down my face. I kept opening my mouth to speak or scream or sob or anything, but it was all used up. I was drained. There was nothing left to feel.

"Yes! Now!" I yelled, unable to control the tidal wave that rumbled through me. Every limb on my body was vibrating. I tried to steady myself and find my center but with everything that had happened in the past forty-eight hours, my center was long gone. I stumbled backward and lost my footing. Two strong, tattooed arms caught me before I hit the ground. I leaned into him and felt his warmth. For a moment, we stood together in silence. His arms, familiar and safe, cradled me.

"Abby," Derrick whispered into my ear, "what is going on?"

"I have to go."

"Where?"

"Home. It's Jacob. He's hurt." It was just three short sentences, but those five words and three periods changed everything. Derrick's body stiffened behind me.

"Can we talk first?"

"No," I said and shook my head, "you can wait until I get back to break up with me."

I shoved myself away from him and shouted an apology to Claire. I didn't bother stopping at the bar to tell Noah what was going on; his fiancée could fill him in. I glanced over my shoulder as I headed for the exit. Derrick stood shell-shocked in the middle of the dining room. His eyes locked on me. This time I didn't look away. I searched his face for a hint of strength that I could steal and take with me, but all I saw was hurt. I'd somehow managed to hurt him again.

In all the warnings that had been given to me about him, no one had given him the same courtesy.

CHAPTER THIRTY-SIX

I yanked my suitcase from the top of my closet and lost my grip on the handle. "Shit!" I screamed into the dark closet as it slammed into my foot. Kicking it open, I stared into the emptiness and wondered what one packed for a trip like the one I was about to take. Was I going home to save my ex-husband? Or was I headed home to bury him?

I ripped a few pairs of jeans off hangers and threw them in. My one and only black dress hung in the back of the closet. I stared at it for far too long before deciding I wasn't going to seal Jacob's fate by bringing it. Instead, I grabbed a few floral and brightly colored tops to bring along. I hoisted the suitcase onto my hip and took it into the bedroom. From my dresser, I pulled out enough underwear to last me through the ice age. Satisfied, I zipped it closed and carried it to the front door.

I checked my phone for more messages, just to be sure nothing had changed. Mom's name appeared on the screen as I picked it up. I sighed and answered.

"Mom, I'm on my way."

"I know," she said. "Melissa told me. I was calling to see if you were okay."

"No, Mom, I'm not okay."

"Are you planning on driving?"

"How else would I get home?"

"You sound upset. Are you sure you should drive? Why don't you call Alan? Maybe he can bring you? I can send you money for a bus ticket if not."

"No, Mom, I'm fine to drive. You don't get to worry about me, not now." I was angry, but I knew she didn't deserve the brunt of it. "I'll be okay."

"Please be careful," she whispered. "I love you."

"You too, Mom. I have to go." I hung up before she could say anything else. Her kindness gutted me. It was bad. I knew it was. Between Melissa's sobbing and my mother's tenderness, it had to be worse than I'd imagined.

Jacob had never had so much as a broken bone. In all his years of playing football, he'd never been injured. He rarely got sick and never had headaches. He was the picture of health. It was hard to envision him in a hospital bed, much less unable to make decisions about his own health. Melissa hadn't said, but I assumed he was in a coma.

I needed to know what I was about to walk into. I opened the web browser into my phone and typed *Jacob Rhodes car accident Missouri.*

A news article from early this morning popped up. *Local man critically injured, driver arrested.* I held my breath as I tapped the link. I skimmed the article. From what was available, a teenager had been driving well above the speed limit and crossed the center line on Highway 5. The accident happened just three miles from the Wishing city limits. The teenager, whose name was being withheld, had walked away from the accident, but Jacob was taken by helicopter to Cox South in Springfield. He was in critical condition. No other details were given, but that was enough.

I dropped my phone onto the counter and leaned over it. I buried my head in my hands and tried to catch my breath. It all came back to me in a rush. Leaving Jacob. Losing his baby. Destroying our life— destroying him. Melissa was right. I was selfish. It was that selfishness that had hurt the people I loved the most. Mom, Dad, Derrick, Jacob. They'd all been victims of my inability to think of anyone but myself.

Now, I may never get the opportunity to set things right with any of them.

I should come with a warning label.

For the first time in what felt like days, I stopped and took in the silence. It didn't last long. Niles meowed at my feet and rubbed against the suitcase. I'd completely forgotten about my cat in my rush to leave. *Yet another casualty of Abby Monroe.*

"Oh," I whispered and wiped my eyes, "I should leave you food, huh?"

"I'll feed him," a voice said from the doorway. I started and jumped back.

"Derrick?" I looked up, confused. "Dad? What are you doing here?"

"Your mom called," Dad said with an embarrassed smile. "I should've known something was wrong when you rushed out of the bar."

"Dad," I said with a sob and fell into his arms. Until that exact moment, I hadn't realized how much I'd needed him. He rubbed my back, and I let him console me. My phone rang again, and I considered taking it and throwing it out the window. "I have to get going."

"You shouldn't be driving right now," Derrick said. His voice was raw with an emotion I couldn't read. I broke free from Dad's embrace and stared up at Derrick.

"I'm fine." It was a lie that no one believed, not even me. Dad and Derrick looked at each other as if to confirm the lie.

"He's right," Dad said, "I'll drive you."

"What about work and Jenny and the boys?" *And Mom and every other mess waiting back in Missouri?*

"I already called Jenny," he said and reached for my suitcase. I started to argue again but he stopped me. "I'm taking you home."

"What about Niles? I can't leave him. I don't know how long I'll be gone for."

Derrick pulled my keys from my hand and said, "I'll stay with him or stop in and make sure he's fine."

"Why would you do that?" I asked. Dad, sensing things were about to get even more weird or awkward, took the suitcase and nodded for the door.

"I'll meet you downstairs." He pulled the door shut behind him, leaving me alone with Derrick so he could take my heart and deal the final blow.

"You don't have to do this," I whispered. "I can get Claire or Jessie to stop in and check on Niles. He's a cat; he'll be fine."

"I want to, Abby." He took a tentative step forward, lifting his hand to me.

"Why? After what I did and said? I assumed the worst and hurt you. I wanted to hurt you." I shook my head and moved back, afraid I'd completely break if he touched me.

"You didn't know because I didn't come to you; that's on me." He matched me step for step, seemingly unafraid.

"He did that because of me." I winced as I took in his black eye again. My fingers twitched, begging to caress his face.

"No, he did this because of who he is."

"I'm sorry." I was sorry he'd grown up with an angry father who took it out on him and his mother. I was sorry I'd hurt him. I was sorry that he'd gotten punched over a ring he'd never give me. But most of all, I was sorry I'd doubted him for even a second. "This is all my fault. I ruined what we had."

"Please don't," he whispered. My back hit the couch just as he reached me. I didn't have anywhere else to go. Derrick lifted his hand and gingerly touched my face. I closed my eyes and sighed. That one touch said so much. "I'm not breaking up with you."

"But you left one cupcake. One single cupcake. And you scratched out my name. You—" He pressed one finger to my lips to stop me.

"I didn't scratch out your name, Noah did. I told him I had to sing solo tonight. I had to play that song for you."

"To say goodbye."

"No," he said, shaking his head. He rested his forehead against mine, and we stood connected in silence. Neither of us capable of finding the right thing to say. I breathed him in, again and again, my chest aching and tugging with each inhale. The emptiness inside me grew deeper with every exhale. My eyes were closed, but I could see him clearly. I didn't dare move. With every passing second, I felt like we were getting closer and closer to becoming one again.

"You're not your dad," I whispered. "You're nothing like him."

"I'm not. I never will be. Not with you."

"I never should've said that. I wanted to hurt you, and I did. I saw you with Claire and immediately assumed the worst. I let my fear scream louder than anything else. I understand if you don't want anything to do with me. You said you were no good for me, but that wasn't true. I'm no good for you. I'm too selfish."

"Abby, I—"

My phone rang from across the room. I glanced up at him and started to apologize again but stopped. Another *I'm sorry* wasn't going to change anything. "I have to go."

"I'll take care of Niles." He lingered in front of me and traced his finger over the side of my face as though he were trying to memorize the curves. Leaning down, he sighed as he kissed my forehead. "I won't say goodbye."

I lifted my gaze to meet his. The sadness in them jolted me. "Then don't," I said and broke our gaze. I slipped out from under him and rushed to the counter to grab my keys and purse. As much as I didn't want to leave, Dad and Jacob were waiting on me. I didn't look back or say goodbye. I wasn't sure what had just happened, but I wasn't going to risk it ruining it by turning around and seeing our ending plastered on his face.

Dad's car was waiting for me out on the street. When he saw me exit the building, he rushed out of the car and came to open my door. "Everything okay?" he asked.

No, I wanted to scream at him, but I just shook my head. "Thank you for doing this."

"I should have done it a long time ago," he said with a twinge of remorse.

I clicked the seatbelt into place and laid my head back against the seat. When I closed my eyes, all I could see was Derrick's bruised eye and broken look. His words echoed through me; *I won't say goodbye.* I wanted to ask what he'd meant by that. Goodbye for now or forever. We had so much to worth through. I felt like an unraveled ball of yarn left scattered on the floor. The beginning and the ending tangled together so neither was clear.

I'd left Derrick to run home to Jacob. My past was once again colliding with my present. I suddenly understood his turning to Claire when his past reared its ugly head again. He hadn't gone to her because he couldn't trust me, he'd gone to her because it made sense in his panic and fear. I didn't know what I was going home to. All I knew was Jacob needed me. Melissa needed me.

But all I needed or wanted was to be back upstairs with Derrick. What I needed didn't matter right now.

CHAPTER THIRTY-SEVEN

"We're about thirty minutes out," Dad said as he gently shook my shoulder. "Do you want to stop and freshen up first?"

I rubbed my eyes and checked the time. It was just after four in the morning. I'd fallen asleep before we made it out of Nashville. "Have you stopped at all?"

Dad shook his head. "I wanted to get you here as fast as possible."

"Can we stop for coffee? Is anyone open for coffee?"

"There's a Casey's on the next exit if that works?" I nodded and reached into my purse. I'd thrown my travel toothbrush and toothpaste in along with a hairbrush and extra ponytail holder. I was fairly certain I'd forgotten everything else I'd need if this visit lasted more than a few days. "I'm guessing you and Derrick didn't get everything worked out?"

"Why do you say that?"

He hesitated before saying, "You kept apologizing to him in your sleep."

My face flushed. I had vague memories of dreaming about Derrick, and I was fairly certain none of them involved apologies. *Please don't let me have said anything else.* "We didn't really get to talk."

"His song was beautiful," Dad said and glanced at me.

"I'd never heard it before last night."

"I can't pretend to know or understand what happened between you two, but something tells me you'll find him right where you left him when we get back."

"I hope so," I said and stared out the window. It had started raining overnight and tiny droplets raced down the glass. I traced them and watched as they each raced towards their demise.

"Playing Racing Raindrops?" Dad asked. I could hear the smile in his voice.

"How'd you know?"

"I taught you that game, remember?" I shook my head. It was something I'd always done, but I didn't have any memories of playing it with him. "When you were little, you'd sit on my lap, and we'd watch the rain falling. I'd always ask you which would finish first. If you guessed right, I'd let you go outside and play in the puddles once the sky cleared."

I remembered the splashing in puddles part; it was one reason I loved the rain so much. Rain always made me think of Dad. "You let me even if I didn't."

"That's true." He laughed and cleared his throat. He pulled into the gas station and said, "Are you ready for this? To see him?"

"No, but I have to be."

"Did they tell you anything?"

I shook my head. "I googled and read an article. It didn't give many details, but I know enough to know it's bad."

He looked as though he wanted to say something else, but he just said, "Well, let's get some coffee, then."

"Dad," I said, stopping him, "thank you for coming here with me. I know it won't be easy for you, either."

"If life were supposed to be easy, we wouldn't have been given hearts that could break." With that fatherly nugget of wisdom, he suggested I brush my teeth and pick up some gum.

In the bathroom, I tried to ignore the stench of those that came before me and focused on cleaning the crust and day-old mascara from underneath by brown eyes. I pulled my hair free from the messy bun

I'd thrown it into last night and raked my fingers through the dirty blonde strands. As I brushed my teeth, I unlocked my phone and read the message Derrick had sent not long after I'd left. There was a picture of Niles and him lounging on my couch. My heart tugged, pulling me back to Tennessee.

We'll be here when you get home.

I read the words and stared at the phone. What I wouldn't give to have awoken to his face rather than the road this morning. I'd been so emotionally spent last night that I didn't even remember dreaming about him. Now in the early light of day, his face was all I could see. His final words to me echoed over and over. *I won't say goodbye.* He hadn't been trying to leave me. The song wasn't a farewell tune; it had been one of apology and forgiveness. I couldn't take back my words or reaction to what I'd seen, but as soon as I was back in his arms, I vowed to make it up to him. Over and over again.

"Let's do this," I said to Dad as I climbed into the car. He handed me a coffee and apologized with a shrug.

"It's so bad, I had to add sugar."

I laughed. "Oof." He grinned and put the car into drive.

The last time I'd been on this highway, I'd been on the other side of the road heading toward freedom as I stole a tiny heartbeat from Jacob. At the time, I hadn't cared how much I was hurting him. His heart could've shattered into a million pieces, and I wouldn't have even batted an eye. Coming home now, I wished more than anything that his heart and he were both intact by the time I made it back to him. We hadn't left on the best of terms, and I couldn't imagine he wanted me there. But sometimes our needs and our wants don't care what the other has to say.

Three months had passed since then. I'd changed in the days and nights since. I had to assume that Jacob had, too. The desperation in Melissa's voice had told me all I needed to know about their relationship. It was the same desperation I'd felt when I saw Derrick with Claire, and then when I heard him singing on stage last night. Jacob deserved to be happy.

So did I, I realized. Happiness had always been a moving target for me. First, I'd escaped my small town and headed off to college a few miles up the road. Then, I married Jacob. I fell into a comfortable rhythm with him and confused contentment for happiness. It wasn't until I saw the reality of my future with him appear on the pregnancy test that I understood the difference. It wasn't like he'd done anything particularly damning, but I knew my future would never be with him or in Wishing. So, I left. When I pulled into Nashville without a plan, I wasn't under any illusion that happiness was waiting for me. If anything, I'd never expected to find it.

But I had.

I found it in the new strings on my guitar. In the words I finally let out. In his steel-gray eyes and safe embrace. I uncovered myself as I got lost in him. I finally saw the future I wanted, the future I needed.

The miles passed beneath the tires of Dad's Audi, and the road hummed along. He'd turned off the radio while I slept to give me peace and silence. Now, I wanted nothing to do with quiet. "Do you mind?" I asked and pointed to the radio. He shook his head.

I turned the volume up and scanned the stations until I found a familiar song. I closed my eyes and leaned back, letting Beau Grant's voice singing the words Derrick had written flow through me. Where Derrick sang the words with a bit of tortured passion, Beau added a longing to them. I much preferred Derrick's version, especially knowing the original line. The fact that he'd written it as a goodbye to Claire didn't bother me. It wasn't about her. The song was about him embracing his vulnerability and opening his heart, just as he'd done with me when he shared the story behind it.

"Is this Derrick's song?" Dad asked.

I reached over and turned the volume down. "Yeah."

"I bet we'll be hearing your songs soon."

"You think?" I didn't want to believe him. After all, he was biased.

"I do. Your words are powerful, and the music you and Derrick make is magic." I blushed at the compliment and wondered if Dad really meant it. Before I could ask, he pulled the car into the hospital parking lot. "I'll let you out here and meet you upstairs."

"You don't have to come in," I said. I didn't know for sure if Mom was here, but the odds were good. She'd always loved Jacob.

"I'll be fine," Dad replied, reading me. I gave him one last look before climbing out of the car. "I'll find you."

Nodding, I waved him off and made my way into the emergency room entrance. A security guard stopped me and waved me through the metal detectors.

"I'm here to see Jacob Rhodes," I said. My voice shook with a fresh wave of anxiety.

"Are you a relative?" the woman at the triage desk asked.

"I'm his," I said, pausing long enough to pull my driver's license from my wallet, "I'm his wife." The words caught in my throat, and I swallowed back the lump that had stopped them.

"One moment, Mrs. Rhodes." She glanced down at my license, then turned her attention back to the computer in front of her. "He's in ICU. Do you know where that is?"

"No."

"Take the elevator to the fourth floor and then left at the nurses station. Room 421."

"Thank you." I glanced around the room behind me and tried to find an isolated spot to gather myself before going up to see him. I avoided the mother with the screaming baby and the man coughing up a lung. I chose the wall across from the triage desk and leaned against it. I leaned against the wall and closed my eyes. I took a few slow, steady breaths to center myself. I wasn't sure I could do this.

"Abby?" The familiar voice made my heart lurch.

"Lillian," I said and turned to greet Jacob's mom.

"You have a lot of nerve showing up here," she said, glaring at me.

"I—"

"She's here to sign the papers, Lil," Eddie, my former father-in-law, said as he took hold of his wife's elbow. "We'll take you up. Our lawyer is on his way to witness and notarize. We've been waiting for you all night."

"I came as soon as I heard," I said. I felt myself sink back into the timid girl they used to know. The desire to please wormed its way through me, strangling in its hold. I hated the feeling.

"You never should've left," Lillian spat at me. "Neither my son nor I will ever forgive you for that."

If Mrs. Edward Rhodes were a cursing woman, she'd likely have called me a bitch or worse. But she wasn't. She was a proper woman and instead chose to use her eyes to convey her hatred. As I did when I was her daughter-in-law, I ignored it. We rode up the elevator in silence as I prayed to find Jacob alive and recovering. I wished Dad had found parking faster.

"Right this way," Eddie said. He placed his hand on my back. I stiffened as he guided me forward. He led me into a waiting room where my mother, Lindsey, Melissa, and a few of Jacob's friends had gathered. They'd been in the middle of a conversation but fell silent when I walked in.

Melissa jumped to her feet, her bright red hair bouncing behind her as she ran to me. She threw her arms around me and buried her face into my shoulder. I pulled her into a hug and let her sobs be enough for both of us. I didn't want to cry anymore. "I'm so sorry," I whispered into her ear and hoped she understood that I meant the words for so much more than the moment we were in.

"He keeps saying your name," she said as she pulled back. I searched her eyes for a sign she was hurt by this but couldn't find anything other than longing. She wasn't jealous. She knew our history almost as well as I did.

"Is he okay?" I asked. She shook her head.

Before she could answer, Eddie put his hand on my shoulder and handed me a pen. "Let's go out into the hallway and get this taken care of."

I took the pen and fell into step behind him. I didn't bother offering him an apology or explanation. His blue eyes, as bright as Jacob's, told me he didn't give two shits about what I had to say.

"Sign here and then initial on the lines marked with an *X*."

I did as he said and was taken back to the night when Jacob had hovered over me pointing at all the places I needed to sign to approve the end of our marriage. My hand didn't shake now. I signed with confidence and handed the paper back to Eddie.

"You can see him if you want. They'll be slowly waking him up as soon as I give the approval." Shocked by his offer, I didn't know what to say. He gave me a final nod and took the papers over to a man in a suit. The bowed their heads together to confer.

"Abby," my sister's voice felt warm in my ears. I turned to find her and mom standing together. Behind them, Dad was getting off the elevator.

"Maybe we should go outside," I said. Mom followed my gaze and turned. Her back stiffened at the sight of the man she hadn't seen in twenty years.

"Alan," she said in a soft exhale, "thank you for bringing my baby home."

The pain in her voice broke my resolve. I reached for her and pulled her into my arms. "I'm sorry, Mom."

CHAPTER THIRTY-EIGHT

I stared at my sister as she paced in front of me. Her hair, dirty blonde and mousy like mine, fell in a short bob that framed her round face. Seeing her now, I saw so much of our dad in her. The way she wrung her hands as she spoke reminded me of how he'd stood as he told me the truth about the money and gifts.

"Have you seen him?" I asked.

"Jacob?" When I nodded, she said, "No. But I talked to Melissa this morning. It sounds like he's improving. I've tried to give them space, given, well, you know …"

"Me."

Lindsey shrugged. "How are you, sis?"

"I'm here," I said, unsure of what to say next. I glanced up at the hospital and counted the windows up to the fourth floor. My first love was up there somewhere, unconscious and unaware of my presence. There wasn't a rule book for how I was supposed to feel in this situation.

"I can't believe he's actually here," she said, pausing in front of me. "What's he like?"

"He's great." The words felt both forced and true. I was grateful to shift the conversation away from Jacob but wasn't sure this was the direction I wanted it to go.

Lindsey snorted. She sounded like Mom. "Sure, Abs, whatever."

"He really is," I said and grabbed her arm. She was making me dizzy with all of her pacing. "Did Mom tell you?"

"About the gifts and money?" I nodded. "She did yesterday. I still can't believe it, but she's not wrong, you know? He still left."

"He did, and she lied."

"So did you."

"Mom told you, huh?"

"She did. Why didn't you tell me, Abby? You could trust me, you know? I wouldn't have told him. You're my sister, you're supposed to tell me stuff like that."

"Linds, I didn't tell anyone." She sat on the bench beside me and rested her head on my shoulder. "I was scared and confused. I didn't know how to tell you, and I was afraid you'd talk me into staying."

"I would have."

"And that's why I couldn't tell you. My mind was made up, and I didn't want to put that burden on you."

"I still can't believe you and Jacob are over. You guys were the one stable part of my childhood."

"No," I said, shaking my head, "we were a mess. I just hid it well."

Lindsey sat up as Mom and Dad approached us. "Oh, by the way, I saw your open mic performance on your Instagram. You're amazing, Sis."

"Thank you."

"Who's the hottie singing with you?" She bumped my shoulder.

My cheeks flushed, and I said, "That's Derrick."

"*Derrick*." She mimicked me and said his name with a sing-song voice. "He the guy Jacob caught you with?"

"What guy?" Mom asked. I glanced up at her and noticed her eyes were brimmed with tears. Her face was splotchy and red.

"Abby's new boyfriend," Lindsey said. I punched her arm. "Ow! What? I know that look. You're smitten."

"Smitten? What grown woman says smitten?" I laughed.

"Derrick is a good guy," Dad offered.

"You've met him?" Mom asked, wounded.

"Yes, I've been going to watch Abby sing every week, and Derrick is there." Dad met my gaze and shook his head. He wasn't planning to tell her about the family dinner we'd had.

"I see." Mom didn't even bother to hide the resentment in her voice. "Lindsey showed me the video, Abby. I liked the song."

That was the closest she'd ever come to a compliment, so I took it. My phone buzzed in my pocket. I pulled it out to see if it was Melissa with an update. It wasn't.

I miss you. Have I told you that yet? I think I miss you more than Niles does. Not that it's a competition. Derrick attached a photo of Niles asleep on my bed.

I miss you, too. And I'm sorry. Have I told you that yet?

I smiled as I watched the bubbles that indicated he was typing a reply appeared.

You did. Once or twice. You can stop apologizing. He added a heart-eyes emoji. I smiled as I read and reread the message.

"Who are you texting?" Lindsey asked and grabbed my phone. "We're in the middle of a big family moment, here."

"Give that back!" I said, laughing as she turned away from me. My face flushed as she read the message aloud.

"Oooh, he sent a kissy face," she said and held up the phone, showing another text from him.

"Jealous?" I asked and took my phone back.

"I'm happily married, remember. I mean, not to a hunky, bearded, tattooed guitar player, but I'm satisfied."

"Gross."

"Girls," Mom scolded. "Stop embarrassing yourselves."

"Sorry," Lindsey and I both mumbled.

"Well," Mom said, clearing her throat. "Your father and I talked, and I owe you girls an apology. I shouldn't have lied to you girls. I knew it then, and I know it now. Alan didn't deserve that and neither did you two." My mouth fell open. I turned to Lindsey and found her just as shocked.

"It's okay, Mom," Lindsey said. "It was a long time ago." My sister was always quick to forgive. It's one thing I loved about her, and it was a trait she shared with Dad.

I wish I could have given my mom the forgiveness she wanted, but I wasn't ready. But, I was more like my mother than my father. I didn't find my way to forgiveness as easily. The hurt was still buried deep inside Dad's eyes. He studied Lindsey and tried to rectify the memory of the seven-year-old little girl he'd left behind and the grown woman standing in front of him. I recognized the look because it was the same one he'd given me the day I showed up at his house.

"Susan showed me photos of the twins," Dad said, offering Lindsey the olive branch she would always take. "I'd love to hear about them."

Lindsey looked up at our father with a wide smile. Pride filled her eyes as she launched into a story of the twin's latest hijinks. Dad sat beside her and listened intently as she spoke. Seeing the two of them together felt like sliding the final piece into a puzzle. Our picture was finally complete.

"Hey, Mom, do you mind going back inside with me? I want to check on Jacob," I said. I patted Lindsey's knee and nodded toward Dad. I wanted to give them space and time.

"Still scared of Eddie and Lillian?" she asked with a laugh. She reached down and took my hand, helping me to my feet.

"Always."

"You and Alan get to know each other, okay?" Mom said to Lindsey. My sister nodded slowly and looked to us for final approval. "Go, Lindsey. You don't have long."

"Thank you, Mom," I said as she linked her arm through mine and walked back into the hospital with me. "Thank you for telling Lindsey the truth and for giving him a chance."

"I had no intention of doing either but seeing Eddie and Lillian hurting and knowing Jacob might not make it, I couldn't help but wonder what I'd do if it were you or Lindsey in that room. I realized that I didn't want to lose you or her without the chance to come clean. I owe you more than that, but it's what I've got."

"I can't say I'll ever understand what you did or why, but as Dad says, I can't change the past. All I can do is be here now and do better."

"Maybe you should take that advice and go talk to the Rhodes."

"Do they know about the—" I asked and swallowed back the rising lump that appeared every time the topic arose. "Baby?"

"I don't think he ever told them. Lillian hasn't mentioned it to me, and neither has Jacob. I'm not sure they need to know. At least not know. They have enough hurt."

She was right, of course. I gave her hand a quick squeeze as we rode up the elevator in silence. When it opened, she led me into the lobby and down the hall. Lillian and Eddie weren't in the waiting room when we arrived, so I sat down next to Melissa while Mom went to find coffee.

"Was that your dad?" Melissa asked. Her voice was strained and tired.

"Yeah," I said. Melissa had been there when he left. She'd watched me go through the loss and disappointment. My answer may have been just one word, but she knew the full story behind the single syllable.

"You look like him."

"I know."

She nudged closer to me until our arms were touching. "I didn't mean for this to happen, you know?"

"It's okay. I want him to be happy." I didn't need to tell her I'd been hurt when I first heard the news. She didn't need to hear that now. Or ever. I left, as he'd said; I didn't get to be hurt by this. And the truth was that I did want him to be happy.

"We are," she said. "Are you?"

I sighed. "I'm getting there."

"You're singing again." She wasn't asking. She shifted and sat forward. "Jacob showed me the videos. I really liked the one about breaking rules; it reminded me of your bachelorette party."

"Oh my gosh! I'd completely forgotten about that night." I

laughed. We'd spend the night going from bar to bar in Springfield, trying different shots and drinks until we passed out in the hotel room. "That was a fun night."

It was hard to deny how proud I felt knowing that my friends and family back home had gotten to hear the songs Derrick and I had created.

"I never imagined we'd end up here," she said, biting back a yawn. "I always pictured us raising our families together. You and Jacob and me and whoever I was able to con into marrying me."

"You wouldn't have to con anyone; Melissa, you're an amazing woman and an even better friend. I let you down and hurt you. I hurt everyone."

"I love you anyway."

I started to reply to her but was interrupted by Lillian sulking into the waiting room. Her eyes were bloodshot, and streaks of black mascara ran down her face. My heart stopped. Melissa leaped to her feet. I joined her and took hold of her hand.

"Is he—"

"He's awake," Lillian whispered. She pulled Melissa from me and wrapped her arms around her. Melissa melted into Lillian's arms, and the two women sobbed together.

I shifted on my feet and searched the room for my mom. I didn't belong here. A year ago, I might have, but not now. Now I was the odd man out. I took a step back and moved toward the door. A strong hand gripped my shoulder and stopped me. I flipped around and looked up into the deep blue eyes of my former father-in-law.

"He's asking for you," he said softly so as not to disturb Melissa or Lillian. "I'll take you back."

CHAPTER THIRTY-NINE

I STOOD OUTSIDE THE WINDOWLESS DOOR AND DREW IN A DEEP BREATH. The sterile air tasted like metal as it burned in my throat. I placed one hand on the handle and the other at the center so I could be as gentle and quiet as possible when I opened the door. It creaked slightly under the pressure, and I winced. The room, dark and filled with the steady beeping of monitors, wasn't at all inviting. I glanced over my shoulder and met Eddie's eyes. He nodded, urging me forward.

I passed through the door and gently closed it behind me. The click echoed through the room. I waited for the echoing to stop before I stepped forward. Fear took hold and locked me in place. I wasn't sure if I was more scared of seeing how injured he really was or knowing he'd still be angry with me. It was likely the latter. While I'd never seen Jacob with so much as a papercut, I knew he was tough. He could pull through this. I wasn't so sure I was strong enough to handle his anger and disappointment in me again.

"Abby?" His voice was hoarse and heavy with sleep, but I'd recognize it anywhere.

"Hey," I replied and stepped up to the side of his bed. My eyes strained to adjust to the dimly lit room, and when they did, I wanted to close them again. Jacob's head was wrapped in a blood-stained bandage and bruises decorated his face. I didn't dare look down at the rest of him. I'd never seen him look so fragile, not even when I'd been the one to break him. Those injuries had all been internal.

"Please don't look at me like that," he said. I forced my eyes to open fully and looked down to meet his gaze. My smile felt unnatural, but I plastered it on anyway. "They gave me good drugs. Nothing hurts right now."

"I'm sorry it took me so long to get here."

"It's a long drive."

"I should have been here."

"No, you're exactly where you need to be."

"Your mom hates me," I said to lighten the mood.

"She's always hated you." The retort made me smile, and Jacob laughed. "Ow."

"Are you okay? Can I help."

"Just hurts to laugh." He pushed himself back and propped himself up against his pillows, wincing as he did. "You look good."

"So do you."

"I'd say you were a terrible liar, but we both know that isn't true."

I pulled my lip into my mouth and bit it. "Jacob, I'm so sorry about all of that. I knew it would hurt you, so I can't say I didn't mean to cause you pain. I did. I can't take it back or undo any of it, but I need you to know how sorry I am."

"I forgave you before I made it out of Tennessee," he said. His voice was rough and hoarse. "Can you hand me that water?"

I grabbed the cup off the table and guided the straw into his mouth. I slid up onto the edge of the bed and watched him take a painstakingly slow sip. When he finished, I placed the cup back on the table. If things had gone differently, we might still be sitting in this hospital but with the roles reversed. My hand found its way to my stomach. I pressed against the soft flesh and closed my eyes. I tried to imagine my belly big and round, ready to pop. I had no doubt that Jacob would've sat exactly where I was. He'd have held my hand and let me squeeze it until I broke a finger. He'd have fed me ice chips and said cliched things like "You can do it, babe."

But he'd have been wrong.

I couldn't have done it. I never wanted to do it. As much as the emptiness ached, I knew none of it was right. Not Jacob. Not the baby. Not us. We weren't meant to be. I was okay with that. Even now, seeing him fragile and so close to—I couldn't even think the word—I had no regrets. Leaving was the right thing to do. Even if it hurt like hell.

"You'd have been due soon," he whispered. He placed his hand on top of mine.

"August 31," I said without thinking. Tears pricked my eyes. I scrunched my nose to stop them. "I dream about her sometimes."

"Her?"

"I never knew for sure, but I felt it. We always said we'd have a girl first. She'd have your blue eyes."

"The light blonde curls you used to have."

"I miss that light blonde hair." I offered him a weak smile. He was one of the few people who had known me when my hair was still sun-kissed and practically white. It darkened into the mousy shade it was now as I grew older.

"Me too."

"Things were so much easier back then."

"Abby, don't do this."

"Do what?"

"Reminisce about the past. We both knew things weren't working. Me lying here on the other side of a close call with death doesn't change that. You weren't happy here."

"Were you?" I asked.

"I thought I was, but I wasn't. When you left, I realized I'd done to you what my father had done to me. I projected my wishes and plans onto you without a single care or question about what it was that you wanted."

"We both used to want those things."

"We did. I stopped paying attention to you along the way. I saw your dreams and talent as a threat to what I wanted." The more he spoke, the stronger he became. There was a new clarity in his words, and I hoped it wasn't from the pain medication. I wanted to believe what he was saying. I hadn't realized that I needed or wanted closure with him until he started to give it to me. "It never occurred to me that you'd resent me for it."

"I didn't resent you."

"Abby," he said and locked his eyes on mine. "Don't lie. You may think I didn't notice the changes in you, but I did. You packed away your guitar and stopped waking in the middle of the night to write things. You kept your eyes open when we kissed. You had one eye on the door and the other on me. You slipped away slowly, and I saw it happening but didn't do anything. I let you go. I didn't fight for you."

He took my hand into his and ran his thumb over my ring finger.

"I never wanted you to see that," I said. "I thought it made me weak. The longing and the wanting? I thought it made me like *him* and at the time, I didn't want a thing to do with my dad."

"You're one of the strongest women I know. I wish more than anything that you didn't have to go through that alone. I can't imagine what that was like for you."

"It was hard," I admitted. "But my dad was there for me. He took care of me."

"Good." He yawned and then started coughing. It was a deep, rattle inside his chest. I handed him the water. It took him a minute to catch his breath. "Thanks."

"You scared the hell out of everyone, you know that, right?"

"I do now." He laughed and added. "If it brought you home, it might have been worth it."

"You didn't have to get hit by a car and almost die for me to come home." Even as I said the words, I knew they weren't true. "Why didn't you transfer the power of attorney and everything over after I signed the papers?"

"I didn't think it was necessary."

"Is it wrong to say I'm glad you didn't?" I was only partially joking.

"I'm glad I didn't either. Abby," he said and took a deep breath. "I want you to be happy. Does he make you happy?"

"Who?" I asked, blushing.

"Derrick," he replied. I didn't realize he knew his name. When he saw the surprise on my face, he said, "I watched the videos."

"You and everyone in town."

"We had a viewing party at the drive-in. We watched all of them."

"You're joking, right?"

"I wish I was," he said with a laugh. "But your sister and Melissa arranged the whole thing."

"No, they didn't."

"Rayna closed down Lace & Grit for the night and served up fried pickles and Boulevard Beer in your honor." He grinned, the edges of his mouth twitching with mischief.

"Now I know you're full of shit. You had me there for a minute." One of his favorite things to do was create tall tales and take them so far into the ridiculous that no one ever believed him.

"You're avoiding the question. Does he make you happy?"

"He does," I said unable to hide my own smile. "I am happy in Nashville. Not just because of Derrick, though. Playing and writing is my calling, Jacob. I wish with all my heart that I could have done that here with you."

"It's okay; it really is. If you'd have stayed, I probably would've cheated on you with your best friend."

"You and Melissa, huh?" I gently nudged his side. "It makes sense, you know. You and her? You two fit." I could've chosen to be jealous and focus on the tiny sliver of truth in his statement, but I didn't. Nothing good would come of it.

"We're okay," he said after a minute of silence. "You and me. You'll always be my first love."

"And, you'll always be mine."

CHAPTER FORTY

I called Derrick when Dad stopped for gas on the other side of
Wishing. He'd offered to drive through town, but I didn't want to see
it. I'd already said goodbye to those who I needed to. I'd given
Wishing a decent farewell the night I left. There wasn't anything left
there for me.

"Hey, you," Derrick answered. I could hear the smile in his voice.
We'd texted a few times over the past couple of days, but it was
comforting to hear his voice. Hearing it made me long for Nashville
even more. I needed more than his voice. I needed to see and touch
him to confirm he was still real.

"I miss you," I said and rested my head against the window.

"I miss you too." Niles mewed in the background. "Niles misses
you, too."

"We just passed Wishing and should be home by four."

"We'll be ready for you."

"Derrick," I said.

"Abby."

"I—" I shook my head. I couldn't say this over the phone. I needed
to tell him in person. "I'll see you soon."

"I've got some news to share when you get back," he said.

"I can't wait." We both hung up without saying goodbye. He was still boycotting the word, and I wasn't mad about it.

"Ready to go home?" Dad asked and handed me a coffee.

I lifted it to my lips and smiled. Of course, he'd gotten my order right. "Yes."

"Was that Derrick on the phone?"

"It was. He and Niles are eagerly awaiting my return. Did you talk to Jenny?"

He nodded. "Last night. I FaceTimed with the boys."

"I bet they miss you."

"I think they miss me helping them with their video games and sneaking them ice cream after dinner."

I laughed and settled in for the long drive home.

"Your mom invited us for Christmas."

His words completely took me by surprise. I'd just taken a sip of coffee, so when I coughed, it came out of my mouth and nose and covered the dash. He pulled a napkin out of the center console and handed it to me. I dabbed up the spill and tried to ignore the burning in my nose. "What?"

"Jenny, the boys, me, and 'that handsome troublemaker my daughter is dating.'"

"No way." I refused to believe it. At dinner last night, Mom had referred to Jenny as "Pilates Polly" the instant Dad excused himself for the bathroom. "I don't buy it."

"She did," he said and handed me his phone to show me the text. I read the words and shook my head.

"I'll be damned."

"Anything is possible, kiddo, even your mother forgiving me and you and Jacob finding common ground."

Dad had a point. I knew coming here would shift something in the cosmos. Either I'd see my first love lying near death and fall for him all over again, or I'd find closure. What I found was the forgiveness I so desperately needed from him and from myself. Happiness, at least for now, had been a pleasant surprise. I'd conjured up this image of him and Melissa wallowing together in their shared misery of losing me—as narcissistic as that sounds—but that wasn't at all the case. They'd found each other in my absence, but it hadn't been in bitterness.

When I said goodbye to them this morning, I left the room knowing that chapter of my life was closed. Jacob and Wishing were my past. I used to think I'd regret both, but I didn't. I was grateful for the time I'd spent with him. I was thankful for the support and love I'd always find in my home, even if it wasn't my home anymore. In the few short months I'd been in Nashville, it had become my home. I still had so much to learn and explore in my new city, but it was where I belonged. It was the place where I'd found myself and my second chance.

Nashville brought me more than a fresh start, though. It brought me full circle. I'd arrived broken and alone. I showed up at my dad's place as a lost daughter. Now, I was sitting next to him discussing the life lessons he'd never taught me. He was getting his second chance, too. Mom wasn't fully ready to forgive and forget, he and I both knew that, but she was closer. Inviting all of us to Christmas was the first step. I wasn't sure Jenny would accept the invitation. She was under no obligation to, neither were my brothers. Same went for Derrick.

Derrick. He was far more than I ever expected to find in Nashville. Until this week, I didn't realize just how important he'd become. He was more than a lover or a writing partner; he was the defibrillator that restarted my life. He'd provided me with the jolt I needed to pull myself out of the dark cloud I'd pulled over myself to protect me from the bright light of the sun. I didn't think I deserved a second chance after everything I'd done. He showed me, more than once, that I did.

Dad put the car in reverse and backed out of the spot. "Ready for another eight hours in the car with your old man?"

"More than you know," I said and smiled up at him.

We spent the drive reminiscing about our short time together in Missouri. He told me stories about him and Mom that I'd never heard. I laughed as he regaled me with the antics he pulled with Mom and her brother, Adam. As we made the long, winding drive through the backroads between Missouri and Kentucky, he shared details of the night he left.

"I spent most of the driving looking in my rearview mirror," he said. His gaze went there instinctively. "I think maybe I was looking to see if you or Lindsey had climbed into the backseat and decided to come with me."

"If I'd known you were leaving, I would have," I said. We'd gone to bed that night just like every other night. Dad read us a few Shel Silverstein poems and tucked us in. Mom came in and sang with me. Neither of them appeared at all distressed or worried. As far as I knew then or remembered now, it was a normal night.

The next morning was anything but normal. It was a Tuesday. That I knew for sure. No one woke Lindsey or me up for school. When I opened my eyes, the first thing I noticed was how bright the sun was. It was fall, so the sun usually woke up later than I did. The next thing I noticed was the smell of cigarettes wafting into my room. I remember gagging at the scent and then following it downstairs.

"Your father left," Mom had said when she saw me. She had a cigarette hanging from her mouth and another burning in the ashtray. A small glass of whiskey sat beside. At the time, I thought it was apple juice. Over the next few months, I learned that "Mommy's juice" wasn't at all like the juice Lindsey and I drank.

I studied her face and waited for her to finish. He left to go where? To the store? To work? I didn't understand then what *left* really meant. My dad wouldn't just leave without saying goodbye. He wouldn't. I knew it then, and I knew it now. I spent the morning searching the house for a letter or a sign that he might have left just for me. All I found were a few shirts he left behind and a Van Morrison cassette tape. He used to sing "Brown Eyed Girl" to me when we were in the car. That album was ours.

"Did you leave the *Moondance* cassette for me?" I asked.

I watched as a slow smile spread across his face. "You found it."

"I did. Mom was useless that day, so I made Lindsey and I breakfast and called the school to tell them we wouldn't be in. After Mom fell asleep on the couch, I went into your room to see if I could find anything that would reassure me you weren't *gone* gone. I found it in your dresser."

"I did leave it for you," he said, sniffling. "I stopped in Paducah and picked up another copy at their Best Buy. I listened to it all the way to Nashville."

"So did I," I said and swiped away my own tear. "Not the cassette, of course, I wore that thing out a long time ago."

I'd listened to the album on repeat after he left. Mom hated it and would yell at me to "turn that shit off!" every time she heard it, but I refused. Dad had given me the gift of music, and I wasn't letting her take that from me.

"I always hoped that record would lead you to find me."

"Did you know when you left that you wouldn't see us again?"

He shook his head. "No, I assumed I'd be home for holidays and that you two would spend the summers with me."

"Why didn't that happen?" I asked even though I could assume the answer.

Dad sighed and gripped the steering wheel tighter. His jaw clenched and unclenched over and over as if he were trying to speak but didn't know what to say.

"It's okay," I said. "I think I know the answer."

"I wanted it more than anything, Abby. I wanted you and your sister in my life. Being your father was and still is the greatest joy and privilege of my life, you need to know that. I never wanted to hurt you, but I did anyway. I believed your mother when she insisted that shuffling you back and forth between Missouri and Nashville would do more harm than good."

"She was wrong."

"I know that now."

"I forgive you, Dad," I said, hoping those words healed as much in him as they did in me when Jacob said them. "I forgave you the day you took me to the hospital and stood beside me without judgment. You were there for me without question when I needed you most, and you're still here."

"I love you, my brown-eyed girl."

"I love you, too, Dad."

CHAPTER FORTY-ONE

THE SWEET SCENT OF FRESH-BAKED VANILLA AND SUGAR GREETED ME when I opened the door of my condo. I closed my eyes and breathed in the welcoming smell. When I opened them, I found Derrick standing in the middle of my kitchen wearing my apron. Niles was perched on the counter, wearing the face of a cat who knew he was breaking the rules.

"Hey," I said. My body warmed at the sight of him.

"Hey," he replied.

"Nice apron."

"I considered wearing nothing under it, but Niles didn't like the idea of my naked ass being near his food."

I pouted and dropped my suitcase onto the floor. "Niles would've gotten over it."

Derrick shrugged and turned back to stir something on the stove. When he lifted the lid, the tangy aroma of tomatoes and garlic wafted towards me. I inhaled and sighed. "It smells amazing in here."

I walked into the kitchen and stopped behind him, wrapping my arms around his waist. I nuzzled my face against his back and breathed him in. "Thank you for taking care of Niles."

"I think we really bonded." He slipped out of my grasp and turned to face me. He placed his fingers under my chin and lifted my head up to his. He smirked as he leaned down and pressed his lips to mine. "I didn't get to kiss you goodbye," he whispered as he pulled away.

"You said you didn't want to say goodbye."

"I didn't, but a kiss would've been nice."

"Doesn't it just make this one sweeter?" I asked and brushed my mouth over his, teasing his lips with my tongue. "I'm so sorry for how we left things. We had so much to talk about, and I just bolted."

Beep. Beep. Beep. The timer on his phone interrupted us. Derrick groaned and pulled away from me. "Let's talk over dinner."

I reached up and tousled his hair. "I'm going to freshen up. I smell like the road and bad coffee."

"You smell delicious," he said as he bent down to kiss my forehead. "Dinner in five."

"Yes, sir." I saluted him on my way out of the kitchen.

I decided to take a quick shower to rinse off Missouri and all that I'd left behind. The deep pelting stream massaged my aching muscles. I could've stayed under the steam of hot water for hours, but Derrick was waiting for me. Knowing he was a few feet away soothed what aches the shower didn't. I opted for a lightweight sundress and skipped the bra. I had a feeling Derrick wouldn't mind one bit.

"Oh," I exhaled when I saw him. He had the apron back on but had ditched his jeans and shirt. Disappointment filled me when he turned around and I saw his boxers. "I see you and Niles reached a compromise, but I'm afraid I'm overdressed."

Derrick smiled and said, "You're perfect." His eyes scanned me, from head to toe, lingering in all the right places. I blushed and kept my gaze on him. "Hungry?"

"Starved."

He took my hand and led me out to the balcony where he'd added a second chair and a small table. On it, he'd placed a few candles and a plate for each of us. A single vanilla cupcake was arranged at the center of each plate. There wasn't a single drop of frosting on his, but mine was piled high.

"Did you make those?" I asked, my eyes wide.

"I did. I talked the lady at the bakery into sharing her recipe."

"I'm sure you charmed it right out of her." I swatted his backside and leaned into him. "This is exactly what I needed."

"Dessert first or second?" he asked.

I was desperate to dive into the cupcake and him, but we needed to talk first. "What's the main course?"

"Ah, my specialty. Spaghetti and marinara and cheesy garlic bread."

"Sounds amazing." He pulled out the chair for me and helped me down. I sat in silence while he poured us both a small glass of wine and served dinner. When he took his seat across from me, I sat back and admired him for a moment.

I tore off a piece of bread and dipped it into the sauce. I took a small bite and let the flavors meld together in my mouth. I moaned lightly. Derrick raised an eyebrow. "I need a minute. This tastes so good."

"Would you like me to leave you two alone?" he teased.

I shook my head. "Don't you dare."

"How was Jacob?" he asked after shoving a forkful of spaghetti into his mouth.

I turned away from him and looked out over the city that had just welcomed me home. The familiar song of cars and laughter drifted up to us, bringing a smile to my face.

"He's good. I mean, he was hurt pretty bad, but he was in good spirits when I left. He seems happy with Melissa."

"Melissa?"

"Yeah, the three of us grew up together. She's my best friend."

"Are you okay with all of that?" he asked as he raised his glass to his lips. A pigeon swooped down and landed on the railing. Derrick tossed a piece of bread to him.

"I am." I set my fork down and reached across the table and took his hand. "Are we okay?"

"I won't lie, Abby, what you assumed and what you said to me that night hurt."

Hearing him admit to that confirmed every fear I'd had. I dropped my head and said, "I wish I could take it back."

"And I wish I'd come to find you rather than waiting for Claire to show up."

"I get why you didn't." I thought of my last words to Jacob and how true they'd been. *You'll always be mine, too.* I couldn't fault Claire or Derrick for being that to each other. I trusted both of them to know that's all it was. History.

"I wanted you that night. I wanted to lie in your arms and hear your voice. You're my safe place to land. Whether it's good or bad, you're the one I want to share everything with."

"I want that too," I said as my heart pounded loudly in my chest.

"I love you, Abby."

I swallowed hard and leaned into the ache in my chest. "I love you, too, Derrick."

He stood up and squeezed between the table and the railing. I slid my chair back and stood with him. "Do you know why I left one cupcake?"

"I thought it was your twisted way of dumping me."

He shook his head. "I left you one because I angry-ate the second one on my way back to your place. Icing and all. It's still fucking nasty, but I wanted to taste it like you did. I wanted to remember the look on your face that night as you watched in horror as I scraped the icing off. But mostly, I wanted to feel your lips on mine for the first time again, to know that you were craving me as much as that cupcake. I wanted to show you how much I loved you."

"Can you show me now?" I asked. My breath hitched as he took my face into his hands and cradled it. He brushed his lips over mine, tender and slow at first, then his desire took over, and he pressed into me with his full weight. When he broke away, I sighed. "Definitely better than a cupcake."

I reached up and touched my finger to the fading bruise on his cheekbone. He flinched and looked away. "Do you want to talk about it?"

"No," he said and sighed. "But I owe you an explanation for that night."

"You don't have to."

"I want to, Abby. I don't ever want to keep things from you. You deserve honesty." He closed his eyes as I kissed the mark left by his father. "I don't know where to start."

"The ring would be a good place," I offered. Mostly because after a few days, the curiosity had driven me insane, but also because he needed to know that I already knew.

"You know?" If he didn't have a beard, I was certain I would've seen splash of red creeping up his skin.

"Noah told me."

Derrick nodded and retreated back to his seat across from me. He gave a shy smile and said, "I wasn't planning to propose to you anytime soon, but I knew one day I'd want to. Dad's been having some financial struggles, and I wanted to get the ring before he had a chance to do anything with it. Turns out, I was too late."

"And then, I blew up everything, and you got punched in the face for nothing."

He shook his head. "No, don't do that. We both could've handled everything differently, but this wasn't your fault. My dad's an asshole."

"Still," I said. "I'm sorry it happened."

"Me too. So, now that we have that settled, are you ready for the good news?"

"That wasn't it?" Hearing the man that I was completely head over feet in love with profess his own love for me felt like the best news imaginable. Whatever came next was just the icing on top.

"A buddy of mine from Sony was at open mic a few weeks ago. He's friends with Beau and a few other artists and helped me get my first cut."

"When we sang 'Mama Said?'" I asked. Derrick nodded in response. "Was it the dude in the suit who kept ordering soda water and left a ridiculous tip?"

Derrick nodded and laughed. "Yes. His name is Chris, and he stuck around for our set. He called the morning after you went home and asked to meet. He didn't want to wait, so I met him for lunch that day."

I took a bite of spaghetti and nodded for him to continue. The corners of his mouth lifted into a wide smile that reach his eyes. How I'd missed those lips.

"He wants us to come in and cut that song and a few others that I played. I hope it's okay, but I played "After Everything" for him, and he loved it. He thinks the songs have potential."

"What?" I asked, my eyes lighting up. "Are you serious?"

"Yes. That's not all."

"I mean, I don't know how it could get any better." Even if it didn't amount to getting a song cut, this was exactly what I'd hoped for when I made the decision to move to Nashville.

"He wants us to play a showcase for the label in October." My mouth fell open. That meant he wanted more than just our songs.

"As in us performing as a duo?"

"Yes, he sees potential in you and me, together."

I sat back and considered his words. I let them roll through my mind as I recalled his past with Claire, Noah, and their band. "Is that a good idea? I mean, I love our music and us together, but what we have is more important. I don't want to lose that along the way."

"We won't," he said.

"How do you know?" I left off the *it happened to you and Claire* part.

"Because I know me, and I know you. This," he said and took my hand into his, "is so much more than anything I've experienced before, Abby. I'm not the same kid I was back then. You've shown me that."

"Good," I said. "Because making music with you is all I ever want to do. You're my melody."

He leaned across the table, and when his lips found mine, I knew I'd found the kind of love people like us write about. Our past was a deep part of us, it had shaped us into the people we both needed to be.

EPILOGUE
ONE(ISH) YEAR LATER

I wiped my hand across my forehead. I watched as Derrick did the same and marveled at his freshly trimmed beard. Sweat beaded along my hairline. My freshly dyed, curled, and perfect dirty-blonde hair fell limp in the humidity. We cleaned up nicely. Even if we sweated away the evidence after ten minutes of stifling Nashville humidity.

"Ready?" he asked. I nodded as he started to strum the intro. The soft chords started slow and then ramped up. We'd rehearsed for this exact moment for weeks, but I couldn't shake my nerves. It was just us on that stage. My blue guitar and his beat-up black one. We could've had a band, but we preferred to keep things simple.

I took in a deep breath and scanned the crowd that had gathered at the Riverfront Stage to watch B. Monroe. perform at their first CMA Fest. I smiled as I spotted Noah, Claire, Jessie, and Leah gathered at the front of the stage. They all wore T-shirts with our faces plastered on them. *My eyes are on their boobs*. That was one detail I'd never thought to include in my dream, and I tried not to focus on how ridiculous it all felt.

Mom and Dad stood behind them with Jenny and my brothers, Adam and Eric, who were quite possibly our biggest fans. Well, more

Derrick's than mine. They adored Derrick, especially now that he'd offered to teach them both how to play the guitar. Dad's face beamed with pride as he gazed up at us. He locked his eyes on mine and smiled. Mom bumped her shoulder against his as if to say *look what we made*. I smiled out at them both and marveled at how far we'd all come in a year. They weren't best friends or anything, but they'd called a truce for the sake of their daughters. Now, they both fought over who was B. Monroe's most ardent supporter. I'd never tell Mom, but Dad held that title. He hadn't missed a show yet.

Just like when we were kids, I was all his and Lindsey was all Mom's. She hadn't made it today, though she'd wanted to be here. Her twins proved to be less effective birth control for her than they had for me, and she was due any day now with a baby girl she promised to name Grace after me. I was flattered but still accused her of lacking creativity in coming up with her own name.

Jacob and Melissa had wanted to come but had opted for a honeymoon in Hawaii instead. I couldn't blame them. I was happy for them. Earlier today, Melissa had sent me a photo of the sun rising over the ocean outside her hotel room along with a good luck message from the two of them.

I found Dad's face one last time before clearing my throat and leaning into the microphone. I let his confidence in me infiltrate my mind and soothe my anxiety. *I can do this.*

"How are we doing, Nashville?" I said into the microphone, hoping no one heard the shaking in my voice. "I'm Abby, and this is Derrick, and we're B. Monroe."

Right on cue, Derrick strummed the first chord of "Doin' What I Shouldn't." He smiled at me as I started to sing the very first song we wrote together. It was just the beginning of our happy ending.

THE END.

ACKNOWLEDGMENTS

As I sit here and reflect on the journey of this book, I'm reminded of those who've been fierce supporters and cheerleaders of mine.

Leah, thank you for being my biggest fan, a constant sounding board, a dear friend, a source of laughter and smiles when I need it the most, and for simply being you. This book wouldn't exist without you.

Maria, you're a badass. Pure and simple. Not only are you an AMAZING writer, but you're a talented artist, a kickass mama, and a great friend.

May, between you and Leah, I know that my words will always have a soft place to land. You've read nearly every one of my books (the good and the meh), and you've answered countless questions and worked to help squash to my insecurities. How lucky am I to have found such a beautiful friend in a Facebook Mom Group?

Rea, I will forever and always be a beta reader for you. Your words, kindness, courage, and honesty have been an inspiration to me over the year or so I've known you. Thank you for reminding me why I write and for giving me a swift kick of confidence when I needed it most.

To my husband, you may not always read my words or understand the quirks of a writer, but you love me and support me. You've given me a life I wasn't always sure I deserved. I love you. Thank you. (And, thank you for putting up with all my indecisiveness around cover designs and my website.)

My dear sweet/mischievous children … where do I even begin? Your giggles fuel me. Your imaginations inspire me. Your cuddles and kisses revive me. You are more than the air I breathe, you are my lungs and my heart. I love you. Also, maybe don't read Mama's books until you're MUCH older.

To my Badass Author Babes, I LOVE you all and appreciate the advice, wisdom, sarcasm, and support you give each and every day.

Lastly, to all the Bookstagrammers who have welcomed me into the community and have helped to lift up so many authors, you all are a gem. There are too many of you to name and I'd never forgive myself if I left someone out, but know that I love you all and appreciate all you do.

Thank you to each and every person who picks up this or any of my books. Whether you love it or like it or hate it, know that I appreciate the time you spent with my characters in their world. And, if you'd leave a review on Amazon or Goodreads or wherever you review books, I'll forever be indebted to you.

ABOUT THE AUTHOR

Andrea is the author of Life is but a Dream, Happily Ever Never, and Lie Baby Lie.

Andrea currently lives in Nashville with her husband, Jeff, and their two children, Jackson and Annabeth. She has a BS in Mass Communication from MTSU and an MBA from the University of Memphis.

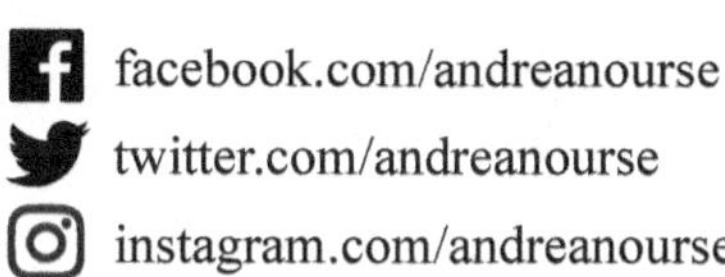

ALSO BY ANDREA NOURSE

Life is but a Dream

Happily Ever Never

Lie Baby Lie